Graham Cawley joined Lloyds Bank in 1954 in South Devon, and retired as Senior Manager of the St James's Street branch, London. He has published several financial articles and short stories. *Chain of Events* is his first novel about banking, which also features his love of golf, football and jazz.

GRAHAM CAWLEY

Chain of Events

To Mike
With my very best wishes

Graham Cawley

Matador
9 De Montfort Mews
Leicester LE1 7FW, UK
Tel: (+44) 116 255 9311 / 9312
Email: books@troubador.co.uk
Web: www.troubador.co.uk/matador

ISBN 1 904744 46 X

Cover illustration: ©Photos.com

Typeset in 10pt Stempel Garamond by Troubador Publishing Ltd, Leicester, UK
Printed by The Cromwell Press Ltd, Trowbridge, Wilts, UK

Matador is an imprint of Troubador Publishing

*In memory of Donald, Lillian
and our dear friend James*

Acknowledgements

My thanks to all those who have encouraged, helped and supported me in the writing of this book, particularly Sara Cowan, Hazel Fawkes, Dr Hilary Johnson, Professor John Tibbetts, David Trower, Jasmyn Turton and my family, Ian, Lisa and especially Shelagh who has been such a staunch supporter.

PROLOGUE

It was not the best of days to be confronting death. He had never liked this road with its dangerous hairpin bends, but now he loathed its debris-strewn path, incited by the raging storm.

Gale force winds plucked dead leaves from the roadside and adjacent fields, swirling them round his vehicle like confetti at a wedding. At least the noise of the storm shut out the screeching gulls that inhabited this stretch of coastline, and he was thankful to be on dry land; it was not a time to be out at sea.

Rain engulfed the windscreen and the leaden skies mocked the fact that lighting-up time was still two hours' distant. The ten-inch blades, hardly adequate to clear the lightest drizzle, all but gave up on the unequal task. There was scarce hope of seeing anything ahead, let alone the rear lights of the cars in front which appeared and faded as the vehicles wound their way up the twisting road towards the top of the hill.

Despite the need to concentrate, he could not prevent his mind wandering. It was as if his whole life was being laid bare before him. Ups and downs, highs and lows, elation and despair. His mind was as active as the 998cc engine of his beloved Austin A30, as it struggled to conquer the steepening road. Yet it coped better with the notorious Devon hills than his previous Morris 8, a wartime relic, replaced a year ago when a successful 1955 had enabled him to buy his first new motor. The compact nature of the A30 would ordinarily have been too restrictive for his bulk, but he relished its cosiness, especially with Peg sitting beside him.

Peg. Would she ever forgive him? They may have been good for each other, essential for their disparate needs, but how could he have so manipulated her? As a man of the world, he had taken advantage of someone whose lifestyle had been effectively trussed up in the most constrictive of parental girdles. She did not deserve his sordid manipulation.

Consumed by guilt, he reached the brow of the hill and entered the cliff-top car park. He used to enjoy the area's contrasting views of distant Portland Bill and the wild terrain surrounding Dartmoor's Haytor peak, but now the rain was so torrential that he could hardly see the flimsy restraining fence which separated the parking area from the five hundred feet drop to the shore below.

As he glided forward, his life collapsed before him. How could it have got to this state? One thing had led to another, but if only he had not begun to gamble. He knew exactly when it had started. On a cold, forbidding winter's day at primary school, he had bet a friend tuppence that it would not snow. It was a classic win/win situation. If it failed to snow, he would win the money – enough to spend in the sweet shop on the way home – and if it did snow, the financial loss would be worth the resultant snowballing and tobogganing. It had taken him forty years to learn that gambling was a lose/lose fool's occupation.

But his gambling was one thing; the rest was something else. How could he have become so involved? He had to put an end to it now.

He stared vacantly through the windscreen, his mind as blurred as the images created on the glass by the continuing rainstorm. Why had he influenced Peg so selfishly?

He prayed to God that she would never be found out; she did not deserve that. Thank goodness she only knew of his gambling. But even that was too much. He should have cherished her, not preyed on her vulnerability.

Tears coursed down his cheeks in a flagrant act of self-pity. Only he knew that his outward show of muscle belied an inner weakness that had dogged him all his life. He could never resist temptation, no matter what the consequences. But the time had come to draw upon all his resolve and do what must be done. His body quivered from an involuntary shiver, the thin lining of his trouser pocket failing to insulate him from the cold steel nestling against his thigh. It really was the only way; he had to end his torment once and for all.

His eyes strained to search the car park and, through the murk, he discerned the familiar shape of a solitary car. At that moment, his nerve failed him. But it was too late. Speeding down the natural slope of the car park, with no other option available, his vehicle shattered the restraining barrier and plummeted to the craggy rocks far below.

CHAPTER 1

'If you value your life, don't even think about it.'

David Goodhart had no need to look up from the lunch table; such an admonition would be accompanied by a twinkle in Sarah's eyes. His threat to get home late from work might have led to acrimony, but on this of all days, Sarah had accepted his teasing at face value.

After all, a tenth anniversary was cause for celebration. How could he let National Counties Bank hamper that? Not always did he put the bank before Sarah and Mark – though Sarah was not one to share such sentiment.

'I could meet you at the pub,' he said. 'Go there straight from work.'

Why not continue the mild ribbing? He had got off to a good start that morning by actually remembering their anniversary. Not only that, he had done his research: tin was the order of the day and he had felt pleased when Sarah had looked askance when presented with what appeared to be an empty can of baked beans. But her hazel eyes had sparkled with pleasure at seeing the replacement contents of a pair of pearl droplet earrings. She promised to wear them that evening.

'You'll be there on your own, David,' she answered. 'And wouldn't that be a waste of those earrings?'

'Come over here, best wife,' he urged, getting up and giving her a bear hug when she fell into his arms. 'Of course I won't be late. Nothing much happened this morning. And after that huge helping of soup, it'll be feet-up time this afternoon.'

'Here or at the office?'

'Don't tempt me,' he replied, releasing her and making for the hall to get his trench coat and hat. 'I don't fancy the walk back. That storm's still raging outside.'

'But you're sure you won't be late home?'

Had he not just said that? But any hint of sarcasm would hardly be appreciated. Instead, he simply asked, 'You're still happy for Dad to babysit tonight?'

He knew the likely answer and shared Sarah's concerns. Yet it was the best option. They had tried youngsters, but their maturity was little better than that of eight-year-old Mark. At least Dad would impose a modicum of discipline. It was just that he was becoming so confused, even though he was not yet seventy.

Sarah shrugged. 'I suppose so. But we mustn't be late home. So please promise to leave the office by five.'

Not again! He had better leave, but Sarah was now adjusting his tie. 'It's time you got a replacement,' she said. 'This one's getting shabby – hardly fitting for the smartest bank manager in town.'

He shook his head. What was it about women and ties? Not ever would he change his old school tie; this one was like an old friend. Not that he gained any esteem from wearing it; Torquay Grammar was not like Eton or Harrow. But it was an attractive tie, not too bright, nor sombre, and he did wear it with pride.

As he at last left their semi-detached house, thoughts of ties evaporated, his coat almost rendered impotent by the cutting wind. Rain slashed into him and he was soon viewing Sarah's "smartest bank manager" comment with irony. But he would have to be at his smartest that after-noon, though not in the matter of his appearance.

Not much had happened that morning, but he still had

a problem. Would he have to bounce the cheques of one of the town's most prominent traders? People seemed to think bank managers took such action with undue relish whereas, in reality, it was always an act of last resort. He was certainly loath to do it in this case.

Bouncing cheques did not encourage amity and he much preferred to avoid bad feeling. In a small town, especially, reputation was sacrosanct and gossip proliferated. But no one ever heard the bank's side of the story; rules prohibited such disclosure. This was an aspect of banking which had never crossed his mind when he joined National Counties as a raw sixteen-year-old, leaving behind what his housemaster had described as "an inglorious academic achievement". (Yet, after twenty-four years, he wore his tie with pride; time was such a healer.) He had originally seen the job in clerking terms – confirmed later by his wartime drill sergeant who disparagingly called him a lopsided pen pusher. But, in management, he soon learnt that banking was about people dealing with people – and bouncing cheques certainly put a strain on customer relations.

But what should he do this afternoon? He did not need today's appalling weather to tell him that November was a forlorn time of year – especially for a popular seaside resort like Barnmouth. Visitors were gone, shutters pulled down and cafes closed. Yet it was also the time when the bank accounts of traders should be at their healthiest.

Approaching the town centre, he noticed the deteriorating décor of the seafront hotels and boarding houses, likely to be made worse by the salty atmosphere thrown up by the winter's storms. But it had been a good summer and the prudent business people would have put aside sufficient takings for such renovations and to see them through the winter. So what was George Broadman up to?

He turned into the High Street and faced a building of some grandeur. As if according it the respect it deserved, the adjacent properties shared its dignity. Highly-polished brass plates announced their occupants as Ponsonby, Charles and Outhwaite, chartered accountants, on one side, with Ducksworth, Brown and Sargeant, solicitors and commissioners for oaths, on the other. He could not wish for more highly-respectable neighbours for his branch of National Counties Bank. In particular, Stuart Brown, the solicitors' prominent senior partner, was a great friend of the bank. Not only was he a first-class lawyer, but he also seemed to relish having a younger, more go-ahead manager in charge. It was a relationship David was keen to nurture, knowing that the more business Brown put his way, the more his branch profits would increase.

But Brown was Broadman's solicitor and would hardly appreciate his client's cheques being bounced. Such action would clearly have to be both correct and justified and before lunch, David had left his assistant, Jane Church, to do some digging around. That was another worry he could do without. Was she up to it? He wondered about the quality of staff the bank would have employed when it had been built fifty years ago. It was one thing to display the outward trappings of impressive York-stone walls, with well-scrubbed marble-like steps leading to a solid oak front door, but it was the staff inside who could make or break a banking business.

Before mounting the steps, he cast his eyes to the roof and was relieved to see in place the white wooden flagpole he had erected shortly after his appointment. Apart from days like this, a chosen flag would flutter elegantly and its sight had become a focal point – on special occasions, a rallying call – for the whole town. He always took great care to fly the correct flag for the right event and although the bank's crest often took pride of place, the Union Jack flew proudly on state celebrations, while the crosses of each patron saint had their annual airings. A committed supporter of Torquay United, he even aired the club's pennant when the club enjoyed moments of major success.

On entering the bank, he could not but admire the mahogany counters, which followed the contours of the building. His cashiers occupied positions to the right of the front door, while on the left, other clerks dealt with securities, safe custody items and foreign transactions. In the public area, matching chairs sat alongside tables furnished with inkwells, steel-nib pens and blotting paper contained in leather-bound rectangular holders. He always insisted that the paper be changed each morning to remove the previous day's unsightly blobs, but he wondered if this practice might be nearing an end with the rising popularity of the ballpoint pen.

Behind the cashiers, a couple of male clerks occupied high desks on accompanying stools and he noted how smart they looked from the public area, fastidiously clad in starched-collared white shirts and three-piece suits. At the back of the office, rose a clatter of mechanical mayhem as his young girls flexed their fingers on complex machines which had become essential to deal with the mounting volume of cheques to be processed. Hand-written ledgers and statements were now a thing of the past, a welcome move for those customers who had increasing difficulty in deciphering the legibility of the writing of modern-day bank clerks.

Overseeing the whole office, on the back wall facing the front door, a massive oil painting depicted an imposing gentleman of Edwardian times. The founder of the bank, eventually taken over by National Counties in the twenties, scowled down on customers as if daring them to enter his building, let alone enquire about the possibility of a small advance. Not for the first time, David wondered if it might be wise to remove this painting to make his bank appear less austere.

It was then that he saw his deputy, Norman Charlton, waving frantically to catch his attention. Norman was a man of rare emotion and on seeing the concern etching his face, David's curiosity turned into mild alarm, especially as Norman was clearly doing his best to conceal his actions from the other staff. This became even more apparent when he signalled David to join him in a room to the rear of the main office.

'What's going on?' David demanded, once they were behind the closed door.

'The police have just rung,' Norman replied agitatedly, belying his background as a composed Spitfire pilot in the war. 'It was the station sergeant up the road.'

'And?' This had the makings of a long, drawn-out explanation, but he needed to get himself dried out post-haste.

'They've spotted some strangers in town,' Norman replied, making David feel he was in a scene from a western. 'Just a couple to start with, but there are about six now. With long overcoats and hats down over their eyes.'

'But why call us about that?' David asked, having just been thankful for his own coat and hat.

'It's the way they're lurking... at the top of the town... near the church. The police aren't doing anything yet – just keeping an eye on them. But they've contacted all the banks – in case they might be mounting a raid.'

CHAPTER 2

David finally sat down behind his desk and reflected on whether he had covered everything. Constant guard was vital against possible bank raids and, rare as they were, he welcomed the opportunity to ram home to his staff the need for extra vigilance. All surplus cash in tills had been stowed in the strong-room, cashiers would carefully watch for strangers in the banking hall, and Norman Charlton would conduct a regular lookout from an office window adjacent to the High Street. David had also rung the police who confirmed their satisfaction that their covert surveillance operation was sufficient action at this stage.

While needing to take every precaution, he doubted trouble from these strangers. They would be foolish raiders indeed to have advertised their presence, a quick-mounted attack being a far more likely modus operandi. But he would still have an anxious half an hour until the front door was closed at three o'clock.

He was also bothered about the wet collar of his shirt. Sarah had urged him to keep spare clothing at his office and he feared an "I told you so" reaction. Discounting the dampness at his neck, he still had to counter her biased opinion of his appearance. "Well-presented" rather than "smart" might better apply. Being six feet tall gave him a good start, but an expanding waistline hardly complemented the cut of his suit, while the state of his shoes and trouser legs bore evidence of his traipse back to work. He was thankful he had no customer appointments that afternoon, leaving Jane as his priority – about those cheques he might have to return.

Before calling her in, he eyed the "in" and "out" trays which sat on either side of his oak and leather-inlaid desk. He loved this desk, even if it was too large for his room. It meant space for only two chairs facing him, but, in practice, he rarely saw more than two customers together. Wives might accompany husbands, while business meetings were usually limited to two directors or partners. His banking business reflected Barnmouth as a small provincial town, with large companies gravitating to Exeter or Plymouth.

Apart from the return of a couple of letters he had dictated that morning, his "in" tray was empty and he reached for his telephone to call in his assistant. Almost immediately, a knock on the door announced the arrival of a young girl in her early twenties, clutching a number of cheques in one hand and a pen and pencil in the other. She stood nervously in front of his desk until he motioned her to sit down.

'Ah, Jane,' he said. Why was she still so apprehensive of him? Two months as his assistant, yet it might have been only two days. Was he that much of an ogre? 'Are those the cheques?'

Jane nodded, blushing, and set out the cheques in two piles.

'And?'

'These are all right,' she answered, picking up the first pile. 'The Smiths paid in at lunchtime, so did Mr McCarthy and Mr Charlton has agreed an overdraft for Mrs Gregg.'

'And the others?'

'They're Mr Broadman's.'

David frowned, taking the remaining two cheques from her. What was George up to? These cheques looked decidedly dodgy. 'What do you make of them?'

Jane reddened even more at being put on the spot. Yet he needed her to be an effective assistant. If her previous training had been inadequate, he would have to teach her, guide her. But she should also use her initiative, try and work things out for herself.

'Let's start with the payees,' he continued when she remained silent. 'Good Meat Supplies for £700, and £300 payable to cash.'

It was now Jane's turn to frown. 'Good Meat Supplies could be his wholesaler.'

That was better, George Broadman being the town's principal butcher. 'And the amount?'

'His weekly supply?'

'Fair enough. But for £700 exactly?'

He watched Jane wrestle with the point he was trying to make, but she simply shook her head.

'It's a round amount,' he eventually said. 'If it's his weekly supply, wouldn't it be an odd amount? Like £712 or £697?'

'Perhaps that's the way the wholesaler works it out. He rounds the amount up or down. Then he adjusts it the next week.'

'You're on the right lines, but you're not quite there. The round amount is probably because he's in debt to the wholesaler. And he's paying it off in instalments. What do you make of that?'

'It sounds logical. Is that a problem?'

'At this time of year it could be. It's the end of the main trading season. He should be set up for the winter. Yet he's in debt?' This would be bad news indeed. He only hoped he was wrong.

'But he can't be in trouble. He's such a good butcher.'

'And you couldn't wish for a nicer man,' David added, having found the company of the butcher particularly agreeable. 'But what about the other cheque?'

Jane studied it in her hand. 'It's payable to cash, so it's probably for wages – or something like that.'

'Have a look on the back.'

She turned it over in her hand and then back again. 'There's nothing on the back.'

'Exactly!' His staff controller had assured him that she was a high-flier, but had she flown too quickly through some of her training programme? 'And what does that mean?'

She looked blankly at the cheque and made no reply.

'Remember when you were a casher?' he asked, trying to avoid any hint of sarcasm. 'When you cashed a cheque, you marked it on the back with a breakdown of the notes and coin you paid out. You also impressed your till stamp on the front. In this case? Nothing.'

'He could have cashed it somewhere else. With a friend?'

'The most respectable butcher in town? Why would he do that?' This was cloud-cuckoo land. George would hardly cash his wages cheque anywhere else. This was getting most disturbing – and for how long had it been happening?

'So what are we going to do?'

That was better – including herself in the decision. 'If he still hasn't paid in and I can't reach him on the telephone, we're going to bounce his cheques.'

Jane visibly winced as she took both cheques into her hand.

'And by tomorrow morning,' he continued, 'I want you to look at his cheques for the last three months – to see if this is part of a pattern.'

When Jane had gone, he rang through to his secretary to try to get George Broadman on the telephone. Miss Harding: another cross for him to bear. Talk about the old school. On his arrival at Barnmouth, she had made it clear that first-name terms were out – from him or any of the staff. In her twenty-five years in the bank, she had always been Miss Harding and Miss Harding she would stay. It was out-of-the-ark stuff, so pathetic. But there was nothing he could do about it and his initial urge to make mischief by ignoring her demands was long gone.

Within a minute, she rang back to say that Broadman was unavailable.

'But I need to speak to him,' he stressed. 'Where is he?'

'I don't know,' Miss Harding replied indignantly. 'And no one at the shop knows. It seems he's disappeared.'

'Disappeared? He can't have disappeared.'

He almost heard the sigh at the other end as Miss Harding added, 'He's not been seen all day.'

This was crazy. Where could the man be? 'Well, I need to speak to him or I'll bounce his cheques.'

This time the exclamation was audible. 'Bounce his cheques? You can't do that.'

Who was the decision maker here, the manager or the secretary? 'Why not?'

'Because he's one of our most respected customers. What about his reputation? What would the Chamber of Trade say? You'd be ostracised. And what about me? He always gives me the best cuts of meat.'

David smiled, grateful for the visual anonymity of the telephone. He could almost see the steam rising at the other end. It would be all his fault that Miss Harding might now get a bit of scrag instead of her usual best end of neck.

But she did have a point. Well-respected customers do not expect their cheques to be bounced. Nor do the recipients. Hard-earned reputations could certainly be lost in an instant. But he could do without admonishment from a secretary concerned more about her future cuts of meat.

'If any customer,' he replied, pronouncing his words precisely, 'not just the highly-respectable George Broadman, decides to go substantially overdrawn without arrangement, he must accept the consequences. Why should the bank be put in such a position? Why should we have to take the risk?'

'It's not just about risk,' Miss Harding spat out. 'What about our reputation? We'd be a laughing stock.'

'That may be your view,' he said. Why must he put up with this? 'But we're the custodians of the bank's money – our customers' money. Why should we throw it away on someone who doesn't have the courtesy to put us in the picture – to ask first? George has effectively walked in here and put his hands in the till. If I pay his cheques, he'll have filched £1000.' He shook his head, realizing that the amount equated to his annual salary. 'No, if I can't speak to him, I'm most certainly going to bounce his cheques.'

The reaction at the end of the line was the slamming down of the receiver. From his first day, Miss Harding had tried to rule the roost – as, apparently, she had with his predecessors. But he was not prepared to endure her intimidation. Yes, he would listen to her views and consider her proffered advice, but the final decision was his. This latest contretemps was clearly a further blow to her yearned-for past prestige.

Having made his decision and arranged for Jane to deal with the cheques, he cast Miss Harding to the back of his mind and allowed himself the luxury of more pleasant thoughts. He really must make tonight an evening to remember. Sarah deserved nothing less. Admittedly, he had not booked a table at the poshest of venues, but it was a place that had special memories for them. Their very first meeting had been at the thatched Royal House Inn, a popular hostelry in the nearby village of Leigh-in-Barnhead. Where better to celebrate their tenth anniversary? Being only three miles away, it would also ease their minds over Dad's babysitting, especially if they got to the inn early in the evening.

It was, therefore, a major blow to his plans when, at ten past three precisely, he heard the front doorbell ring, quickly followed by Jane putting her head round his door and hissing, 'The inspectors are here.'

CHAPTER 3

Inspectors. Of course! He could not suppress a grin, making a mental note to let these uninvited guests know at an appropriate moment that the police had deemed them to be villains.

Realizing that Jane must be curious as to the cause of his amusement, he wiped the smile from his face and asked if the front door security chain had been properly used when the inspectors were let in. Pursed lips and a shake of the head told him the worst. How could they get it wrong? For two years, he had been drumming into his staff the necessity for strict adherence to all security procedures, emphasising the vital front door opening routine. How often had he stressed that the chain must be kept in place while the identity of any caller was established? Otherwise, a flung-open door would be the perfect welcome to would-be raiders, or a valid reason for a black mark at the beginning of a branch inspection. He shook his head in despair. Just the start he had hoped to avoid for his first inspection at Barnmouth.

He tried to hide his disquiet from Jane who remained transfixed in his doorway, but before he could quiz her further, another figure overshadowed her and hovered expectantly at her shoulder.

'Mr Goodhart?' the man boomed, as if Jane's slight frame might somehow restrict David's awareness of his unexpected visitor. Jane almost jumped out of her skin before carrying out an impromptu two-step with the inspector as they tried to synchronize an ungainly entry and exit.

When she had gone, the inspector stepped inside, pushed the door closed behind him and, as David stood to greet him, he shed his sopping top coat, dumped it unceremoniously on the floor and sprawled into one of the two chairs on the customers' side of the desk. David immediately realized that this interloper was not as large as he had first seemed. In fact, much of his apparent girth had been represented by his coat, which he now feared was soiling the room's Axminster carpet.

He was a slight man, bordering on being skinny, and could not be more that five-feet-six tall. His three-piece charcoal grey suit seemed to have creases in all the wrong places, while the knot of his tie was either soiled from too many a liquid lunch or was deliberately fashioned of a different shade from the rest of the material showing above the top button of his waistcoat. He was of indeterminate age, possibly because the top of his head resembled a mature conker. The wrinkles extended down his face like the lines of a busy railway junction, harbouring steely-blue eyes that now locked on David with the intent of a vulture regarding its prey. David felt certain that this man, despite his unkempt appearance and apparent disregard for normal conventions, was not to be underestimated.

'My name's Parker,' the inspector said, using the built-in amplifier so often favoured by little men. He then thrust his arm across the desk to give him a knuckle-breaking handshake.

'Welcome to Barnmouth,' David replied, sizing up whether or not to make light of the expression, bearing in mind bank inspectors were never the most welcome of visitors. He decided better of it. There would be plenty of time to gauge Parker's sense of humour, without taking a chance at this initial meeting.

'Hmm,' Parker grunted, sinking back in his chair and then plunging his left hand into the pocket of his trousers where he immediately started to jangle what must have been a handful of half-crowns, florins and sixpenny pieces. 'I can think of a better time of year to sample the questionable delights of Barnmouth. You might imagine how cold and wet it was outside, congregating up the road, waiting for you to close your front door.'

One day, David thought, this archaic practice of mounting a surprise offensive would end. He had only discerned the full significance of bank inspectors some years after joining National Counties. In his junior days, they had seemed like tyrants, carrying before them a fearful reputation for destroying all who had the temerity to cross their paths. He had heard of many a promising career becoming becalmed following a typical inspectorial squall, blown up over seemingly insignificant banking misdemeanours.

But now, he fully accepted the practical role they played. They were an adjunct to the outside auditors that banks, like other public companies, employed. It was their duty to ensure that no one was cooking the books. Cash being cash, it was essential that it did not go missing. He had often smiled as he recalled his old customer, Edna Jones. A couple of years before she passed away, her son had persuaded her to open a bank account, rather than keep all her savings at home. She had complied, albeit reluctantly, but most weeks thereafter she had struggled to the bank and cashed a cheque for the balance, only then to pay the money back in. Eventually, having been pressed by the cashiers to explain her actions, she confessed that she had been worried at having to deposit all her money in the bank and she regularly wanted to check that it was still there. David well knew that other customers would not take such extreme action, but they would certainly not wish the bank to lend foolishly if there was any risk to their own balances.

Theory was, however, one thing, but in practice he had come to learn that inspectors did not just inspect – they also spied. They constantly checked behind the backs of unsuspecting branch staff, eager to pounce on any flouting of the bank's rules. For this reason, he and his staff would never welcome the dreaded, unexpected ring on the front doorbell, shortly after closing time.

Yet they should all be batting on the same side. Parker would have been a branch manager before his inspectorial appointment, and David knew that should promotion come his own way, a spell as an inspector could be possible. But there were inspectors and inspectors. He had come across some who might have the humility to remember their heritage within the bank, but others enjoyed encouraging managers and clerks to view their visits as wars of attrition. He wondered if Parker was one of those.

'Anyway,' Parker continued, still watching him closely, 'I wasn't expecting to come here and enjoy myself. But waiting up the road was soul-destroying, to say the least.'

David wondered if this was now the time to broach the involvement of the police, but thought better of it. Yet they ought to be rung. He hoped Norman had used his initiative to do this. In any case, if they had continued their surveillance to the front door, they would know their fears had proved ill-founded.

'Perhaps a cup of tea would help,' he said, thinking this might warm the man up, physically and mentally.

Parker shook his head. 'Later, maybe. I must get on. First days are always the worst. So much to get through – especially this time.'

David groaned inwardly. It was not just the last comment that had an ominous ring to it. The whole inspection team had much to do on its arrival, particularly in taking control of all items of intrinsic value to ensure that nothing was missing. He visualized Parker's four or five assistants beavering away in the general office as they tackled the not inconsiderable task of counting every note and coin in the branch. Being Monday, weekend takings would make it worse, extending the operation into the early evening. He would be lucky to leave by seven. Goodness knows how Sarah would react to that. At the best of times, she hardly shared his dedication to banking, but on this of all days...

'Especially this time?' he queried, dwelling on the inspector's terminology. What could be different about this inspection from all the others Parker must have conducted?

The inspector slumped further into his seat, his posture contrasting sharply from a facial alertness that convinced David he was a man of singular perception. 'What I'd like you to do,' Parker said, ignoring the question, 'is to give me a run-down of all your staff.'

'So soon?' David blurted out, immediately regretting his response on seeing the inspector's eyes narrow at such apparent questioning of his request. It was just that staffing matters were usually deferred until after the first day's checking procedures had been completed.

'Most certainly,' Parker snapped, jangling his coins even louder, reminding David of the neurotic Captain Queeg in The Caine Mutiny; or of a rattlesnake about to strike. He tried not to dwell on that as Parker added, 'Let's start with your deputy.'

'That's Norman Charlton,' David replied, still puzzled at what was going on. 'He's been here about ten years now – arrived straight after the war.'

'Ten years? And no promotion? Isn't he any good?'

'On the contrary,' David answered, nevertheless wondering how Norman was getting on out there with the rest of the inspection team, 'he's a good sub-manager; just not ambitious.'

'And why's that?'

David frowned. It was a question he had asked himself. 'I'm not really sure. He had a distinguished war record – Spitfire pilot. I just wonder if he burnt himself out.'

'Has he talked to you about it?'

'No, never. But I just wonder if... after all the excitement and fear... whether he decided to settle for a more humdrum life in civvy street.'

Parker pursed his lips. 'I suppose that's possible.'

'But someone of his acumen could have achieved a very good career. Perhaps he doesn't want the responsibility.'

'You mean you don't know?'

The sting in the reproach shook him. He would clearly have to choose his words more carefully. 'I meant the responsibility of running his own branch. It's not everyone's cup of tea.'

Parker nodded, as if accepting the point. 'Is he married?'

What on earth was the man up to? Why the third degree? He's only been here five minutes and already had poor Norman in his sights.

'No,' he answered, wondering as to where this was

leading. 'A confirmed bachelor, I'd say. Yet he seems to like the ladies. He gets on particularly well with the elderly ones. They always seek him out for investment advice.'

'What about when you're away – on holiday? Can you rely on him to cope in your absence? Lending decisions, that sort of thing?'

On to lending already? Is that what this was all about? But lending was his own responsibility. Parker knew that. Why start asking about Norman's ability? And so soon. Norman was not the most confident of lenders; in fact it seemed to scare him rigid. But this was not information he wanted to volunteer so early into the inspection. 'Yes, he's fine,' he answered, as neutrally as possible. 'If he's in any doubt, he'll defer a decision; wait till I get back.'

'So he has your seal of approval?'

'Yes. He's an able deputy and that's what he'll probably stay – until he retires. But if he's perfectly content in the job...'

'And who's his deputy?' Parker interrupted.

David took a deep breath. So it was not just about Norman. Parker was clearly seeking the low-down on them all. 'That's Bernard Groves – my head cashier.'

'Age?'

'He must be in his late forties. No, he was fifty – in the summer. I was away at the time, but everyone was agog at his sumptuous party. Outsiders could hardly believe he was only a bank cashier. We all assume his wife has private means.'

'Assume? You mean you don't know?'

David blanched at the implied criticism. Yet, to an extent, he knew it was valid. He had always made a point of knowing as much as possible about all his staff – their personalities, traits, strengths and weaknesses. That way he could guide them, nurture them, even cajole them if it was to help their careers. But delving into matrimonial matters was never easy, especially if it was seen to be prying into the affairs of spouses. It could be a most sensitive issue – particularly in the case of Celia Groves.

'Normally, I certainly would,' he eventually replied, miffed at being put on the defensive, 'but she's a very private person, apart from their social extravaganzas. Doesn't even have her own bank account, not here anyway. And not even a joint account with Bernard.'

'Any children? Outside interests?'

'No children and they probably never wanted any. Children would have cramped their style. Bernard and Celia like to host big occasions and not only on birthdays. They also enjoy luxurious holidays. Makes my wife quite envious. She can't understand why a cashier should enjoy a better lifestyle than his manager. But we do have a child.'

'Um,' Parker muttered, as if weighing up the comparative benefits of children and expensive holidays. 'I don't have any children either,' he added.

David could hardly imagine the dishevelled heap in front of him being a doting father. But he was starting to understand his tactics, his questioning technique: put the adversary on the defensive, then direct short, sharp verbal volleys at the target. He could imagine Parker being an effective army strategist – though he would need a dedicated batman.

'Anyway,' the inspector continued, 'is he a good worker?'

'There's no doubt about that,' David replied, pleased to get the questioning back on the topic of work. 'He's accurate to a fault and always organizes our cash requirements efficiently. He can also be a good ambassador.'

'Can be?'

There he goes again. Another single shot hit home. This was not a man to be under-estimated. He was able to pick out the subtlest nuance. 'Put it this way, Bernard knows all the right people in the town: solicitors, accountants, local councillors. Socially, I mean, not just as customers here in the branch. The trouble is that he thinks that mixing in such circles sets him apart from the rest of us.'

'Arrogant, eh?'

David nodded. 'Not so much outside the bank, but certainly here in the office. It doesn't make him popular.'

'With you? Does that include you?'

'No, no,' David replied, smiling. 'It doesn't bother me. I can take it or leave it. But he doesn't have a natural affinity with the others.'

At that, the telephone rang. He listened for a moment and then asked Parker if he would now like a cup of tea. Getting a nod, he asked for a tray for two and put down the telephone.

'My secretary, Miss Harding.'

'One of your youngsters?'

'Goodness, no,' he said, unable to conceive of Miss Harding ever having been a youngster. 'She's been with the bank twenty-five years. Has more in common with Bernard Groves than the youngsters.'

'Arrogant as well?'

'Let's just say she has a mind of her own. Likes to think she runs the place.'

'One of a breed,' Parker acknowledged from apparent experience.

'But there are mitigating circumstances. She lives with a domineering mother – totally under her thumb. So, when she gets here...'

Parker shrugged and David wondered if he might be under his wife's thumb at home. But before he could pursue that line of thought further, there was a sharp rat-a-tat-tat on his door.

CHAPTER 4

David watched his secretary's entrance with some fore-boding, all too familiar with her expression of withering disapproval. He had faced it on many an occasion after having had the temerity to cause her displeasure. He only hoped that he had not betrayed his concern to Parker who had his back to the door and had chosen not to turn round to meet the new arrival.

Miss Harding moved past the inspector's chair and placed the tea tray she was carrying on the desk between the two men. David attempted to make introductions, but her mind was clearly focused elsewhere. Rather than proffer her hand to the inspector, she used it instead to reach for his coat, which was still lying in a crumpled heap on the floor beside him. Picking it up, she pointedly grasped it by its lapels and shook it hard to rid it of its remaining rainwater, and the myriad creases caused from what were probably years of misuse. She then took it to the coat cupboard adjacent to the desk and hung it on the spare wooden hanger kept for the use of customers who took a little more pride in their appearance.

On completing this tidying-up operation, she moved back to the desk and took from the tray her shorthand notebook and HB lead pencil which had been warming themselves against the pale-blue Poole Pottery teapot. Then, apparently fully equipped for duty, she stood still and fixed David with a purposeful stare.

'Thank you, Miss Harding,' he responded. 'That will be all for now.'

But his secretary remained stationary and silent, giving no outward indication that she had even heard him, let alone acknowledging any comprehension of his words. Her thin lips pursed and a narrowing of her eyes indicated a determination that there would be only one winner here.

'I'll call you a bit later,' David added, fearing a scene in front of Parker. 'Probably in about half an hour.'

'In half an hour?' she echoed. 'No, I need to take the rest of your dictation now.'

'In half an hour, Miss Harding, if you don't mind,' he repeated wearily, not relishing a battle of wills in front of the inspector.

'Well, actually, I do mind,' she replied indignantly. 'If I don't take your dictation now, I shan't be able to get it finished for your signature before we go home at five.'

'I'm afraid no-one will be leaving by five today,' Parker interjected, clearly irritated by the scene evolving around him. It reminded David of the latest Agatha Christie novel he had just finished where the police inspector refused to allow anyone to leave the scene of the crime before he had checked all their credentials. He only hoped that the comparison would not turn out to be too close for comfort.

He also felt that Parker's statement would leave Miss Harding in little doubt about his position of authority. It would not do her any harm to appreciate that during the next couple of weeks, any contrariness on her part would meet resistance from the inspector, as well as himself. But he did not anticipate her immediate reaction. 'As you wish,' she said petulantly and flounced from the room without saying another word.

When she had gone, Parker gave a world-weary shrug, which David hoped was not a silent criticism of his handling of the situation. But what more could he have done? He had attempted to make a proper introduction and had made it clear that the inspector's arrival needed to take precedence over his dictation.

'So, that was Miss Harding,' Parker mused. 'You could say she has a mind of her own. But is she any good as a secretary?'

David started to arrange the cups and saucers on the tray as he considered his reply. He was rather taken aback by the inspector's mild reaction. Was this another ploy? 'Surprisingly enough, yes,' he replied, stirring the tea in the teapot. 'It's just a little delicate. She's not easy to handle – as you've seen. How do you like your tea?'

'Milk and two sugars, please,' Parker answered, making no further comment, as if expecting additional insight into Miss Harding's psyche.

'She does like her routine,' David duly obliged. 'But it's her mother who tries to impose that leaving by five business. She likes to think of what's thought to be a nine-to-five job in literal terms.'

'That's not going to make me very popular,' Parker said, his eyes swapping their intensity for what David thought might be a mischievous twinkle. But then it was gone, as he added, 'Tell me more about her home life.'

This was getting intriguing and not a little disconcerting. Would Parker's probing into the home lives of his staff also extend to himself? 'It's difficult to know where to begin. I suppose it goes back ten years – when her father died. She's an only child and her mother's taken advantage of that. Playing on her emotions. You know the sort of thing.'

'I'm not sure that I do,' Parker said, leaning forward in his chair, further lines appearing on his face as it contracted in concentration. 'It must have been an emotional time.'

'Yes, yes, of course it was,' David acknowledged, hardly able to conceive that Parker might have a more sympathetic nature than his own. 'But I gather it was the way her mother went about it. She's denied her daughter a life of her own – in the guise of mother and daughter facing their loss together. Over the years, it's developed into emotional blackmail. Mother insisted that this was how her husband would have wanted it; that they must maintain a close family bond – in memory of the loving man they'd both lost.'

'And it's grown into a neurosis?'

'Exactly! Her mother even sets a table place for her departed husband when they celebrate birthdays or Christmas. What other fantasies she gets up to, goodness knows.'

Parker shook his head, as if in disbelief.

'To start with,' David continued, 'Miss Harding was happy to be the doting daughter; it was the natural thing to do. But now, she's effectively imprisoned by her mother's influence. It's made her into the archetypal spinster; in her forties, dowdily attired, socially immature and with no sign, interest or hope of marriage.'

'But she's an able secretary.'

David smiled at the statement, not question. Parker getting to the nub of the situation again. 'It means we get through the work pretty well. No idle chit-chat.'

'Anyway, away from the office she's clearly under her mother's thumb. Is that domestically and financially?'

'Financially?'

'Who controls the purse strings? How much income goes into the household? Are they dependent on Miss Harding's salary? What are their outgoings? Are they hard up?'

David could hardly believe what he was hearing. What possible interest could Parker have in Miss Harding's financial circumstances? Was it because she made her disapproval of him so obvious? If so, it hardly justified this sort of inquisition.

'I'm not sure I'm with you,' he said, at the same time realizing he had not yet poured the tea. He now did so, handing over Parker's cup across the desk. 'That, surely, has no bearing on Miss Harding's proficiency as my secretary.'

'I need to know what you know. And as her manager, do you not consider it your duty to know everything possible about Miss Harding – and about all your other staff, for that matter?'

'Well, of course...'

'And is it not your role to ensure that you're well aware of any possible financial problems which might affect a clerk's judgement in carrying out his or her responsibilities?'

'Yes, but...'

'And if Miss Harding – taking her as a hypothetical example – has serious financial problems, would you not want to know about them? Don't forget your responsibility to your customers, never mind the bank.'

How patronizing! 'I'm well aware of that, but...'

'Mr Goodhart, there are no "buts" about it. It's your job, man, and if I see fit to enquire about Miss Harding's financial position, I am only doing what you should have been doing every day since you were appointed manager of this branch.'

How dare he! David could hardly comprehend Parker's contemptuous outburst as he watched him take a sip of tea, almost basking in the stunned silence that had enveloped the room. How dare he make such overt criticisms so soon after his arrival, before he could have any idea about whether or not he was doing his job properly? What was to be gained from acting so aggressively?

Every day since his arrival at Barnmouth two years ago, he had scrupulously examined every transaction passing through the accounts of each member of staff. These were the rules. He dutifully checked on all payees of cheques issued by his clerks to ensure that payments were being made in keeping with their positions. Small amounts payable to Littlewoods Pools might not raise an eyebrow, but he could not countenance his less-than-generously-paid staff being in hock to bookmakers and the like. And credits to their accounts must not defy his eagle eye, particularly if deemed to relate to other employment. Such additional labour was strictly forbidden. As for staff anticipating their long-awaited paid-in-arrears monthly salary – he had to make it patently clear that such temporary overdrafts were definitely off-limits, no matter where his personal sympathies might lie.

Yes, he was doing all that was required of him, yet Parker had taken it upon himself to lambaste his alleged neglect of managerial responsibilities. Rage coursed through his veins at the sheer injustice of it all, but he knew that, somehow or other, his response must be considered. At all costs, he could not afford to appear rattled.

'And you really don't think I've been doing that?' he answered, his tone calm and measured. 'You can hardly expect me to think that's fair.'

'Life isn't always fair, Mr Goodhart,' Parker replied wearily. 'But I hope you get my drift. And I know my job – just as I hope you know your own. Now, I think we both appreciate where we stand with your Miss Harding. Who else can you tell me about?'

David was pleased that he had stood his ground. He could easily have buckled under Parker's intimidation and he might even have gained some respect. But he still felt distinctly uneasy at the early course this inspection was taking and would not be at all surprised if Parker's initial sniping led to some kind of bombshell. In the meantime, he would certainly give him a rundown of his other staff.

'Jane Church is my MA. Still too wet behind the ears to be an effective manager's assistant. But she's willing and keen to learn.'

'How long has she been here?'

'Only a couple of months. She was rather foisted on me – by the staff controller. I gather he wants more girls on the managerial treadmill.'

'A sign of the times.'

'But I think it's a good thing,' David countered, deciding to make his position entirely clear about the like-lihood of girls playing a more significant role in what had always been a male-dominated business. His only stipula-tion was that girls with management ambitions must also become qualified by way of the stringent professional qualifications set by the Institute of Bankers. Some of his older managerial colleagues in the region heaped their scepticism over this happening, but a number of female clerks, including Jane, had duly enrolled at night school, as if determined to give their male counterparts a run for their money. 'Given the right encouragement, there's no reason why girls shouldn't be as able as men.'

'Um,' Parker grunted, giving David the option of deciding whether or not the inspector agreed with his views. 'But what's she like with customers? Does she have an easy rapport with them?'

33

'Jane? Good heavens, no. Not yet, anyway. That was her in the doorway when you came into my room. She's still like a frightened rabbit. But she'll grow out of that. Just needs to gain some self-confidence. At least she's prepared to listen and she's certainly intelligent.'

'What about her integrity?'

David could not help but gape. 'Integrity? What do you mean by that?'

Parker shrugged. 'Just wondering. Still waters and all that. Who's next?'

What with questioning Norman's deputizing ability, Bernard's home life, Miss Harding's finances and now Jane's integrity. To where was it all leading? David could not help but frown as he replied, 'Barbara Bolton, I suppose. Our supervisor – you could call her the office linchpin.'

'Oh? Why's that?'

'Long service for one thing. She's been here over thirty years – continuously from way before the war and right through it. Knows our customers intimately. Not on a personal basis, but from their accounts and files. She's totally dedicated, works long hours and hardly ever takes her full holiday entitlement. I don't know what we'd do without her.'

Parker shook his head. 'Sounds too good to be true. But you've already taken me to be a cynical old codger, eh?'

David was too astounded to respond. And had his eyes deceived him or had he really glimpsed a cheeky glint. Whatever, the moment had come and gone, the inspector's ascetic demeanour returning as he took from his jacket pocket a small black leather-bound notebook and started writing what were probably cryptic comments about the staff under discussion.

After a couple of minutes, he put the notebook away and his steely gaze returned. 'I imagine that's all your senior staff. I shan't need to know about the others at this stage. But how many are there? About half-a-dozen?'

'No, seven, actually.'

'Perhaps you'd better give me their names,' Parker said, retrieving his notebook from his pocket.

'There are three men. Trevor Smith's our number two cashier, Douglas Dallimore's in securities, and Roger Singleton's our junior.'

'And the girls?'

'Our ledger clerks are Jilly Sheffield, Daphne Dewhurst and Maureen Summers. That then leaves Katie Tibbs, our copy typist.'

'I'll catch up with them as the inspection progresses,' Parker said, putting away his notebook and standing up. Then, like a caged tiger, he started to pace back and forth on his side of the desk, before returning to sit on the edge of his chair. Foregoing his previous sprawl, he leaned forward intently, his eyes locked on David's.

'You were right,' he said, 'earlier on. I wouldn't normally deal with staff matters so soon. I ought to be outside, helping my lads count all that cash. But... and this must remain confidential between the two of us, you understand?'

David nodded. What on earth was this all about?

'We believe,' Parker continued, 'Head Office, I'm talking about – we believe that something's going on down here in Barnmouth... something untoward.'

'Untoward?' David could not disguise his surprise, and concern, at such a pronouncement. The arrival of inspectors was bad enough at the best of times, but the last thing he expected, or wanted, was an additional agenda.

'You'll appreciate I can't say anything more at the moment. In fact, there's little more I can say. But if, indeed, something untoward is happening down here, it could well involve the bank and your customers, never mind your staff.'

'I can't believe that...'

Parker held his hand up. 'Say no more. There might be nothing in it, anyway. But I have to know, as soon as possible, everything about your business – and about everyone involved with it. And that means everyone.'

CHAPTER 5

David did not know whether to be livid or disconcerted at Parker's attitude, while his parting shot was most disquieting. Everyone? He tried to concentrate on his driving as he turned his Hillman Minx from the cliff-top coastal road into the mud-strewn single-track country lane that led to the cosy hamlet of Leigh-in-Barnhead. At this time of year, it seemed even narrower than usual, the high hedgerows still awaiting their pre-winter shear. He winced as the wet red Devon soil splattered the sides of the car; it would no longer resemble the pristine two-tone model he had bought last month.

Despite its white top and pale-blue body giving the car a feminine air, he much preferred its compactness to his previous tank-like Morris Oxford. But he still retained a sentimental attachment to the Oxford, his first-ever car, and having sold it to a local garage, he enjoyed seeing its new owner driving it around the town.

He would have to endure the muddy lane for about half a mile as it meandered down to the village, one of four routes from opposite compass points. In the rainy season – much of the year in Devon – he often felt the lanes resembled raging rivers as they converged to create havoc in the village centre. Sandbags featured prominently in doorways, but the main problem for the Royal House Inn related to its thatched roof. He was aware of three serious fires, the latest two years ago caused by a stray firework. Since then, the village council had banned fireworks in Leigh and bonfire-night revellers now had to travel to Barnmouth.

Sarah had not spoken throughout the journey, her vexation matching his, but for different reasons. Arriving home at six-thirty, not as late as he had first feared, he had apologized profusely, but had failed dismally to lift the frost-laden atmosphere. Like most people, he rarely responded kindly to criticism – even when justified – but when it was unwarranted, he could be forthright in his response. Sarah's way was to clam up completely and then hum unrecognisable tunes through pursed lips as she busied herself around the house, insignificant tasks suddenly taking on monumental importance. It was so childish.

Now, beside him in the car, the humming had stopped and he was glad that her glacial stare was directed through the windscreen, rather than at him. At times like this, she seemed unable to accept his work responsibilities, but in lighter moments, she actually acknowledged his gentle ribbing that her own biggest responsibility rested on which hat to wear on which occasion. He was sure that this was not the time to resurrect that particular line.

As the car approached the bottom of the hill, they passed the village hall on the left and, on the right, the quaint tearooms that served hungry visitors delicious cream teas. He could not resist licking his lips just thinking about them. The Royal House Inn, standing resplendent under its latest thatched roof, then faced them at a T-junction, giving him the choice of turning left towards Torquay or right for Newton Abbot. He turned right and then immediately left into the car park, set between the back of the inn and the Norman church which overlooked the village from the south.

They entered the inn from the rear, David immediately getting into his routine of ducking carefully under each doorframe. At his height, he normally had no problems in doorways, but this old building had previously caught him unawares. Once inside, a wall of warmth hit them from the bar's roaring log fire. As much as anything, the aroma of burning apple wood attracted him to this particular hostelry and he immediately felt the tension easing from his body.

Low oak beams featured throughout the bar and into the adjacent restaurant area. Attached to them and to the complementary pillars built into the cob walls, an array of antique farming implements told the story of the agricultural heritage of the village. But a major feature for him and any respecter of fine ales was the line of porcelain handles, which drew a wide variety of brands from their casks.

Presiding over the bar, Charles, a big bear of a landlord, chatted animatedly to a group of dark-suited customers perched on high bar stools. Their sharp Cockney accents contrasted markedly with Charles's soft West Country burr, the overall effect being a far cry from the locals' dialects which David often had difficulty in deciphering. As soon as they walked in, Charles broke off his conversation and stepped forward to envelop Sarah as if she were a long-lost sister. Eventually, he let her go, grinned at David and pumped his hand enthusiastically.

'Glad to see you both again,' he said, then adding with a wink at Sarah, 'Although why you don't let Sarah come on her own, David, I'll never know.'

'On her own?' David echoed. 'With you lot down here? You must be joking.'

It never failed to amaze him how a modicum of flattery from another man could lift his wife's spirits while he, the one she had chosen to live with for the rest of her life, could cause such despair by arriving home a little late from the office. Now, the dancing flames from the fire reflected in her hazel eyes, which sparkled with a warmth that he hoped he might share once he was able to wrest her away from Charles's attention. Matching his own improved mood, the tension encasing her whole body appeared to be released like a broken spring and her changed demeanour reminded him of the first time he had met her in this very bar.

Eleven years ago, he had first noticed her lively eyes, but within minutes he had made an overall assessment of a young lady he knew he must get to know better. There was nothing angular about her: round face, cheeks and eyes radiating openness and honesty. A petite five-feet-two, her body curves complemented her facial features. He must, surely, have had some influence as now, so many years later, the only change he could see in her were added laughter lines stretching from her eyes to her ears which – he had previously failed to observe – now showed off the pearl droplets he had given her that morning. So, she could not really have been too cross with him as she prepared for their evening out.

Her eyes were still shining as they sat down at their table, but this time, they were directed at him. 'I do love you, really I do,' she whispered, out of earshot of a nearby couple. She then reached across the table to take his hand in hers. 'Happy anniversary, darling.'

In keeping with this new mood, he lifted her right hand to his lips and kissed it tenderly.

'Well, kind sir, we are being formal tonight,' she chided gently, then adding with a knowing grin, 'I hope you'll be able to do better than that later.'

At times like this, he could hardly believe how cross words ever passed between them. It did not happen often and disagreements were usually trivial. He could not recall experiencing a major marital crisis and most minor upsets arose at times of Sarah's frustration at being tied to the house and its attendant chores. But much of this was of her own making. She, too, had been enjoying a promising career with National Counties, but after Mark's birth, was adamant that her place was with him at home. When he turned five, she had tried to return to the bank, part-time, but they would have none of it, despite their previous high regard for her. They did offer full-time employment, but she refused, insisting on taking Mark to and from school, rather than entrusting him to others. David much admired her maternal principles, but deeply regretted that the bank's intransigence had resulted in her subsequent antipathy towards his employer. This often led her to believe that he had conflicting loyalties and it pained him that his assurances to the contrary could fall on deaf ears.

A waitress, clearly anxious to take their order, interrupted their good-spirited banter, even though he had still not organized their drinks. Monday evenings were never the busiest for eating out and perhaps she was hoping for an early night, but he was determined not to be rushed on this of all occasions, although with Dad babysitting, they would certainly not dally once the meal was over.

'First of all,' he said to the waitress, 'I think drinks are called for. And tonight it has to be champagne.'

After she had scuttled off, Sarah grasped his hand again. 'Have you had a pay rise? We've not had champagne in ages.'

'A special occasion with a special lady,' he replied, squeezing her hand before picking up a couple of menus for them to study.

The fare at the inn was straightforward English

cooking and he plumped for a medium-rare rump steak, while Sarah chose lamb chops. They decided that a bottle of Charles's house red would be a suitable accompaniment and he duly gave the waitress their order when she returned with two glasses of champagne.

'So,' Sarah said, after taking her first sip, 'it was a bad day at the office?'

'Um,' David grunted, replacing his flute on the table. 'It was all right until after lunch. Then things went from bad to worse.'

But he was reluctant to expand further. The convivial atmosphere of a pub was not the place to have a confidential discussion, especially with the other couple nearby. He was also conscious of the strangers at the bar and felt unnerved at the passing thought that they, not the inspection team, might have been the subjects of the police surveillance. He tried to overhear what they were talking about, but in the absence of Charles who had left them, they had their heads together in intimate conversation.

'I'll explain later,' he added, cocking a head to the other couple, although more concerned at the trend of his thoughts. 'But it seems that all might not be as it should be in Barnmouth. Anyway, you're the last person to want bank talk to interfere with our celebrations. Let's forget about it for the evening.'

'I'll drink to that,' Sarah replied, raising her glass. 'But I can't help worrying about your father babysitting.'

'Oh, he'll be all right. Mark will enjoy it.'

'Only because your Dad forgets to bed him down for the night. His memory's getting worse than ever. Surely he's not old enough to be getting senile?'

David shook his head. It seemed unlikely. 'I think he's just become terribly distracted – with life generally. And he's never got over Mum's death.'

'But that was six years ago,' Sarah replied, taking a sip of champagne just as the waitress returned with their bottle of wine. She waited as David declined to taste it, simply asking for it to be poured, before adding, 'I don't want to sound callous, but life must go on eventually.'

'Would you ever get over such a car crash? And he must still be feeling guilty.'

'But it wasn't his fault. Why should he feel guilty?'

'Because he got out of the car unscathed. I reckon that's how I'd feel if it happened to you and me.'

'Well, let's make sure it doesn't happen to us,' Sarah said, pointing at the bottle of wine. 'Perhaps I'd better drive home.'

But an hour-and-a-half later, he resisted that particular offer and took the wheel of the car. He felt fortunate that while he much preferred to drive, Sarah would normally opt for being driven. The only time when this arrangement failed was when they drove in unfamiliar territory and Sarah needed to navigate. It inevitably led him to stop, wrest the map from her grasp, turn it the right way up and try and memorise the remainder of the route to their destination. But it was not a problem this evening; the car could find its own way home from Leigh.

'What did you mean when you said things had gone from bad to worse?' Sarah asked when they were underway. 'You're not getting the push, are you?'

'Good heavens, no... well, I certainly hope not. On the other hand, you can never tell with inspectors. And I wouldn't put anything past this one. His name's Parker and he certainly has a nose for things. And talk about the third degree.'

'In what way?'

'He gave me a right grilling – about everyone in the branch. Then he dropped the bombshell: Head Office thinks there's something funny going on in Barnmouth. It could involve the bank – customers and staff. But that wasn't all, earlier on I had to bounce a couple of George Broadman's cheques.'

'You what? You can't do that. He's our butcher.'

'You sound just like Miss Harding. She said I'd be drummed out of Barnmouth – ruining the bank's reputation and all that. And then she had the nerve to say she'd no longer get the best cuts of meat.'

'I think she has a point. What made you bounce his cheques?'

'Because it's my job to do what's right,' he replied, not relishing what looked like becoming another interrogation. 'Let's change the subject. We don't want to spoil the evening. Anyway, we're home now.'

As he stopped the car in front of their house, he leant over to give Sarah a kiss and was relieved when she responded and then gave him a cheeky grin. But as she made to get out of the car, her smile vanished and she froze in her tracks.

'David, there's something wrong. There aren't any lights on. There's no way your Dad would have gone to bed yet. In any case he'd have left the lights on downstairs.'

He felt an ominous air of foreboding cut right through him as he opened his door and stepped into the road. And then he shivered involuntarily as he saw that the front door of their house stood wide open.

CHAPTER 6

He could almost smell the whiff of fear permeating the air as they rushed to the front door. Thoughts of accident, burglary, kidnapping – even death – transcended his mind, expunging all the pleasures of the evening. He knew his inner turmoil would not only be shared by Sarah, but be stretched to breaking point in her single-minded dash to Mark's bedroom.

Mark. Their only child. How they wished it otherwise, but it was not to be. It made their disquiet and parental feelings even more acute as they rushed into the house and flicked on the light to bathe the hall in welcome illumination. Sarah led their frantic way up the stairs, almost stumbling over the risers in her haste to get to Mark's bedroom. On reaching it, she paused at the door which stood slightly ajar. She glanced back at David as if to draw strength from him to enter the room and realize her worst fears. But he felt impotent to ease her anxiety as she pushed the door open. The light from the landing seeped into the room like a beam from a torch and fell on the candlewick counterpane that covered Mark's bed virtually from top to bottom. Sarah's gasp of relief instantly told him that she had discerned a tell-tale lump in the bed and he could now see that it was topped by an unruly mop of dark hair which adorned the fraction of pillow showing at the top of the bedspread. A snort and an asthmatic wheeze confirmed that all was well with the otherwise inert body and Sarah turned to collapse with relief into his arms.

But where was Dad? As they retraced their steps

downstairs, the somnolent house told him that not even a perfunctory search would be needed to establish his absence. It was not that it was normally a noisy house – Dad especially hated loud music – but it was odd not hearing his incessant wireless and mindless chatter, whether or not anyone was with him. It could be infuriating, particularly after a hard day's work. At such times, David had often despaired of the chance to relax to the dulcet sounds of his jazz heroes, Lester Young and Coleman Hawkins. On one occasion, he had even eschewed pangs of guilt by switching on his HMV stereogram and dropping the stylus on to Duke Ellington's rousing version of "Rockin' in Rhythm", later accepting that it had been an infantile attempt at getting his own back. Now he would relish the comfort of Dad's wireless and loquacity, rather than experience this ghost-like version of the family home.

'Where on earth has he got to?' Sarah demanded. 'There's no way he's going to babysit again.'

'Steady on, darling,' David replied, not normally prone to drawing such impulsive conclusions.

He had often thought it strange how two completely opposite temperaments could fashion a perfect union. Although he was a natural sceptic on astrology, he held a grudging respect for some aspects of the zodiac. Characteristics relating to his own birth sign of Cancer were the complete opposite of those associated with Sarah's Sagittarius. So many times he had used his water to douse her fire.

'Let's try to think about this rationally. There may be a good reason why he's not here. We were worried enough that Mark might have had an accident, so why not Dad?'

'But leaving Mark alone upstairs in bed? And there were

no lights on, never mind the front door being wide open.'

David put a comforting arm around her shoulders and led her to their Grieves and Thomas settee, a safe haven at times of stress. He was not sure that its baby-yellow colour rested easily against the maroon flock wallpaper they had inherited when they bought the house, but following the opening of a Chinese restaurant in the town, he had made a mental note that if anything had to be changed in the lounge, it would be the wallpaper. As he drew her to him on the settee, he stretched behind him to put on the standard lamp, hoping that the added illumination might shed some light on their problem.

'We must call the police,' Sarah urged.

'The police? But it's only ten o'clock – and we're talking about a grown man. They'd hardly be interested, especially with no sign of an accident.'

'What else can we do?' Sarah protested. 'At least we must report he's missing. We've got to do something, David.'

'Okay, okay,' he replied, getting up to go to the telephone, grateful that they did have one recently installed. 'It's just that I don't want us to appear stupid. It could be a wild goose chase. And you know he's been acting strangely recently. That's why you were concerned about him baby-sitting.'

When he got through, he gave the police a rundown of events, still thinking that it sounded thin, but the duty officer took it very seriously and pressed him on many points. He needed to know the estimated time of Dad's disappearance, his likely movements, what he was wearing and his present state of mind. David became increasingly concerned on being then asked further questions. Did Dad have any health worries? Were there difficulties at home?

Had he any financial problems? Was he suffering from depression? Several minutes later, he put the telephone down and returned to Sarah, his face ashen.

'There's been a terrible accident,' he said, drawing her close to him, needing every ounce of her support. 'They're coming round to see us. They're anxious about anyone who's missing. They've just discovered a vehicle on the rocks – smashed to bits. It seems it went over the cliff.'

'Oh, my God!' Sarah exclaimed.

'But it can't possibly be Dad. He's never driven since the accident. And how would he have got hold of a car?'

'When did it happen?' Sarah asked, drawing back and looking at him intently. 'This evening? But they wouldn't have found the wreckage until the morning – when it's light. So, it can't be your father.'

'They don't know when it happened, but they've found the wreckage. A fishing boat crew saw it glinting in the moonlight. There must have been a break in the clouds. But I still don't see how...'

He stopped short as they both heard the familiar creak of the sitting room door being opened behind them. As one, they swung round to face the incomer.

'What's going on?' Mark asked, rubbing sleep from his eyes. 'You weren't having a row, were you?'

'Of course not, darling,' Sarah replied, getting up and gathering him into her arms, before returning to rejoin David on the settee. 'It's just that we have a problem – with Grandpa. We don't know where he's got to. And he might have been in an accident.'

'What sort of accident?' Mark asked. 'He only said he was going out to look for the black baby.'

'The black baby?' they exclaimed in unison, David then adding, 'What on earth are you talking about?'

'I don't know,' Mark answered, starting to cry. 'That's all he said and then he put the light out.'

'All right, all right, darling,' Sarah soothed, using her hanky to dry Mark's eyes and cheeks. 'It's just that we don't know where he is. But let's get you back upstairs to bed. We'll get it all sorted out in the morning.'

As she took Mark to his bedroom, David could hardly share her optimism. What did Dad mean by looking for a black baby? He was becoming increasingly bizarre. Was it his memory? He remembered a previous infamous lapse when Dad had actually asked Sarah who she was and had she come in to do the cleaning. Her pithy response was hardly worthy of someone of her intelligence. It had certainly been disconcerting, leading to an early appointment with the doctor. He found nothing physically wrong, suggesting it was probably psychological – following the car crash. His parting shot was that "he'll get over it eventually".

But that had not yet happened. Instead, he had almost reverted to childhood, the most infantile things amusing him. And his inability to concentrate only matched his complete lack of organization. Then there was his inane chattering and, for some reason, he had developed an infatuation for Elvis Presley, of all people. David could hardly believe that Dad could idolize the so-called king of rock and roll, especially as he had acquired an aversion to noise, and loud music in particular.

Sarah came down the stairs and joined him on the settee. 'Mark's fine. He's sleeping like a baby. After I'd assured him all would be well, he just smiled at me, nestled his head in the pillow and was off. As for me, I can't even contemplate sleep. What are we going to do now?'

'Wait for the police, I suppose,' he replied, knowing

that neither of them felt like sitting around doing nothing. 'I just don't understand what Dad could have meant when he told Mark he was going out to look for the black baby. Has he gone off his rocker? But even if he has, I can't believe he'd get in a car and drive it over a cliff.'

They drifted into a contemplative silence, as if fearful of airing further speculation, but their reverie was broken by the sound of a car stopping outside.

'That must be the police,' David said, getting up and moving into the hallway to let them in. On opening the front door, he faced a tall uniformed officer and another figure standing behind.

'Good evening, sir,' the policeman said, before stepping aside and adding, 'I think I have the answer to your problem.'

'Dad!' David gasped, as his father moved forward sheepishly.

'We found him wandering up the High Street,' the policeman said. 'Then your call came through and we put two and two together.'

At that, Sarah came rushing to the door. On seeing her father-in-law, she was unable to contain an outburst of pent-up emotion. 'Where the hell have you been? How dare you leave Mark on his own with the front door wide open? Haven't you any sense of responsibility? You'll never ever babysit again.'

'Hang on, Sarah,' David interrupted, putting an arm around her, if only to restrain her. 'There'll be plenty of time for that. Let's get him inside and find out what happened.'

'Well, I'll leave you to it,' the policeman said. 'No point in my getting involved in a domestic wrangle.'

'No, wait a minute,' David said. He needed to know

what Dad had been up to. 'What was he actually doing?'

'As I said, just wandering around – as though he was looking for something. But when we first saw him, he was singing...'

'Singing?'

'Yes, and giving a pretty fair impression of that American – the one who's all the rage these days.'

'You mean Elvis?' David groaned. There could be nobody else.

'Yes, that's the one,' the policeman agreed, clearly bemused at some of the goings-on in Barnmouth.

'Heartbreak Hotel,' the old man interrupted, giggling like a schoolboy. 'I'm sorry, David, but I didn't realize anyone was around – let alone a policeman.'

'You never know where we might be lurking,' the policeman said, good-naturedly, then added, 'I'll be off then. At least he's home now, so don't be too hard on him. He hasn't done any harm, just appears to be totally confused.'

David gritted his teeth as he closed the door. You can say that again. But what a relief that it was not Dad who had driven over the cliff, not that Sarah, from the look in her eyes, seemed to be harbouring such thoughts.

'Well?' she demanded, as they moved into the sitting room. 'No harm done? There but for the grace of God. What possessed you to leave Mark like that?'

'I'm sorry. I didn't think.'

'You can say that again! How old are you? And you haven't got an ounce of responsibility in you.'

As her voice rose, David watched his father cringe at her verbal onslaught and recalled doing the same as a small boy when he had upset his parents. He decided the time had come to show some compassion; Dad was clearly not in full control of his faculties. But before he could do so, Dad raised his hands in the air, as if by way of surrender.

'I'm so sorry,' he said, his eyes pleading for forgiveness. 'I don't know what's wrong with me. One moment I seem to be all right and then I'm doing something irrational.' Pausing, he clenched his right hand into a fist and tapped his forehead in frustration. 'Of course I shouldn't have left Mark. But when I go off like that, I can't seem to get my mind round two things at once. I decide to do something and everything else seems irrelevant. I'm so, so sorry.'

His contrition clearly struck home with Sarah who visibly relaxed. She placed her arms around him and led him to the settee where they sat down together. She rocked him to and fro as though he were a child and tears trickled down her cheeks. She attempted to say something, but the words remained choked in her throat.

'Don't worry, Dad,' David said for them both. 'It's over now. Let's get you upstairs to bed. A decent night's sleep will do you the power of good.'

Twenty minutes later, he poured out a couple of whiskies and handed one to Sarah as they sat down in relief. 'Happy anniversary, darling. What an evening!'

'You can say that again,' Sarah replied, before leaning across to kiss him gently on the lips. 'I'm so sorry I got cross, but...'

'Don't worry about it. You had every right to. The thing is, what do we do now?'

'Go to the doctor – as soon as possible. Do you think your father's losing his mind? Would the doctor know about such things? Or is it a job for a psychiatrist?'

'Questions, questions. I don't know the answer to any of them. He's become so bizarre. As for this business of looking for a baby – let alone Elvis Presley...'

He stopped in his tracks, mulling over the words of Presley's hit record.

'What's wrong, darling?' Sarah asked, frowning.

'I don't know. Probably nothing. But why did he pick that particular song – Heartbreak Hotel? I've just been going over the opening line. Could it be significant?

'I don't know. I haven't a clue about the words.'

'I'm sure it starts with "Since my baby left me..." That can't be linked to that black baby business, surely?'

CHAPTER 7

Jane Church was at her desk by seven-thirty the next morning. A few minutes earlier, she had clearly shocked a bemused Mrs Smithers, the office cleaner, who would normally have completed her duties before the arrival of any staff.

'Hello, my love,' Mrs Smithers had exclaimed when she opened the front door. 'Why are you here so early?'

'I've so much to do,' Jane replied, with a sigh. 'What with the inspectors and...'

'Inspectors?' Mrs Smithers interrupted, closing the door behind them once they were inside. 'I didn't know they were here.'

'Didn't know?' Of course, Mrs Smithers only worked mornings. 'They arrived yesterday afternoon. So make sure you open the front door with the chain, and check their credentials. Poor old Roger got it in the neck when he let them in without a why or a wherefore. He was so unlucky. Jilly had just popped out for some stamps and he thought it was her coming back.' She could not help but grin. 'Instead, there were these men in dark overcoats and with hats down over their eyes. He thought they were raiders. He'd never heard of inspectors – after all, he's only been in the bank a few weeks.'

'I'll be gone by the time they arrive. They won't be up at the crack of dawn.'

'Don't you believe it,' Jane replied. 'They're probably sussing us out this very minute.'

She got on well with Mrs Smithers. It was as if the

cleaner, now in her late sixties, understood her insecurity, even though her role as manager's assistant should have suggested otherwise. It was only later she had learnt that they lived on the same council estate and, unbeknown to her at the time, Mrs Smithers had, apparently, admired the way she had worked hard to achieve a worthwhile job, despite the taunts and jibes from her peers on the estate. It was strange that now, four years after leaving school with her three A levels, those same youngsters held her in genuine esteem, several of them having confessed that they wished they had worked harder at school to get some meaningful occupation. To give them credit, she knew that some of them had even enrolled at night school to try and make up for lost time.

But this episode had severely affected her self-confidence, not helped by her entry into the world of white-collar workers. It had been far easier to relate to Mrs Smithers than to some of the so-called professional people employed in the bank.

Strangely enough, despite blushing profusely whenever he spoke to her, she had more affinity with Mr Goodhart than with some of the others in the office. He still tended to unnerve her – after all, he was the manager – but at least he had no airs and graces, unlike Bernard Groves and Miss Harding – arrogant pair. How dare they make her feel so inferior! If only she had the nerve to hit back. But better to keep out of their way, although this was not easy in such a small office. It had been different in Torquay where she had started in the bank. With over forty staff, it was not hard to avoid people who worked in different sections. But it was all rather claustrophobic in Barnmouth.

That was why she wanted an early start this morning, without the distraction of others as she tackled the task set for her by Mr Goodhart. The arrival of the inspectors had thwarted her yesterday, but she had spent time in the strongroom to scrutinize the old ledgers covering Mr Broadman's account. Mr Goodhart had asked her to go back three months, but she had become intrigued and decided to investigate further back than that.

The ledgers had to remain locked in the strongroom overnight, but she had recorded numerous entries on to long day sheets and would now check these with the actual vouchers which were kept in her locked drawers in the general office. Doing this before other staff arrived meant she would be able to spread out the vouchers and be finished before the others came in.

The previous afternoon, she had established that the cheque for £300, which had caused the manager so much concern, was part of a pattern. During the last six months, there had been over fifty cheques in round amounts, in the sums of £100 to £500. They totalled over £20,000 and appeared to be completely unrelated to the innumerable other cheques passing through the account – presumably the normal outgoings of the shop. But why, on each occasion, was there a credit for the same amount being passed through the account a day or two before? It meant that, despite the amounts involved, the account had never become overdrawn. But no such credit had preceded yesterday's cheque for £300 and an overdraft would have arisen if Mr Goodhart had paid it.

She had spent much of last evening speculating about what had been going on and was eager to get the voucher drawers unlocked in order to examine the respective cheques and credit slips. It was good that Mr Goodhart had entrusted her with the job, especially after her stupidity yesterday at not being able to answer his simple questions. Of course she had known the procedure for cashing cheques, so why had she got so flustered? It was always the same – and so stupid. Anyway, he must have confidence in her to do this investigation and she must justify his faith in her.

But how could it possibly be Mr Broadman's account under investigation? In only her short time at the branch, she knew him to be one of Barnmouth's most prominent citizens. His shop was a hive of activity, customers drawn to it because of his fine cuts of meat and also through his larger-than-life personality. As he wielded his knives and saws, he laughed and joked and did everything to encourage his customers to return. And how he buttered up the women, charming them with his good looks and bonhomie. They fell for him completely and it was disconcerting that he even trespassed on her own feelings.

She felt unnerved at her vulnerability – and naivety. Her only experience with the opposite sex had been a cinema visit with a distant cousin – arranged by her mother. How humiliating! She had been far happier doing her studying and did not need her mother to engineer a social life for her. In any case, what boy would have wanted to take out such a gawky, bespectacled stick-insect specimen? No, far better to withdraw into her shell and not harbour any interest in the male species.

And then Mr Broadman entered her world – if only its fringes. As she unlocked the drawers of the desks, she felt a stirring inside her, quite alien to anything she had previously experienced. She needed steely concentration to rid herself of the feelings as she studied the cheques and credit slips which had passed through the butcher's account.

She soon established that the round-amount cheques were either payable to cash or to someone called Jack

Stringer. Bearing in mind Mr Goodhart's admonition yesterday, she scrupulously examined the front and back of each cheque payable to cash, but on no occasion was there evidence of actual encashment. The only marking was the crossing-stamp on the front: the rubber-stamped impression of the bank through which the cheque had been presented. There were only three such banks: Barclays in Exeter, the District in Plymouth and the Chagford branch of National Counties.

She spread the cheques out on the desk like playing cards, immediately thinking of the butcher as her playing partner. She blushed from the roots at the thought and was relieved that no one was around to see her. She took out her cotton handkerchief to wipe her face in a futile attempt to cool down. Did the man have the same effect on all his women customers? And that was a puzzle, how had he remained single? Why had be chosen to remain single? No, this was nonsense. What was coming over her? She would next be speculating on whether he had a particular lady friend. Concentration on the job in hand was clearly called for.

The prime question was why so many cheques payable to cash had been paid into those three banks and into whose accounts? And what about the cheques payable to Jack Stringer? Once again, each one had been paid into the same banks in Exeter, Plymouth and Chagford. But who was Jack Stringer? It was not a name known to her, but why should it be? She did not know anyone who lived in those three places. He might be another trader, but that was hardly likely bearing in mind the amounts involved. In any case, Mr Broadman's main dealings would be through his wholesaler, Good Meat Supplies.

It was extremely baffling and she switched her attention to the credits. The first thing she noticed was that they were all coloured white, not pink, meaning that they had been paid in at Barnmouth – rather than through other banks. Many of the credits clearly related to the shop's takings, but the ones in round amounts always corresponded with Mr Broadman's own cheques and were paid in one or two days beforehand.

What was it all about? There was only one thing to do – refer everything to Mr Goodhart as soon as he arrived at the bank. Gathering the cheques and credits into separate piles, she clipped them together in the order they were annotated on the day sheets and awaited the arrival of her manager.

CHAPTER 8

The aroma from sizzling fried bacon still filled the air as David replaced his knife and fork on the plate and smacked his lips together in satisfaction at the splendour of Sarah's cooked breakfast. What a treat! It was normally cereals and toast on weekdays, but Sarah had forewarned him that lunch might not be forthcoming today. Everything depended on how she and Dad got on with the doctor. She was on the telephone now, trying to make an appointment. He yawned as he awaited the outcome.

The last twenty-four hours had not been conducive to a good night's sleep. Dad, George Broadman and Parker had all conspired to feed his insomnia. He would not normally succumb to such influences, his war service having trained him to banish extraneous thoughts for the benefit of proper rest. But this was different. What had caused Parker to say that something untoward was going on in town? And could it be linked to George Broadman? Surely not. Yet what was the butcher up to on his account? But work was one thing; Dad's behaviour had been something else. It was a family problem, affecting them all. No wonder he had not slept well.

Mark clearly had other things on his mind as he sidled up to him, clasping his arms affectionately around his neck. 'Saturday will never come,' he bemoaned. 'Do you think we'll beat Southend?'

'I don't see why not. They'll probably be tired from the long journey.'

'Long journey?'

'They're from the other side of London. But I was only kidding. They'll probably come down on Friday and stay overnight.'

He was delighted that Mark now shared his infatuation with Torquay United. They had attended every home game this season and had not yet seen the team lose. How different from previous seasons. The improved fortunes seemed to stem from the arrival of one new player – Don Mills, a record signing from Leeds United – and even promotion was now being mooted. But this Saturday would be different – they had been invited to watch the match from the directors' box.

'Anyway, young man,' he continued, releasing himself from Mark's grip and standing up, 'shouldn't you be on your way to school?'

'I'm waiting for Mum. She's on the telephone.'

At that, Sarah came into the room. 'Twelve noon,' she confirmed. 'The doctor couldn't make it earlier, but that suits me fine – I've so much housework to do. I doubt if I'll be back in time to get you lunch.'

'That's all right. I'll get a sandwich. I only hope the doctor comes up with something positive. Make sure he gives Dad a thorough examination. And tell him everything about last night. And don't forget to say...'

'All right, all right, darling,' Sarah interrupted, 'just leave it to me. I've lived with your father long enough to know exactly what to say to the doctor.'

'I know, but...'

'Darling! Don't worry. Just get off to work and I'll ring you when I get back.'

Suitably relieved at Sarah's unfailing efficiency, David donned his overcoat, kissed Sarah and Mark goodbye and stepped outside. He immediately groaned at finding the weather little better than yesterday, but straightaway a black Bentley swept by him. He had to skip smartly from the kerb to prevent his trousers getting soaked, but the car then glided to a halt a little way ahead.

Only one person in Barnmouth owned and could probably afford such a car – Stuart Brown, senior partner of Ducksworth, Brown and Sargeant, the solicitors next door to the bank. David's high regard for the man was tempered somewhat by the flaunting of his ostentatious wealth, but it was not enough to outweigh his natural charm and legal prowess. The man was also a star for stopping to give him a lift on this foul November morning.

As he reached the vehicle, Brown beckoned him to get into the front of the car. 'Morning, David,' he said, as he scrambled inside and slid on to the sumptuous leather seat, even more comfortable than his favourite armchair at home. 'I know you like your walk, but on a morning like this?'

David smiled in relief at being given a lift. 'You can say that again. This storm's going on forever.'

He snuggled his shoes into the car's deep-pile carpet and could hardly hear the engine as Brown engaged first gear and moved the vehicle towards the town. Even the wipers were silent as they cleared the windscreen, a far cry from the rubbers of his old Oxford which protested noisily at a task that was often beyond them. No, Brown had every right to enjoy the trappings of his wealth, even if this could border on pretentiousness, as with his predilection for a personalized number plate. David could empathize with his choice of number one, often envying such owners when he and Mark played their regular "spot the number" game on journeys, but when Brown had bemoaned the unavailability of the accompanying letters SOL or LAW, this was taking his grandeur too far. In the end, unable to obtain a plate bearing his own initial, SB, presumably because it bore only two letters rather than the normal three, Brown had managed to acquire a plate depicting the initials of his wife, Barbara Anne. Many townsfolk cynically believed this to be a sop to his spouse, rumour having it that she was the prime source of their immense wealth.

'Your timing's impeccable, Stuart,' David added, as they got under way. 'If I'd stopped to give Sarah a lingering kiss...'

'More fool you,' Brown interrupted, smiling wickedly. 'But if you choose to shun such a lovely lady...'

David grinned, not surprised at the response, Brown having a reputation for a roving eye. Many believed that, despite an apparently stable marriage, he had achieved several extra-marital conquests in the town, not least with last year's lady captain at the golf club when, after a winning partnership in a foursomes' competition, it developed into a cosy twosome following the evening's prize-giving.

Ladies of all ages seemed to succumb to Brown's easy-going charm and good looks. Perhaps it was envy on David's part, but he never deemed him to be a man's man; he was too effeminate for that. His hair was a shade too blond and wavy; his skin a mite too soft and downy; while his pale blue eyes emitted delicacy rather than strength. That said, he coveted Brown's sporting prowess, which included a golf handicap of twelve and the ability to play an impressive set of tennis despite being in his fifties. He was also a director of Torquay United Football Club and it was at his invitation that they would join the directors at Saturday's match. But David was especially conscious of Brown's standing in the business community, something he fostered for the benefit of National Counties.

'Make sure you get involved with the professionals,' his regional manager had urged on his appointment to Barnmouth branch. 'They're such a good influence on your profits, not just as a source of new business, but also for the credit balances held on behalf of their clients.'

That was certainly true. Without credit balances, he would have no money to lend out, unless he went cap in hand to head office, a far less profitable way to finance his operations. So he had striven to nurture the accountants and solicitors, of which Brown's firm was the largest and most reputable in town.

'I hope the storm clears up for the match on Saturday,' Brown said, as they passed along roads lined with horse chestnuts, sycamores and flowering cherries. The trees had long lost their leaves and now limbs, torn shoots and twigs adorned the roads and pavements like shrapnel dispersed across a petrified battleground. 'And for the golf on Thursday.'

'I might not be able to make the golf. The inspectors arrived yesterday.'

'But it's the Turkey Trot. You can't miss that.'

That might normally be so, but golf was hardly high priority in this of all weeks. He had far more important issues to deal with, not least Parker. His likely reaction to such time out of the office needed little imagination.

'Is this your first inspection?' Brown asked, as if reading his mind.

David nodded. 'That's why I'm doubtful about the golf.'

'Your inspection's nothing to do with this terrible business about George Broadman?'

'George Broadman?' David jerked his head round to

stare at Brown, hardly able to comprehend the solicitor's words. 'What's happened to George?'

'Haven't you heard? It seems he's driven his van over the cliffs – at the car park between here and Torquay.'

'Oh my God! I'd heard something about that last night. But I'd no idea it was...'

'I suppose we mustn't jump to conclusions, but why would George do a thing like that? He was always so hale and hearty. A good customer, wasn't he?'

'Mm,' David simply answered, nodding his head, but not wishing to start discussing a customer's standing, even with Brown who was well versed in matters of confidentiality. But why had Brown waited so long into their journey before telling him about George? It should have been his first topic of conversation. How odd.

'Couldn't it have been an accident?' he asked, trying to gauge Brown's reaction to an event that would shock the whole of Barnmouth. And what about yesterday's bounced cheques? Were they linked to George's death?

'Seems unlikely. Why else would he have gone to that car park? Particularly at this time of year – and on such a wild day.'

They sat in contemplative silence until they reached their offices. Brown then drove the car into the narrow alley that ran between the buildings to the small car park at the rear, where he parked between a Morris Minor and a Ford Prefect. 'Not a good start to the day,' he said, breaking the silence. 'But later on, I'd like to come and see you about another matter. There's some new business I want to put your way.'

Even the continuing shock of George Broadman's death could not stifle a twinge of excitement at such a prospect. Brown was so supportive of the bank and even if many of his clients operated in London, he still liked their banking business to be domiciled in Barnmouth. 'I'll look forward to that. Perhaps we could speak on the phone to fix a time. I'm not sure how my day will pan out with the inspectors.'

As they parted company, he reflected on this latest turn of events. He could hardly grasp what might have happened to George Broadman and whether it might be linked to yesterday's doings. No one had warned him that banking could be like this and he could do without the problems now besetting him – including Dad's strange antics.

Casting aside thoughts of Sarah's noon appointment with the doctor, he reached the front door and rang the bell. As he waited, he heard the chain being put in place on the other side. The door then eased ajar to reveal Roger Singleton, clearly anxious to identify the caller. That done, he released the chain and David entered the bank, almost bumping into Mrs Smithers, who was making to leave after her cleaning shift. 'Hello, Mrs Smithers. Another half-day, eh?'

'Get away with you, dear,' Mrs Smithers replied, clearly enjoying the teasing she often received about her hours of work, even though everyone was well aware that each evening she also cleaned the offices of the solicitors and accountants next door.

After further such banter, David was still smiling as he reached his room. Although he had only known the cleaner for a couple of years, he thought the world of her. He could not imagine a more considerate and helpful person to work with – an opinion he knew his staff also shared.

He had only just time to sit at his desk and unlock its

drawers before there was a knock on the door and Jane inched into the room, trying not to drop a bundle of files and vouchers in her grasp.

'For goodness' sake, Jane, do come in – and be careful with that lot.' He had no wish to see his carpet covered with confetti, but before getting involved with her work, he recounted what he had heard from Stuart Brown.

'Do you think it could have been suicide?' she asked, suppressing a sob and fumbling at the sleeve of her cardigan to retrieve a handkerchief. 'I'm sorry, sir,' she then continued, 'it's just that I've never encountered a death like this before. And what with this business with his account. I've been checking his ledger sheets and vouchers and all the time he must have been dead...'

Her voice tailed off as tears now tumbled down her cheeks. David stretched a comforting hand across the desk and was struck by her vulnerability as he took her limp hand in his. But why not? The younger generation might give the appearance of being mature and worldly-wise – not that this applied to Jane – but they were still children at heart.

'Thank you, sir,' she then said, letting go of his hand and slipping her handkerchief up her sleeve, having wiped her cheeks dry. 'I'm fine now. It's just that...'

David put his hand up in front of him, like the command of a traffic policeman. 'Say no more. It's never easy – this sort of thing. But we'd better get on. What have you found out about George's account?'

CHAPTER 9

He watched Jane carefully as she focused her attention on the cheques and credits that she had placed in separate piles on his desk. She then extracted from a file a number of day sheets that he could see had been annotated with innumerable dates and amounts.

He remained silent and was quietly impressed with the methodical way she had set out her stall. It was patently clear that she had spent considerable time on the task he had only set her the previous afternoon – exactly the response he would expect from an ambitious personal assistant. Perhaps Jane had more about her than he had previously thought, or was she at last blossoming into the role selected for her by the staff controller?

'I've done what you asked,' she said when she was ready to proceed. 'This first pile of cheques relates to Mr Broadman's normal day-to-day business transactions and the others are his round-amount cheques. And I've also dug out his credit slips because they follow a similar pattern.' She frowned before adding, 'But it doesn't make any sense to me.'

'Let's have a look at these first,' David answered, picking up the first stack of cheques and flicking through them quickly. 'Normal trade cheques: Good Meat Supplies, electricity, gas, rent. Nothing strange here – apart from the wholesaler's cheques being in round sums.'

'Yes, but now look at the next lot,' Jane countered, her voice choking slightly as she handed him the pile of round-amount cheques, all of which she pointed out were payable to cash or to Jack Stringer.

He studied the top cheque, which was dated six months ago. It was payable to cash, for £200, and the crossing stamp impressed on the front was that of the Chagford branch of National Counties. He turned the cheque over, but the reverse was blank.

He looked up, his brow furrowed in concentration, but stopped short of posing the question on his lips. Jane had slumped back in her chair and sat staring vacantly at the wall behind him. When she had entered the room, he had hardly noticed she was wearing her normal dowdy straight skirt and matching woollen cardigan, but he was now shocked that her face had become as grey as her attire.

'Jane? I seem to have lost you. Are you feeling all right?'

She gave no impression that she had heard him, but after a few moments, her brown eyes drew away from the wall and registered with his. He immediately knew that her glistening pupils signalled further tears and he foresaw the need for the pristine white handkerchief he kept for such occasions in the right-hand top drawer of his desk.

'Jane?' he repeated, hoping that she would still be able to control her emotions.

'I'm sorry... I'm sorry, sir,' she eventually stuttered. 'It's just that...'

'All right, all right,' he answered gently and, for the second time in such a short while, instinctively stretched his hand across the desk to take one of her hands in his. It was disconcertingly cold, despite the radiators pumping out sufficient heat to counteract the raw morning.

'It's just that this is all so frightening. We're looking at Mr Broadman's cheques as if we're going to have to get him in to explain...'

Her words tailed off as tears started to fall down her cheeks, depositing themselves on her cardigan like early morning dew settling on turf. Handkerchief time had arrived and he took it from the drawer, handing it to Jane who removed her steel-rimmed spectacles to dab her eyes with the soft cotton fabric. At that, there was a sharp knock on the door.

'Not just now,' he called out, not wanting Jane to be embarrassed. 'Come back in five minutes.'

'I'm so sorry,' Jane then said, smiling rather wistfully. 'That was really kind of you. I think I'm all right now.'

'We'd certainly better get on,' he replied, concerned that George Broadman's demise had caused her such distress. 'What with the day's work out there – and not forgetting the inspectors.'

'That might have been them at the door,' Jane suggested.

'I hope not,' he answered. Had he been too curt with the caller? But putting that thought behind him, he sifted through the round-amount cheques and the related credit slips and pursed his lips as he realized what had been going on. But before he could draw Jane into his confidence, there was a further knock on the door. 'Come in,' he called out.

The door eased open and Katie Tibbs hesitantly entered the room, a shorthand notebook and sharpened pencil clasped in her hands.

'Good morning, Katie,' he said, giving the young typist a welcoming smile. 'Was that you who knocked before?'

'Yes, sir,' she answered, beaming brightly. 'I just wanted to know when you would like to give me some work.'

'You, Katie? What's happened to Miss Harding?'

'Oh, didn't you know?' the young girl answered, glancing almost conspiratorially at Jane and then back at him, her hazel eyes alive with excitement. He had always considered her to be a pretty girl, but particularly so this morning, the glow of her round dimpled cheeks almost matching her long auburn hair which cascaded down the back of her well-filled red jumper. In other circumstances, he might have found her presence distracting. 'I'd already arrived before Miss Harding came in. That's unusual for me because you know she's always having a go at me for my timekeeping. But I've much further to come than her and she doesn't have to rely on buses. Anyway, I'd got my coat off and was tidying myself up when...'

'Oh, do get on with it, Katie,' he urged. What a chatterbox; he could well do without it this morning.

'I'm sorry, sir. I just thought that... Anyway, Miss Harding breezes in and then Bernard calls her over and whispers something in her ear. She then rushes to the cloakroom all of a dither like, so I went in after her to see if she was all right. There she was with her head over the washbasin, taking some tablets. She said she had a terrible migraine and would have to go home. She told me I'd have to do your shorthand. It was such a shock. Well, I've never done your work before and my shorthand's not really up to it. But I'm trying to improve with my classes, so I hope you'll understand and...'

'Katie! I'm more bothered about Miss Harding than your shorthand. You mean she's gone home already?'

Katie nodded.

'Then I must give her a ring. She might be all right by this afternoon, so we'll leave any dictation until then. You just get on with your own work for now.'

When she had gone, he shook his head at Jane in mock

71

despair. 'Whatever next? Did you know Miss Harding had gone home?'

'No. I was in here with you before she arrived.'

'Anyway, I want you to start looking at today's work. Examine the clearings for any more of George Broadman's cheques. I know what he's been up to. He's been cross-firing.'

'Crossfiring? What on earth's that?'

'It's something we should have picked up long ago. But it looks as though we've got away with it – unlike those other banks.'

'But this crossfiring – what exactly is it?'

'It's a con,' he replied. 'A con – by people taking advantage of the banks' clearing system. And it can be extremely sophisticated. But let me put it to you simply. A customer has accounts at two different banks and he draws a cheque on one which he pays into the other – let's say for £1,000.'

'But there's nothing wrong with that, surely?'

'Hang on a minute. Be patient. So, he now has a balance of £1,000 at the second bank and he withdraws this in cash. In the meantime, he had already drawn a similar cheque on that account and paid it into the first bank to cover his original cheque. He then goes through that same rigmarole again, probably over and over again.'

'But what's the point?' Jane asked, clearly puzzled.

'That £1,000 in cash is the point. He has that amount in his pocket, but neither of his accounts shows he's over-drawn. Technically he's overdrawn because the cheques going back and forth aren't cleared funds. But the accounts never actually go into the red.'

'So why do the banks let him do it?'

'Because they're lulled into a false sense of security by

the apparent respectability of the customer. They can't believe that he would do anything underhand.'

'Someone like Mr Broadman?'

'Exactly.'

'So what should the banks have done?'

'They shouldn't have allowed the cash withdrawal until the original cheque had been cleared – three days later.'

'I think I've got it,' Jane said, though still looking puzzled, 'but it seems a palaver to go through for £1,000.'

'But that's only a simple example I was giving you. Much more complicated systems would net crossfirers huge amounts of ill-gotten gains – provided the banks don't have their eyes open. But it only needs one bank to act properly for the whole deck of cards to come crashing down. And if I'm right, that bank was us yesterday.'

'Yesterday?'

'Yes, George Broadman's cheque for £300 – the one payable to cash. It follows the pattern of all his other round-amount cheques. But on this occasion, a credit hadn't been paid into his account beforehand to cover it. Maybe it got delayed, so I wouldn't mind betting it's in today – possibly with others. Off you go then. Search the cheque and credit clearings and anywhere else for that matter. Look for any transactions ready to go through George's account. If you find anything at all, come back to me, post-haste.'

Now on his own, he took a deep breath and realized that the palms of his hands were moist. It was a lucky escape. Had he fallen down on his job? It seemed so if George Broadman had, indeed, been crossfiring. It was the sort of thing Parker would pick up in his inspection, but with no money lost, any criticism ought to be muted.

He sat there for several minutes contemplating the

events of the morning, now empathizing with Jane's difficulty in rationalizing the activity on George's account with his untimely death. How could such a thing happen to a man so well known in the town? What could have made him drive his van over the cliff? He shuddered at the thought of it. He had only known the butcher for two years, but the man had been long established in the town and was apparently liked and respected by everyone. Yet why should he be involved in crossfiring? As for Miss Harding, why had she not told him herself that she had a migraine? It was all very odd, but he felt certain he would not have to wait long before Jane returned and, sure enough, a knock on the door announced her arrival, breathing hard from her exertions.

'Look at this lot!' she exclaimed, depositing a pile of vouchers on his desk. 'There's over £3,000 and the credits should have been on the account two days ago. They were misposted to another account. Goodness knows why. Barbara only found the mistakes this morning. I can't tell which banks the cheques in the credits were drawn on, but the crossing stamps on the front of Mr Broadman's own cheques are those same banks as before.'

He took the vouchers from her and smiled. 'I think you might be getting the hang of this crossfiring business. But let's see how it stands now. We've got credits totalling £3,000, which cover his cheques for the same amount. If those credits had been properly posted to the account two days ago, the balance would have been enough to cover these cheques in today and yesterday. And if we weren't on our toes – and we couldn't have been in the past – we'd have probably paid them all. Thank God for those misposts.'

'So we'll bounce all the cheques?' Jane asked, taking

them back from him and picking up a steel-nibbed pen from his desk set and dipping the nib into the pot of red ink. 'What reason shall I put on them?'

'It'll have to be "effects not cleared". On the other hand – no, it doesn't matter...' His voice tailed off, a lump rising in his throat at the image of George's van hurtling over the cliffs. It was going to take time to get over this particular tragedy. 'I was just thinking that if George is dead, we ought to return his cheques "drawer deceased". But we haven't been given specific notice of his death; it's still really only a rumour. So put on "effects not cleared".

'Not "refer to drawer"?'

'No. That would only be if paying the cheques had caused an overdraft. Don't forget we have the credits for £3,000. It's just that we don't know whether the cheques in those credits are good or worthless. "Effects not cleared," tells the other banks just that.'

'If it wasn't so sad,' Jane said, her eyes moistening as she annotated the top left-hand corners of the cheques, 'I'd have found this all rather exciting. But I still can't believe Mr Broadman would have done something like this.'

David was relieved to see her blink away any possible tears and could hardly believe the change in her maturity over such a short period. It was only yesterday that he had cast doubts over whether she was up to the job, and now – less than a day later – she had researched the problem and somehow or other it looked as if they were going to come out of it unscathed – apart from the inevitable admonitions from Parker.

But there was no getting away from it; he ought to have known what was happening on George's account. There must have been faults in the office – by his staff. Why else would the uncleared element of the credits not have been brought to his attention? Had they all been lulled into a false sense of security by "the most respectable butcher in town"? But that did not explain what he had been up to and whether it was connected to his apparent death.

CHAPTER 10

From her kitchen, Sarah Goodhart glanced through the door into the dining room where her father-in-law was tucking into a bowl of cornflakes. She slowly shook her head. Albert Goodhart! He really was the end. Everything had seemed normal enough since he had risen from his bed, shortly after she had dropped Mark off at school. It was only a ten-minute walk there and back, but after last night, she had not relished leaving him alone in the house at all, never mind for that short period.

Despite their occasional altercations, she had always been fond of him. After all, he had welcomed her into his family with open arms from the day she had met David. She knew the feeling was mutual, yet there had always been one problem between them. She had never been able to call him Albert and he had certainly never encouraged her to do so. As an alternative, she was uncomfortable about calling him Dad – if only because he was not her true father – while Mr Goodhart seemed far too formal. After ten years of marriage, she still more often than not ended up calling him nothing at all and when talking about him with David, it was usually "your Dad" or "your father".

Throughout her life, she had found this business of names and titles unsettling and wished that older people would take the lead and be more forthright about how they should be addressed. It was as if they were unaware of the confusion and embarrassment that such lack of direction could cause. It had not been so bad at work where most people were referred to as Mr, Mrs or Miss and the manager of the bank was invariably called Sir. But socially and within the family, she knew she was not alone among her friends in finding the whole question of salutations unsatisfactory.

Albert's wife had been the exception, insisting on being called Mary, yet he never followed her lead. Why have one rule for one parent-in-law and another rule for the other? At least her own parents had been consistent with David. It was Mr and Mrs Darling – full stop.

But they had now passed away and, apart from David and Mark, Albert was the sole remaining member of her family. She looked at him once more from the kitchen, getting ready to carry out their morning ritual. He seemed so vulnerable as titular head of the Goodhart/Darling dynasties. It was not a physical vulnerability. He had kept himself fit – mainly from regular walking – and had certainly not developed a middle-age paunch, so often the preserve of men in retirement. And although he was now over sixty-five, he had maintained a full head of hair – much to the envy and sometime dismay of David who was already thinning on top. No, there appeared to be nothing physically wrong with him, yet he had an air about him that did not stack up. In particular, he had taken on childish habits and although she had known people in their eighties or more almost reverting to childhood ways, Albert was no age for that to be happening to him.

'What time did you say we're going to the doctor?' he called out, wiping his lips with the back of his hand after finishing his Kellogg's.

'Just before twelve,' she replied, moving into the other room to carry out her normal breakfast-time chastisement. 'What's the point in giving you a serviette if you're always going to use the back of your hand?'

78

He grinned at this daily routine, which she knew he relished – just like a small child. His next move would be to rise from his chair, give her a big hug and thank her profusely. 'You're always so good to me, Sarah. I simply don't know what I'd do without you and David.'

But this time, he said it with a catch in his throat and he stayed clinging to her, clearly unwilling to let her go. 'I really am sorry...' he then added, almost tearfully, '...for last night. I don't know what happened to me.'

'Don't worry about it,' she answered, dearly wishing she could call him Albert, or even Ally, which Mary had used when she wanted to show particular affection. 'That's why we're going to the doctor. One way or the other he'll be able to sort things out.'

As she released herself from his grasp, she only hoped that this would, indeed, be the case, but she was not filled with confidence. Since his wife's death in that dreadful car accident six years ago, he had become a different person. He was still the same upright old soldier he had always been, but he was different now – in character and personality. At first, she had assumed he was simply consumed by grief and David now felt it might be guilt, even though he had not been responsible for the collision. And although as time passed the tragedy receded from their minds, the changes in Albert unaccountably increased.

Until the accident, he had always been the most even-tempered husband and father, yet now his fuse was as short as a matchstick standing against a telegraph pole. He had always been meticulously organized, but these days he lived in a self-imposed world of orderless mayhem. Reliability was non-existent; concentration had taken an extended vacation and thoughts and deeds had become increasingly devious. Yet he was still loving and affectionate. He adored Mark and Mark loved him. But he was different now. And as for last night... that had been so disconcerting.

They were due to see a Dr Edwards – not a name she knew, but it was two years since her last visit to the surgery, shortly after they moved to Barnmouth. They all enjoyed good day-to-day health and Mark had avoided picking up germs at school. The receptionist had said nothing about the doctor, except that he was new to the practice. Would he be young or old, off-hand or understanding? She just hoped that he would be someone who would listen, give them time and have a good "bedside manner".

David's father seemed totally relaxed about the visit and that helped to keep her own mind at rest. It was a pity that David could not be with them, but she did not want him to have time out of the office on the first morning of his inspection. It was an important time for any bank manager, but even more so this time, it being his first inspection in Barnmouth. It was too early in his appointment for the outcome to lead to promotion, but it would provide a good indication of how he was doing so far.

Come midday, Dr Edwards turned out to be a young man, probably in his late-twenties, with a ready smile that beamed at them through dark-brown horn-rimmed spectacles which he had possibly chosen to make himself look older. As he rose from behind his desk to greet them – what a good start – he motioned them to sit down in the two upright chairs opposite him. They settled in their seats and Sarah glanced round the room, which was surprisingly homely. Apart from the obligatory plastic-sheeted bed alongside one wall, it was almost like someone's private lounge, with a large mahogany cabinet – surely not for drinks – against another wall and a long matching bookcase under the window. Medical tomes of various sizes and colours crammed the bookcase, while on top of it, a pile of *The Lancet* medical journals lay awaiting ready reference.

Several watercolours depicting famous golf courses hung on the walls and these, together with a bag of golf clubs standing against a coat cupboard adjacent to the door, aptly confirmed the doctor's main outdoor interest. She found the overall impression most comforting, especially when she saw a couple of framed family photographs on one side of the desk. A courteous young family man, keen on sport and with good taste in furniture and personal mementos was, to her, "just what the patient ordered".

After giving the doctor a comprehensive account of Albert's history and current condition, she repaired to his anteroom while he conducted a thorough physical examination. How she hoped he would come up trumps; how she wanted Albert to be his old self. Such wishes and many other thoughts crowded her mind as she sat on the uncomfortable chair in the cheerless closet which was such a contrast to the other room. She again chided herself for getting cross and impatient last night, now realizing more than ever that Albert had become more of a parent to her than her own mother and father. How different they had been with David, almost castigating him for his success in banking and his undying consideration for his family. It was only much later that she had realized her mother, in particular, had been jealous of her and all that David had provided. It had been such a sad episode in her life – and so unjust.

'You can come back in now,' Dr Edwards called from his room, breaking her reverie. She quickly returned to sit at Albert's side, across from the doctor who was poring over his notes.

'The good news, Mrs Goodhart,' he said, looking up and pushing his spectacles on to the bridge of his nose, 'is that I can't find anything physically wrong with Mr Goodhart. In fact, you're clearly doing a great job looking after him. For his age, I don't think he could be in better shape.'

She smiled in appreciation of these comments, but anxiety swept through her, knowing that whenever someone prefaced a statement with "the good news is", there would surely follow an ominous rider starting with "but".

'And the bad news?' she asked, not wanting the doctor to delay his prognosis with any further words of possible false encouragement.

'First of all, I'm not sure it is actually bad news. My problem is that I don't really know what's wrong, but clearly something isn't right.'

Unconsciously, she stretched out her arm to take Albert's hand in hers and gave it a reassuring squeeze, even though the doctor's hesitancy was hardly reassuring her. She had felt sure he would know exactly what was wrong.

'At first,' Dr Edwards continued, looking at her directly in the eye, 'I thought the problem might have been the onset of senility.'

'But he's surely not old enough for that?'

'Not necessarily. It's certainly more usual in older people, but it can afflict some even younger. It's a degenerative disease. To a degree, most people develop symptoms, as they get older. For example, not remembering names – not only of strangers, but also close friends. Other possible symptoms might be regularly losing your keys – or forgetting where you've put your glasses. But don't get too concerned about that last one. It gives me enough trouble and I'm only thirty.'

As he joked about himself, he flashed a smile at her and then winked at Albert. Good man, it was the perfect way of including Albert in the proceedings.

'Anyway,' the doctor continued, 'these things are known as benign memory loss. But a better example of its onset is the inability to recognise and name the famous. I'm talking about really well-known people, such as Churchill or Hitler – or those from the world of show business, like Humphrey Bogart or Marilyn Monroe. But there's no worry there with Mr Goodhart.' He paused, before adding with a knowing grin, 'Particularly in the case of Marilyn Monroe!'

'So you don't think it's senility?' Sarah asked, warming still further to this young doctor who seemed mature beyond his years. But she was still anxious about what more there was to come.

'I'm almost 100% sure. But what I'd like to know is more about the car accident. You mentioned it earlier, but Mr Goodhart can hardly recall what happened. I know it must be upsetting for you...'

'No,' she interrupted, 'don't worry about that. We've been over it so many times. We're almost numb to it – you know, the tragedy of it all.'

'Of course,' Dr Edwards replied, nodding gently, as if understanding exactly what they must have all gone through. 'It's just that Mr Goodhart tells me he came out of it unscathed, but I wonder if you've anything to add to that.'

'Not really,' she said, thinking that the doctor might be sharing the view that Albert was harbouring feelings of guilt. 'They took him to hospital and kept him in overnight – for observation. They thought he might be suffering from concussion.'

'From hitting his head on the windscreen?'

'I really don't know – specifically, that is. The car actually turned over, but Albert walked away from it unharmed. He was in a bit of a daze, but you'd expect that. I think the hospital was just being cautious. The next morning, he appeared fit and well and they suggested he came to stay with us – until he got over the shock. He's been with us ever since.'

'Lucky man, if you ask me,' the doctor said, then looking down at his notes. 'So they didn't take any X-rays?'

'Not to our knowledge. After all, he didn't have any broken bones.'

At that, Dr Edwards rose from his chair and went to the bookcase where he started to thumb through the issues of *The Lancet*. He selected one of the magazines and leafed through its pages until he found the article he was clearly seeking. After reading for a couple of minutes, he returned to his desk and rested the magazine alongside his notes.

'I'm sorry about that,' he said, 'but I've been mulling over what might be the trouble. I remembered reading an article about it recently. I'd rather not say any more just now, because I might be well off beam. But I'm going to make an appointment for Mr Goodhart at Torbay Hospital. I think he needs to see a neurological consultant – with a view to having an X-ray of his brain.'

'Of his brain?' Sarah exclaimed, not aware that such a thing was possible.

'It's only a precaution,' Dr Edwards tried to reassure her, 'but I think it might reveal the reason for Mr Goodhart's problems.'

CHAPTER 11

David slumped in his chair and found it difficult to think of Sarah and Dad at the doctor's surgery. He could only reflect on the interview he had just had with Parker. What a grilling! Talk about the third degree. And he found it difficult to believe that, of all customers, it had been about George Broadman. Merciful release had come by way of a telephone call from Stuart Brown who now wanted his meeting to discuss the potential new business he had mentioned earlier. He was due in five minutes and David would need all of that time to calm down and regroup his thoughts.

Parker had collared him at eleven o'clock, shortly after Brown had telephoned to confirm officially that George had, indeed, been found dead at the bottom of the cliffs. At this early stage, the police were keeping an open mind on the possible cause of death, but the likelihood was suicide. Parker had, somehow, also heard the news and was anxious to learn about George's bank account, particularly about any possible indebtedness.

'No, there's no borrowing at all,' David had been pleased to confirm, but on seeing Parker's expression of relief, he felt obliged to tell him about yesterday's bounced cheques and this morning's revelations.

As he recounted events, he had become increasingly disconcerted by Parker's reaction. The inspector's gaze had been locked on him throughout and his complexion had veered from deathly white to livid-puce when he heard about the suspicion of crossfiring.

'You mean you saw no prior warning on the account?' he demanded. 'No prior warning at all?'

'No, it only came to my attention this morning. But I had an inkling yesterday. One of the cheques I bounced was for £300 – payable to cash. But it clearly hadn't been cashed here or anywhere else, so I asked Jane to delve back into his account. This morning, she gave me all the evidence I needed.'

Parker let out an exasperated sigh. 'You mean evidence that had been there for all to see for some time back?'

David simply nodded, knowing there would be a rider to the question.

'And for how long are we talking about?'

David kept his eyes fixed on Parker's, not wanting to appear ill at ease, but he had to suppress a gulp as he answered, 'I asked Jane to go back three months, but as she got into it, she decided to make it six.'

Parker rose from his chair and started to pace the room, placing the heel of one hand to his forehead. David sighed inwardly. Did the man have to be such a master of drama? Parker then thrust his other hand deep into the pocket of his trousers and jangled his coins and keys. 'And for how long has your Jane been doing this job?'

'Since she came here – two months ago.'

'And before her?'

'That was another youngster – Alan Jones. He was transferred to Exeter. That's when the staff controller insisted I took Jane in his place.'

'And neither of them took it upon themselves to keep an eye on accounts such as Broadman's – looking for unusual transactions?'

'Barnmouth's hardly the place you'd expect a respectable trader to be crossfiring,' David retorted, immediately regretting his impulsiveness.

'But we now know that it is, don't we?' Parker almost snarled. 'Tell me, Mr. Goodhart, where would you expect crossfiring to be taking place?'

David could well do without such overt sarcasm, but he knew he was on the back foot. 'Fortunately,' he answered, 'this is my first experience of it. I've no idea where else it might take place or how prevalent it might be. As for young Alan and Jane, the subject isn't covered in their training manuals. So it's hardly fair to accuse them of falling down on their duty.'

It was all very well having a go at him, but he saw no reason why his assistants should be targeted. If there had been slip-ups, it was down to him, but even so...

'Was crossfiring ever covered in your own training?' Parker asked, continuing his reproachful attack.

'As a matter of fact, it wasn't,' David answered. 'But I've certainly since acquainted myself on such things. And if I'd had the benefit of serving on the inspection staff...' he let the words tail off, knowing he had overstepped the mark.

Parker stayed silent and returned to his seat. He rested his arms on the desk, looking at his fingers, which gently drummed out a silent tune on its surface. After a minute of such contemplation, he looked up. 'Let's just forget about Broadman's crossfiring for a moment. And let's also forget about what might or might not be covered in training manuals. Let's simply deal with the question of uncleared items in customers' credits. Surely, your assistants, your cashiers and your supervisor are perfectly aware of the standard banking procedures for processing credits?'

David could only agree. If George Broadman had paid in a cheque drawn by another customer of Barnmouth branch, he would automatically know if the cheque was good – whether the other customer had enough money on his account to cover it. And the cashier would mark the credit slip that the cheque represented cleared funds.

All other cheques in a credit would be deemed to be uncleared and would be sent – through the clearing system – to the banks upon which they were drawn for payment. How often he had tried to explain to customers that, during this three-day process, such cheques might justifiably be considered as worthless pieces of paper. Paying his own customers' cheques against such items could be an unwarranted risk and he had to rely on the laid-down system within the bank that highlighted which cheques in credits were cleared or uncleared.

'So,' Parker continued, acknowledging his nodded acceptance, 'when a customer pays in a number of cheques, what does your cashier do?'

David tried to hide his grimace when he went through the procedure, but he had only himself to blame for Parker's pedantry. He should not have made that incautious reference about not having been on the inspection staff.

'And when the credit gets posted to the customer's account?' Parker then asked.

'The cleared balance is calculated and I can then decide whether or not to pay the customer's own cheques.'

'Right! Now we're getting somewhere. But if everyone's been doing things properly, how had Broadman been getting away with crossfiring for so long?'

Putting it that way, David found himself empathizing with the inspector – not with his aggressive, condescending manner, but with his conclusion that something was materially wrong with their accounting procedures. And he was disquieted on one particular point: it was clear that someone was doing something wrong, but he knew that it was not himself. Parker, on the other hand, had every right to believe he might well be the culprit. It was not unheard of for a manager to be taken in by a customer; to be seduced by charm and flattery, leading to a general laxity in appraising what was actually happening on his account. But he would have to be patient; let time convince Parker of his innocence.

'That certainly needs investigating,' he answered, not wanting to hazard a guess as to where the problem lay or who was to blame.

'Too true,' Parker said, then adding rather begrudgingly, 'but I suppose I must give you some credit for acting how you did yesterday – not to mention this morning. If you'd paid Broadman's cheques – relying on his supposed integrity – we'd now be looking at a substantial debt.'

David could hardly believe he had heard a smattering of praise filter across the desk, but he knew that it barely offset the earlier criticisms.

'And I think we should have a quiet word with those other banks,' Parker continued, getting out a navy fountain pen to make some jottings in his black notebook. 'Remind me who they are.'

'There's our own branch at Chagford. The cheques I returned today were paid in there. And then it's Barclays in Exeter and the District in Plymouth.'

'And do we know the customers at those banks?'

'No,' David replied, fearing that Parker would have expected him to have established this, 'but we do know that Broadman's cheques were payable to cash or to someone called Jack Stringer.'

'Is that someone you know?'

'No, the name means nothing to me.'

'We'll have to find out,' Parker mused, raising his pen to his lips, almost caressing its end with a light touch of his tongue. 'We won't have a problem at Chagford, but the other banks are likely to be cagey about disclosing details.'

'But it would be in their interest to co-operate,' David interjected.

'I agree, but I think I'd better be the one to make the enquiries. A bit of inspectorial weight might be necessary. If they think there's still a chance to get out without a loss, they ought to be willing to help.'

Now that the interrogation had developed into more of a discussion, David decided to broach with Parker his puzzlement at George Broadman's actions. 'I really don't understand what this business is all about. From your own experience, is there normally a common denominator with crossfiring?'

Before answering, Parker put away his fountain pen and notebook. 'Greed – that's the usual underlying link. An insatiable appetite for money; cash that's needed to feed an ever-growing addiction. Drugs, drink, women, gambling – that sort of thing. And any such vice, for want of a better word, can lead to blackmail.'

So much for "the most respectable butcher in town". But what about the town itself? What was going on behind those panelled front doors and lace net curtains? Were they shielding dens of iniquity, rather than suburban respectability? His mind flirted with lurid goings-on in Barnmouth's inner sanctums and, later on, he would enjoy sharing extravagant and outrageous theorizing with Sarah.

He rose from his chair as Parker got up to leave the room. 'I can't say I've been cheered by this morning's events,' the inspector said, his furrowed brow resembling a newly ploughed field. 'And I hate to think what other fates you have in store for me. But as far as I can see, this particular problem appears to have nothing to do with those other activities I mentioned yesterday.'

When he had gone, David awaited Stuart Brown's arrival knowing that Parker's parting shot was not meant to give him any comfort. After the last twenty-four hours, he would not expect it and he preferred not to dwell on any further problems that might arise. Except that Dad was not far from his mind. The last thing he needed was a continuing domestic problem – his banking ones were bad enough – and he prayed that the doctor would be able to prescribe Dad with something to get him back to normal.

The telephone interrupted his thoughts and Katie confirmed that Stuart had arrived and was waiting in the banking hall. Hearing Katie's voice reminded him that he had not yet contacted Miss Harding and he made a note on his pad to do this when the interview was over.

After collecting the solicitor from the banking hall, he was relieved to be sitting opposite him, rather than Parker and, unlike in the car, Stuart's opening words were about George Broadman. 'I really can't understand what must have possessed George to commit suicide.'

'I think everyone must feel that,' David replied. 'I suppose an inquest will delay the funeral. When do you think it'll take place?'

'The inquest or the funeral?'

'Well, both for that matter.'

'I really don't know,' Brown answered, brushing a loose strand of blond hair back into his manicured coiffure. He was always immaculately turned out and David imagined him gardening in a well-pressed three-piece suit. 'The inquest will be in the hands of the police. I can't imagine them allowing the funeral to be held until it's over. But do you mind if we get on? I'm really pressed for time.'

'That suits me fine, Stuart. Fire away.'

'If you play your cards right,' Brown almost gushed, 'John English's account is yours for the taking.'

'The Esplanade Hotel?' David answered, knowing that English had owned the town's largest hotel for several years and Brown would not have wanted an urgent appointment to discuss a personal account.

'Of course. I reckon it's just the sort of business you should have. It's the best hotel around and deserves the best bank. John's getting fed up with the District. He finds it too small – no bigger than a sub-branch. And he doesn't think the manager's up to it – too inexperienced. John says he doesn't understand the hotel business.

'What about the actual bank account?' David asked, already worried at that age-old criticism made by a dissatisfied customer.

'That's no problem at all. John never exceeds his limit. But he needs to expand – the bar facilities, to be precise. Increased turnover, that's what he wants. But he's worried the District won't go along with it. So I suggested he comes to see you.'

There was certainly no stopping Brown's introductions, even if some potential new business – like English's? – might initially appear questionable, but that could always be properly assessed at interview. And the regional manager had been right; nurturing Brown had not only led to new accounts, but also to substantial credit balances accumulating on the accounts of Ducksworth, Brown and Sargeant. Much of these arose through Brown's own clients who operated elsewhere, particularly in London where his client base seemed to be expanding rapidly.

David could well understand a cut and thrust solicitor like him needing to look further afield from the provincial business domiciled in Barnmouth and if the bank benefited from such a get-up-and-go approach, all well and good.

'Do you know how much he wants to borrow?' he asked, curious as to why English doubted that the proposition would appeal to the man at the District.

'I don't know the exact figure. Probably about £5,000. But you'd have plenty of security. The hotel must be worth at least £30,000.'

David paused before replying. Security would be no problem, but why would expansion of the bar cost a sixth of the hotel's overall value? It was a bit odd, but there would be no harm in seeing English and finding out. 'Do you want me to give him a ring to fix an appointment?'

Brown looked pensive, his forefinger and thumb rubbing the almost-smooth stubble on his chin. 'No, I've a better idea,' he eventually said. 'I owe him a round of golf. We could play a three-ball on Thursday. You could discuss it with him then.'

Oh, no, no, no. Talking business on the golf course never worked. It was fine to meet potential customers socially, but discussing business was strictly off-limits – especially with a third party present.

'I'll do my best to make it,' he said, adding, 'but it'll have to be in the morning. I need to be back here straight after lunch.'

'That's perfect,' Brown replied, beaming. 'I'll let John know this afternoon.'

'But there's just one thing,' David now stressed. 'I never believe the golf course is the place to discuss business...'

'Couldn't agree more,' Brown interrupted. 'But at least

it'll break the ice. And you'll have to let him win.'

'You must be joking! I've never done that. Anyway, it's the Turkey Trot. We're playing for our Christmas lunch.'

Having agreed a tee-off time of eight-thirty and expressed further consoling words about George Broadman, Brown left, leaving David to mull over the arrangements. Playing golf on Thursday was a luxury he could ill-afford. On the other hand, new business was in the offing; although he was somewhat disquieted by what he had heard about the proposition.

Casting such thoughts aside, he decided it was high time to ring Miss Harding, but before he could reach for the handset, the telephone rang and Katie said his wife was on the line.

'David,' Sarah urged, failing to shield her anxiety, 'I really need you to come home. Can you manage that?'

'What, now? I thought we'd agreed I'd have a sand-wich here.'

'I know. I'm sorry, darling. But I must see you – about your Dad. I think there's something seriously wrong with him.'

CHAPTER 12

His immediate reaction was to down tools and rush home, but Sarah stressed that this was unnecessary. Yes, she wanted him to come, but it could wait until his normal lunch hour at one o'clock. Dad was fine, but she would prefer to discuss the doctor's views face to face, rather than on the telephone. He was certainly thankful for those extra twenty minutes – time enough to make his much-delayed telephone call to Miss Harding.

'Barnmouth 3521.' He had only seen his secretary's mother once and had never before heard her speak. But from what he had gleaned from others, her voice exactly fitted that of his imagination – authoritative, even dictatorial. Rumour had it that she had always been top dog (or bitch?) in the Harding household and had driven her husband into submission, even, some said, to his premature death ten years ago. Since then, it seemed she had wreaked misery on her daughter – compounded still further in recent years by an alleged frailty that demanded constant kindred attention.

He had known other women like her – his late mother-in-law springing vividly to mind. He put it down to a basic insecurity and failure to have achieved anything tangible in life – be it success in career, sport or hobby, never mind a normal secure bond in matrimony. So often, he had experienced such men and women endeavouring to dominate committees, seeing it as their opportunity to hold a position of imagined importance and power. The fact that few committee members get selected through achievement –

the lack of other volunteers often prevailed – should curb their alleged right of dominance. But in his experience as treasurer on committees ranging from the local scout group to worthy charities, there had always been one person who tried to lord it over others. For this reason, he did all he could to avoid committee work and he felt rather ashamed at some of the lame excuses he had made in the past.

One thing for certain was that he would never be on a committee with Mrs Harding; her apparent incapacity to leave the house made such a nightmare mercifully impossible. He was surprised that she had found the energy or inclination to lift up the telephone and imagined that her normal response to it ringing would be to bark a sharp instruction to her daughter. For this not to happen now possibly meant his secretary was still unwell.

'Hello, Mrs Harding. It's David Goodhart – from the bank. I'm just ringing to find out how your daughter's feeling.'

'And I should think so, too,' she snapped, making him purse his lips and let the lids slip down over his eyes in exasperation. It was a response he could do without this morning. The cumulative effect of the metaphorical scars left by Broadman, Parker, Dad and now Mrs Harding were getting hard to bear.

'I'd have rung earlier, but...'

'It's outrageous – the way you've treated my daughter.'

'I beg your pardon?'

'It's outrageous. She has a hard enough time looking after me. But to get to work and then for you to make her so upset she has to come home. Well!'

'I'm sorry, but...'

'There's no "but" about it. You just listen to me...'

'I beg your pardon!' he interrupted, now feeling even more outraged than Mrs Harding. 'How can you say such things? I haven't even seen your daughter today – let alone upset her. What's she been saying to you?'

'She hasn't needed to say anything. I can tell. It's so obvious. Anyway, if it wasn't you, who else could it have been?'

That was enough. He had delayed going home to comfort Sarah in order to make a compassionate call to his secretary and all he was getting for his consideration was a load of abuse. 'Mrs Harding, may I please speak to your daughter?'

'No, you may not! She's not in a fit state to talk to anyone – let alone you.'

And with that, she slammed down the receiver. He was dumbfounded and remained seated in his chair, staring at the handset. He wanted to hurl it across the room, he was so angry. Instead, he replaced it carefully in its cradle, put on his coat and strode from the bank to recharge his lungs with some much-needed fresh air.

At least it had stopped raining, while the wind on his face immediately cooled him down as he made for the seafront, passing the amusement arcade that stayed open throughout the year. Even with only a few punters, the cacophony emanating from the pinball machines and one-arm bandits would normally bludgeon his senses, but after the lambasting from Mrs Harding, it was like sweet music to his ears.

He moved on past an ice cream parlour, resisting the urge to cool down further by way of a vanilla cornet, and then went by the fancy goods shop, which specialized in ornaments made from seashells. Customers of his owned the business and spent each Sunday scouring the beaches for raw materials, gluing them together in the evening before painting and being made ready for display in the shop on Mondays. He much preferred his own Sundays to be days of rest.

He tried to obliterate that dreadful woman from his mind and now had mixed feelings about his secretary. Was she behind the vehemence of her mother's outburst? Had she really blamed him for her return home? Or could she possibly be an innocent victim of her mother's vituperation? He shook his head in despair and made his way along the seafront towards his house, turning his mind to what Sarah might reveal about Dad. But his approach to the Esplanade Hotel distracted him and he decided to take a good look at it. If it was to be offered to him as security, a formal valuation would be needed, but there was nothing like a personal once-over to evaluate its location and general state of repair.

He had met John English on several occasions and although he did not necessarily take to him, he had no real antipathy towards the man. Like most hotel landlords and publicans, he was a mite too hail-fellow-well-met – perhaps an essential trait for their choice of business. The hotel, itself, had appeared to be well run when it had been the venue for local dinners organized by the Institute of Bankers, but now, at the onset of winter, it seemed a little tired and in need of a coat of paint – not unexpected at this time of year. Most such properties suffered from the sea air and would be redecorated in the spring, ready for the summer season. This could be a costly exercise for a building as large as the Esplanade and he would have to ensure that this expense was properly covered in the hotel's forecasted outgoings.

He was also curious as to why English wanted to extend the bar facilities. Two popular pubs flanked the property, but their clientele would probably not be enticed into a hotel bar where drinking would normally be confined to pre-meal aperitifs. He would have to quiz English about this.

Leaving the hotel behind him, he turned his mind back to the problem of Dad. What had the doctor said to make Sarah believe there was something seriously wrong with him? He dwelled on this as he made for home, his progress hampered by the pavements being strewn with debris torn from the adjacent trees. There would clearly be much work for the council to undertake once the storm had cleared.

As he entered the front door, Sarah rushed to greet him, her face etched with a concern he had not seen since his parents' car accident. She took both his hands in hers and looked pleadingly into his eyes as she reached up to kiss his lips. 'Perhaps I shouldn't be worried,' she said, drawing back and guiding him towards the lounge. 'The doctor told me not to worry – and that he was only arranging it as a precaution.'

'Arranging it?' he queried, as they sat down on the settee. 'As a precaution?'

Sarah recounted all that had happened at the doctor's surgery, culminating in the proposed appointment with the neurologist and a possible X-ray.

'That does sound serious,' he said, putting an arm around her and frowning at something beyond his comprehension. 'I've never known anyone to have a brain X-ray. Did the doctor explain why?'

She shook her head. 'That's why I wanted you to come home. I needed to talk to you about it.'

He leant back on the settee and tried to grasp what he was hearing. He only hoped the doctor knew his stuff. 'What about the doctor? What was he like?'

'It was a Dr Edwards,' Sarah replied, brightening up. 'He's new to the practice, but he's very nice. He looked too young to be a doctor, but he said he was thirty.'

'Only thirty? He's hardly out of medical school.'

'Oh, come on, David. You're sounding as prejudiced as those people who question your own age as a bank manager. If he's good enough, he's old enough. Anyway, I thought he was great and he was wonderful with your Dad. I think we're in very safe hands.'

It was a relief to hear Sarah's assurances, but he still harboured doubts about such a young doctor. 'If he thinks the brain's the problem, does that mean mental trouble?'

'I don't know,' she replied, a catch in her voice. 'But I'm so upset at how angry I got with him last night. That was unforgivable.'

'But you weren't to know,' he consoled, drawing her close to him. 'You had every right to be cross. But what does Dad think? How did he react to the news?'

'That's the funny thing,' she replied, back in control of herself, 'it just seemed to flow over him. It was that child-like thing again. It was as if he were a child, not showing any reaction to a mother and doctor talking about its illness. It was very odd.'

'When does the doctor want him to see the consultant?'

'He didn't say, but he was getting on to the hospital straightaway.' At that the telephone rang and Sarah looked at him questionably, before asking, 'That surely couldn't be him already?'

He shrugged his shoulders and smiled. 'There's only one way to find out.'

She went to the other room and he could tell from her feint staccato-like responses that it was, indeed, the doctor.

If nothing else, he had certainly acted quickly, fully justi-
fying her high opinion of him.

'Tomorrow afternoon,' she said, on returning to the
room. 'Two-thirty. Can you come, as well?'

'Of course,' he replied, keen to be positive, though
concerned at having further time out of the office on top of
his golf the next day. 'Did he say how long it would take?'

'About half-an-hour – if the consultant's running to
time.'

'That's not so bad, then. I don't want to be out too
long. I'm playing golf on Thursday.'

'Golf?' Sarah answered, clearly surprised. 'With the
inspectors there?'

He nodded. 'Believe it or not, it's business. Stuart
Brown's asked me to play with him and John English.'

'Ugh!' Sarah exclaimed, screwing up her nose. 'John
English? That slimy creature?'

'Slimy? What makes you think he's slimy?'

'Ugh!' Sarah spat out again. 'He gives me the creeps.'

'I didn't even know you'd met him.'

'Ugh!' Sarah replied for the third time, giving a far too
exaggerated shudder. 'Only once, but that was enough.
The girls had a coffee morning at the Esplanade – about
two months ago. I did tell you at the time. I suppose you
weren't listening – again. Anyway, he came across to see if
everything was all right. It was all he could do to keep his
hands off us. As for mentally undressing us... Ugh!'

'I'm sure you were imagining it,' he suggested, before
adding with a grin, 'Or was it wishful thinking?'

'You must be joking!'

'Anyway, Stuart wants me to take over the Esplanade's
bank account. So he thought it would be a good idea for
me to meet up with English on the golf course. A getting-

101

to-know-you exercise.'

'Rather you than me, then,' Sarah said, with mock disdain.

This light-hearted exchange had certainly lifted their mood of anxiety and, on the way back to the office, he felt sufficiently buoyed to buy Miss Harding a box of Black Magic, the only problem being that a visit would mean meeting her mother – not a happy thought. He was still smiling at Sarah's reaction to John English when he was back at his desk, but then realized that he had neither told her about George Broadman's suicide, nor his own spat with Mrs Harding. Oh well, that would have to wait until the evening.

He rang for Jane and when she arrived in his room, her changed demeanour struck him forcibly. Gone was her normal hesitancy, replaced by an alertness that had started to manifest itself that morning. Was it possible for such a transformation to have taken place in such a short time? It was almost a relief to see her revert to the old Jane and blush when she realized he was staring at her.

'Sit down, Jane,' he said, averting his gaze. 'How are you getting on with the day's work?'

'It's been completely straightforward. Makes a change, doesn't it?' She smiled, perhaps in pleasure – or relief – at being able to make a rare quip.

'That's more than my morning's been.'

'The inspector? He was certainly in here for some time.'

'Him – and other things. Needless to say, he wasn't best pleased about George Broadman – not about his suicide, but his bank account. We've really slipped up somewhere along the line.'

'But we haven't lost anything. We bounced his cheques in time.'

'Thank goodness we did. No, we should have picked up what was going on long ago. Mr. Parker knows it and so do I. The question is, why didn't we?'

'I think I know what my next task will be.'

David smiled. Had he been misjudging her? Had her timidity been his fault? Whatever, he was warming to her rapidly and, despite her inexperience he was certain she was not to blame for what had been going wrong. In any case, she had only been here for a couple of months and the problem had existed far longer than that. 'How did you guess?' he replied, before continuing seriously, 'I want you to delve into our systems. Why didn't we know about the uncleared cheques? We both know what should be done, but why wasn't it actually happening? But be surreptitious. I don't want you to ask anyone else. Just dig around a bit. Look at all the relevant vouchers and forms. Then let me know what you've found out. I've got to take my father to hospital after lunch tomorrow, so let's do it in the morning.'

Jane looked worried. 'I hope it's nothing serious.'

'What? Oh, with my father? I don't really know. It's a check-up. But I've another problem – with Miss Harding. I'm not sure what to do.'

'Have you managed to speak to her? Is she all right?'

'That's the point,' he replied. Should he take her into his confidence? On impulse, he decided to tell her of the telephone call. 'I had a problem this morning with her mother. Now, I'm sure you'll understand that this must be confidential...'

'Of course, sir,' she readily replied, though unable to hide an air of indignity.

'I'm sorry, Jane. I didn't mean to imply anything. It's just that in matters concerning staff...'

'Of course I understand,' she quickly acknowledged. 'I

don't want to know anything I shouldn't, but if there's any way I can help...'

'I'm not sure there is,' he replied, smiling in acknowledgement of her offer. 'I tried to speak to Miss Harding this morning, but her mother thwarted me. She seemed to think it was my fault Miss Harding had gone home unwell.'

'But that's ridiculous. You never saw her this morning. It was Katie who told you she'd gone home.'

'I know, but try telling that to Mrs Harding. She even slammed the phone down on me. The upshot is that I don't know if Miss Harding's still ill or on the mend.'

'What are you going to do?' Jane asked, her face indicating genuine concern.

'I'm not sure. But I do know that if I turn up at the house, I'm not going to be made welcome.'

They remained pensive for a few moments, during which time Jane removed her glasses and dabbed her left eye with her handkerchief. Thank goodness, a speck of dust, rather than tears, appeared to be the problem this time – and he had to force himself not to stare. Without her spectacles, she was really rather attractive.

'I've an idea,' she then said, enabling him to cast such thoughts aside, 'why don't I go along to see her? I can then tell her your predicament – once I get by her mother. I could go on the way home. It won't be out of my way.'

He was surprised and delighted at her response. It could certainly work. Once he knew what was wrong with his secretary, he could decide when to see her himself or work out what to do next. 'Jane, that'd be a great help. You're sure you don't mind?'

'Of course not,' she replied, almost glowing with pride. 'But for now, I better get on with my George Broadman investigations.'

CHAPTER 13

Leaving her manager's office, Jane was, indeed, glowing with pride. This was what she hoped her job would be all about: something to get her teeth into, taking on extra responsibility and being treated by her manager as, to coin a phrase, his right-hand man. It had not always been so.

She had joined National Counties four years ago, nervous, apprehensive and self-conscious. She vividly recalled her first day at Torquay branch when she had been so frightened about turning up. She had alighted the bus at Castle Circus, despite it being half-a-mile from the branch in the Strand. She hoped an invigorating walk might provide the inner strength to cross the insuperable threshold from school to work. She was also aware that it would delay the inevitable moment of truth.

At eight-thirty on a Monday morning, Union Street was alive with cars and red Devon General double-decker buses, while workers jostled each other on the pavements. Having passed the Regal cinema in Castle Circus, she soon approached the tiny street that harboured the Electric, its quaintly named competitor. If her starting time had been fixed for the afternoon, she knew she would have entered one or other of these establishments to take refuge in the darkened anonymity of the auditorium.

As it was, she carried on walking and came to the small Union Street branch of National Counties. If only she had been posted there, rather than to the much larger imposing branch in the Strand. There would be fewer staff at the smaller office and it would be far less daunting. How she hated meeting strangers at the best of times, never mind in such awe-inspiring circumstances.

She soon reached Fleet Street – the home of more prestigious stores – arching its way down to the harbour like an outstretched boa constrictor. Unlike Union Street, there was no temptation of darkened cinemas in which to shelter. But there was no hiding place from National Counties and, at one-minute-to-nine, she summoned the courage to ring the front door bell.

If, on that first day, she had been told she would be there for over a year, she would have resigned on the spot. She was a stranger in a coterie. The contrast of her own inhibitions and the sheer camaraderie of her new colleagues was untenable. But as the days turned into months, a gradual coming-together occurred and when she was transferred to the small branch at St Marychurch, she was even a little sad.

Yet her years at Torquay and St Marychurch had not developed her self-confidence. She could not fault her training and must have done reasonably well for her manager at St Marychurch to recommend her selection to the B grade category of staff: the first recognizable training grade for potential managers. Grade A was for high-fliers and was not an option. The staff controller had stressed at her interview that she must first develop her confidence and personality to enable her to fulfil the potential shown in her ability with the work.

At some length, he took her through the bank's marking system used by managers and inspectors in the regular reports they submitted on members of staff. Of the ten assessable categories, she was surprised to hear that only three related directly to the quality of a person's work: accuracy, efficiency and technical ability. Four others comprised personal qualities: manners, appearance, personality and general intelligence. And the remaining three assessed attitudes towards work: resource and initiative, diligence and esprit-de-corps.

This was dispiriting as well as illuminating. The staff controller had highlighted her blatant areas of limitation. So many categories reflected the core requirement of possessing and displaying self-confidence – such a desperate drawback for her.

On being transferred to Barnmouth, she had been determined to come out of her shell, but that was easier said than done. Miss Harding's domineering attitude only increased her insecurity, while Bernard Groves's arrogance seemed intent on taking her down a peg. Thank heavens for Mr Goodhart. Initially, he had seemed to view her with suspicion and he had the knack of saying things that made her blush uncontrollably. But he was always kind – like this morning – and now he was putting his trust in her, not only to delve into George Broadman's transactions, but also to go round to see Miss Harding on his behalf. She could almost feel the adrenalin coursing through her veins. And there was something else – quite alien to anything she had felt before. Was this what self-confidence was all about? Was it possible she might be able to repay Mr Goodhart's apparent new-found faith in her?

She got back to her desk, relieved to find it free of other work. Now she could get on with her investigations. She extracted Mr Broadman's cheques and credits from the drawer and concentrated on the credits, which were now her prime concern.

They went back to the beginning of June and she hoped these would be sufficient for her purpose, not wanting to probe back further. Putting aside the credits that clearly related to shop takings, she started to examine those that included cheques in round amounts. She immediately spotted a pattern. Not only was such a credit paid in every week, but also each one bore Mr Broadman's own signature for having paid it in. Yet his shop's cashier always paid in the normal takings, so why had Mr Broadman paid in these others himself?

It was odd, and even stranger; each credit had been taken in by Bernard Groves. Why had Trevor Smith's till never been used, nor Barbara Bolton's relief till, for that matter? Most transactions would certainly be processed through the number one cashier, but it seemed inconceivable that not once during the six months had a cashier other than Bernard Groves taken in these particular credits.

And what was this? All the round-amount cheques within each credit had been marked as cleared funds. Could they all have been drawn on Barnmouth branch? Of course not. She now knew that crossfiring depended on cheques being drawn on different banks to take advantage of the clearing system. The cheques in Mr Broadman's credits must have been drawn elsewhere – presumably on those other accounts of his and that of Jack Stringer.

She then gasped and raised a hand to her mouth. Bernard Groves must have deliberately marked the cheques as being cleared. Why on earth would he have done that? It meant that no one else in the branch would have subsequently known that the account's balance included a sizeable uncleared element in it. No wonder Mr Broadman had got away with his crossfiring for so long. And Mr Goodhart would never have known about it. He would be so relieved, and Mr Parker should now view things differently.

But she now had to sit tight. Mr Goodhart had told her not to say anything to anyone else. Just as well. She would not have had the nerve to take it up with Bernard Groves himself. No, she would have to wait until she saw Mr Goodhart in the morning.

It was now almost five o'clock and the others were locking the strongroom and drawers of their desks, prior to leaving. The inspectors had already gone, having completed their preliminary checks of the cash, bearer certificates and general security procedures. They had said they would reduce their numbers to three tomorrow: Mr Parker and his regular assistants, Richard Allen and John Fisher. Being so busy, she had hardly noticed the two aides, but Katie Tibbs had already extolled the virtues of Richard Allen, while Daphne Dewhurst and Jilly Sheffield had claimed to be vying for the attention of John Fisher. So far, their feelings did not appear to have been reciprocated.

Although only twenty-two, Jane felt aeons older than the other three girls who were not yet eighteen. Yet they were far more worldly-wise and less inhibited than herself, particularly where boys were concerned. She was never sure whether their alleged exploits were factual or simply figments of their fertile imaginations, but either way, she could only envy their undeniable charms. Daphne's golden hair adorned a face of cherubic, yet alluring, innocence, while Katie and Jilly both oozed a sensuality, which their nubile figures seemed eager to promote. If only she could share such attributes.

Putting aside such thoughts, she turned her attention to her next task – visiting Miss Harding. She could hardly believe how she had volunteered to go and see her. She had no affinity with the secretary and her impulsive offer rested solely on Mrs Harding's outrageous reaction to Mr

Goodhart's sincere solicitations. How dare she treat him so badly!

Like mother, like daughter? From day one, Miss Harding had been the same with her. It was little consolation to learn later that she had denigrated all Mr Goodhart's assistants in the same way. Yet as the weeks passed, she occasionally shed her obdurate veneer and there were times when Jane even sensed a vulnerability in the secretary's demeanour. It was as if her domineering attitude was a front for her own insecurity. Could it be that she suffered from the same inhibitions that she, herself, had to endure? No, it was not possible.

But Miss Harding could never become a bosom pal and it was with some foreboding that she eventually approached the Harding household. What sort of reception would await her – from Mrs Harding? If Mr Goodhart's sympathetic overtures had been dismissed so categorically, what hope was there for his humble assistant now clutching his box of Black Magic?

Even though she could see lights shining behind the curtains of the living room and a bedroom upstairs, she had to ring the bell three times before someone eventually opened the front door. A rather short dumpy lady of about seventy faced her, but although such a shape could portray a jolly disposition, Mrs Harding's face depicted a distracting sourness. Thin uncompromising lips bordered a horizontal slit of a mouth, while her narrowed eyes were bereft of humour. The overall effect was far different from the frail old lady she had expected to meet – someone who apparently needed her only daughter to be at her beck and call. This was a woman of some determination and was clearly a force to be reckoned with.

'Yes?'

At that moment, Jane realized she did not have the confidence or experience to cope with such a hostile reception and bitterly regretted having offered to act as Mr Goodhart's emissary. But there was no turning back and, somehow, she must breech this fortified human defence line and get inside to see his secretary.

'I'm Jane Church – from the bank. I've come to see how your daughter's feeling.'

'Who? Jane who? Church, was it? Never heard of you. How do I know you're from the bank?'

'I'm sorry... but...' Jane stuttered. She had been at the branch two months now, working alongside Miss Harding, sharing Mr Goodhart's workload, yet his secretary had not seen fit to mention her name to her mother? Some vote of confidence in the manager's latest assistant! 'I work with your daughter. Could I come in and see her, please. I won't be long.'

'How do I know who you are?' Mrs Harding snapped, her eyes narrowing still further, as if to establish some form of recognition.

'I haven't any proof, but if I might come in, Miss Harding can identify me.'

There was a leaden pause in the conversation while Mrs Harding stared at her, clearly contemplating her next response. Jane failed to hold her gaze and had to look away, only turning back to this awful woman when she eventually deigned to reply.

'I'll have to check first. I'm not going to let a stranger into my house.' And with that, Mrs Harding slammed the door shut, leaving her standing in the cold, not knowing what to do next.

For two pins, she would have turned tail and gone home, but that would not have impressed Mr Goodhart.

On no account must she fail him, nor herself, for that matter. This was a test of character – the staff controller would certainly have called it that. She must never forget he had shown confidence in her and this was just the sort of exercise she should undertake to justify his faith in her. No, she must wait on the doorstep and hope Mrs Harding would soon return and let her into the house.

When the door eventually re-opened, Mrs Harding stepped aside, threw her head back by way of a wordless "come in" and pointed up the stairs. 'She's up there, in the front bedroom. And don't be long.'

It was to Jane's considerable relief that she was not followed up the stairs and when she tapped her knuckles on the slightly open bedroom door, Miss Harding, almost inaudibly, called her to enter.

Her first surprise was that Mr Goodhart's secretary was not in bed, but sat fully clothed in a small Lloyd-loom chair at the side of a walnut dressing table set under the window. Her second surprise was that Miss Harding actually smiled at her – a sad, wistful smile that caught her completely unawares.

'Jane, do come in. I'm sorry, there's only one chair in here. Just sit yourself down on the end of the bed.'

What was happening? Miss Harding apologizing, making her welcome and even smiling?

'We were worried about you,' she replied, settling on the bed. 'Mr Goodhart tried to ring you at lunchtime, but...'

She stopped in her tracks as Miss Harding started to cry. There was no sobbing, no blubbing, just a plaintive gentle weeping which tore at her emotions.

After what was probably only a few seconds, but seemed considerably longer, Miss Harding dried her face with a handkerchief and asked her to close the door. 'I'm so sorry,' she then said. 'This really is embarrassing.'

'Oh, don't worry, Miss Harding. I'm always bursting into tears. It happened this morning in front of Mr Goodhart. That was terribly embarrassing.'

'It's not just the tears. I'm embarrassed about everything. I know Mr Goodhart tried to speak to me. I heard this end of his telephone call. And I could hear what happened with you on the doorstep just now. I feel so humiliated.'

'Don't worry...'

'It's been going on for years now. My mother's so domineering – she's become a Svengali. I can't take it any longer. And I know it's made me so awful – at the office...'

Her words tailed off as fresh tears formed in her eyes. Jane was totally bemused. Was this the same Miss Harding who treated the bank as her fiefdom? The one who had lorded it over her since her arrival? The secretary who saw herself as the boss, rather than Mr Goodhart? No, this person was different. The woman sitting in front of her was a normal human being, displaying the whole gamut of female emotions. She could even grow to like this particular Miss Harding.

She had heard of cases of character change, as when a meek and mild employee might bully his wife at home, or a hen-pecked husband would develop aggressive tendencies at work. She supposed it reflected a person's metabolism and was an inherent inner weakness. It was putting on a front, one that could all too easily be over-hyped in a vain attempt at boosting self-esteem. And in Miss Harding's case? She probably left home each morning so shell-shocked by her domineering mother that she could not help but take it out on her work colleagues. It was a fake show of strength from someone she could now see was the opposite of how she portrayed herself at the office.

'And I've done something so, so dreadful,' Miss Harding then blurted out. 'I simply don't know what to do.'

'Don't worry,' Jane said for the third time and then passed over the box of Black Magic. 'It'll all work out. And these are from Mr Goodhart. He wanted you to have them tonight. He was really worried about you. But are you feeling any better now?'

Miss Harding took the chocolates, looked away from her and suddenly blushed. Jane was astounded to see Miss Harding react in a manner so like herself. Should she pinch herself to see if she were dreaming?

'Please thank Mr Goodhart for these,' Miss Harding replied, now looking shamefaced. 'They're my favourites, but I don't deserve them. And it's not a question of my feeling any better. I'm not ill, Jane. I never have been.'

'But you came home this morning. I was told you had a bad migraine.'

'No, that wasn't true. I did take an aspirin, but it wasn't a migraine. I suppose I just ran away. I was simply devastated by the news – about poor old George.'

'George? George Broadman?'

Miss Harding nodded, tried to speak, but the words would not come out. Jane was not sure what to say, if anything at all. Why would Miss Harding feign a migraine? And run away because of the news about George Broadman?

'Jane,' Miss Harding eventually managed to say, 'I'm too embarrassed to say anything more. Embarrassed and humiliated. But it's worse than that – much worse. I couldn't even tell Mr Goodhart. But I've decided what I must do. I need to see Mr Parker, as soon as possible – like tomorrow morning. Would you tell him I want to see him? I don't want to come into the bank and it'd be no good seeing him here. I think the Seaway Café would be a good place. Would you ask him if he'd meet me there at ten?'

'But would he do that?' Jane asked, thinking that Mr Parker was not the sort of man to be dictated to in this way.

'I think he will, if you tell him it's absolutely vital – and that it concerns his inspection. And Jane – I've only ever had one true friend in my whole life and I'm so lonely now. Do you think... oh, this is so difficult for me to say, but would you be prepared to be my friend?'

Jane could not help her eyes moistening as the pathos of the moment enveloped her. She could hardly believe what she was hearing.

'And just one more thing, Jane,' Miss Harding continued, almost in a whisper, 'please stop being so formal. I'd much rather you'd call me Margaret.'

CHAPTER 14

'The Seaway Café?' David could not believe what he was hearing. And the day had got off to such a good start. He had woken after a long dreamless sleep – much to his surprise after Tuesday's traumas. Mark had behaved himself at breakfast, while Sarah had been particularly amicable, no doubt relieved that he was accompanying them to the hospital that afternoon. He had then noticed a stillness in the atmosphere outside; the light suddenly brightened through the window by a hazy orange ball which memory told him must be the sun. Quite irrationally – and he would never dare admit this to Sarah – his immediate thoughts did not dwell on crossfiring, Miss Harding or, even Dad, but that the improvement in the weather could well dry out the course for tomorrow's golf.

But golf was not on his mind now as Jane recounted her meeting last night with Miss Harding. 'And she said she wasn't ill – and had run away?'

Jane nodded and pursed her lips. 'It was extraordinary, but I felt really sorry for her. She was so forlorn.'

'Forlorn?' he echoed, hearing a word that could not possibly apply to his secretary. 'Are you sure you went to the right house?'

'She needed to unburden herself,' Jane continued, ignoring his last question which he now regretted posing. It was not a time for flippancy. 'And she really took me under her wing. She even asked me to be her friend – and call her Margaret. And do you know what? At that particular moment, I did want to be her friend. She was desperate for support.'

David could not prevent himself from exhaling a pensive sigh as he leant back in his chair. He clasped both hands behind his head, elbows splayed outwards, and contemplated all he had heard. A terrible foreboding hung over him. What did Miss Harding want to tell Parker that she could not say to him, or even Jane – especially as they would now appear to be on such intimate terms? Margaret, indeed. Even if he had been given permission to be that familiar, he doubted he could ever contemplate calling his secretary anything other than Miss Harding. Some people simply did not personify such a spirit of informality.

'It all seems to involve George Broadman,' he mused, encouraged by Jane's nod of her head that they were on the same wavelength. 'Do you think he was that friend – the one she said she'd only ever had?'

'It sounds as though he might have been.'

A sudden thought crossed his mind. 'She's not pregnant, is she?'

The look of surprise on Jane's face made it clear she had not contemplated such a possibility and he immediately retracted his question. 'No... no, of course she isn't. In any case she'd not want to confess that to Mr Parker. Didn't you say she needed to see him because it was linked to his inspection?'

'Yes, but she didn't say how.'

'And does Mr Parker know she wants to see him?'

'Yes – and I'm sorry. I had to tell him before letting you know. Just after he arrived, I saw him put his coat back on, ready to go out. I thought I'd better catch him straightaway. I didn't know how long he'd be and ten o'clock was not far away. Anyway, I could only give him the gist of what had happened, but he readily agreed to meet her.'

'How did he react to such a strange request?'

'He didn't really react one way or the other. He seemed in a hurry to leave. He just wanted to know where the Seaway Café was and said he'd be there.'

David could hardly believe this situation might have anything to do with George Broadman's crossfiring, but perhaps something personal had been going on between him and Miss Harding. Yet that was so unlikely. But whatever it was, she was apparently too embarrassed to discuss it with someone she knew, preferring to disclose it to an uninvolved party. Not that a bank inspector could be deemed to be uninvolved. But if it was a personal matter between her and the butcher, no wonder she became upset when she learnt of his suicide.

But thinking of George reminded him of the other task he had set for Jane yesterday afternoon and he asked how she had got on with her investigations. It was extraordinary that her revelations about Miss Harding should have taken precedence over his concern about how George had got away with his crossfiring.

Jane hesitated before answering, as if finding it difficult to switch her mind from Miss Harding's problems. 'I've certainly got somewhere,' she eventually confirmed and then described what she had discovered. 'I couldn't believe what I was seeing, but didn't think I should go any further until I'd referred it all to you.'

David nodded, grateful that she had not taken it upon herself to tackle Bernard Groves, a difficult man to handle at the best of times. Bernard had always been an excellent cashier, each day balancing his till to the penny, something David could hardly claim for himself when he was a cashier, his confusion with half-crowns and florins often resulting in small differences in his till. But what had possessed Bernard to mishandle George Broadman's credits?

'No, quite right,' he replied. 'Leave that to me. And you'd better get on with your other work now. But hang on a minute – let me check my diary.' Flicking through the pages, he frowned when he reached today. 'John Jackson? I'm seeing him at eleven. I've never heard of him. Do you know who he is?'

'It's a new account – for us, anyway. It was transferred from Loughborough – about two weeks ago.'

'Well, before you do anything else, you'd better let me have his file. I must do my homework before he arrives.'

When she had gone, he tried to plan out the rest of his day. He must give some dictation to Katie and then he had the interview with John Jackson – whoever he was. That should take no more than half-an-hour, by when Parker ought to be back from seeing Miss Harding. Fearful of what the inspector might reveal and how long he would need to say it, he was conscious that he must not leave it late to get Dad to hospital by two-thirty. As for Bernard Groves, that would have to be dealt with later.

In no time at all, it was eleven o'clock, by which time he had studied John Jackson's file and a rather flushed Jane had ushered him in, then leaving in some haste to her desk. As Jackson took his seat, David was not unimpressed by this tall, broad-shouldered young man, probably in his early twenties and whose grooming splendidly comple-mented his sturdy build. Brylcreemed hair, as sported by Denis Compton, crowned a craggy face that radiated sunshine from homely hazel eyes. A Harris Tweed sports jacket strained to embrace what looked like a forty-four inch chest, while well-pressed grey flannels and highly polished brown brogue shoes under-pinned the entire ensemble. No wonder Jane appeared flustered when she had shown him in.

'I see your account's just been transferred from Loughborough,' he said, impressed with the assured way Jackson's eyes held his attention. 'How come you've moved down to this part of the world?'

'I've come back to live with my parents,' Jackson replied, grinning. 'The only trouble is, they're fed up with keeping me and I've had to take a job. They think I've been sponging off them for far too long.'

'Sponging?'

'The perpetual student – so they say. I'm twenty-two and they think I should be gainfully employed by now.'

David nodded his head in affirmation. 'I think your parents and I might have a lot in common.'

Jackson smiled, his eyes twinkling. 'But I have been trying hard – since university. I got a sports degree at Loughborough and I'm hoping to get my golf card.'

David raised his eyebrows, eager to hear more.

'I want to become a professional,' Jackson continued, 'but no joy yet. So I've taken the job of assistant pro here in Barnmouth. It'll be good experience – and help pay my way. My parents are rather pleased about that.'

'I'm not surprised. But many congratulations. I'm a member there and we do need a keen assistant. But you didn't come here just to tell me that.'

'No, I need a loan – for a car. I can't depend on buses to get me to and from the club. And I'll be playing away at tournaments and at other clubs.'

'What sort of car are you looking for – and what will it cost?'

'I'm not really fussed – so long as the boot's big

enough for my clubs. An estate car might be the answer. As for cost, I reckon I could go to about £400.'

'Do you have anything to put towards it?' David asked – the salient point with any lending proposition, the bank never wanting to put up the full purchase price. A meaningful contribution by the customer always helped to concentrate the mind.

'I've managed to put together about £100,' Jackson replied, and then adding with a rueful grin, 'I've not been totally dependent on my parents.'

'So, you're looking for £300,' David mused, working out a few calculations on his jotter. 'Over two years, that would mean repayments – including interest – of about £14 a month. Is that the sort of figure you can afford?'

'I'm sure that won't be a problem.'

How many times had such an assurance been given in this room, only minutes then being needed for him to prove the fallacy of the answer? It was all about writing down a few sums on a piece of paper, something that so many customers chose not to do. They much preferred to keep figures in their heads leading, either vicariously or innocently, to a false belief in their ability to repay. He hoped that Jackson was not one of these, but just in case, he started to write down the answers this personable young man gave to his questions about his income and expenditure.

'It's a bit tight,' he concluded, having completed his totting up.

'But it'll be boosted when I get my tournament winnings,' Jackson added, optimistically.

'When or if?' David countered. 'Much better to stick to your known wages. In any case, you ought to be able to afford the repayments. But there's still an element of risk and I think we need to look to some form of security.'

He often found this matter of security – or collateral as the Americans preferred to call it – to be a vexed question with some customers who took the view that the bank was being paid interest for taking the risk. But any such earned interest would never equate to the loss that would arise if customers failed to repay the capital. The prime area of risk must lie with the customer, not the bank. But it might still be possible to grant a loan if some form of security was available.

Jackson's upper front teeth bit gently into his bottom lip as he contemplated his reply. 'The only tangible thing I'll have is the car – and my job. Would that be enough?'

'I'm afraid not. The car might end up being worth nothing and you could lose your job. No, when we talk about security, we mean items like houses or stocks and shares. All right,' he added, seeing Jackson's look of incredulity, 'I know such things are normally beyond the reach of impoverished graduates – and many bank managers, would you believe? The only alternative would be for you to provide a guarantor – someone like your father. Do you think he'd be prepared to support you?'

'Of course. I'm sure he would, especially as he's been enthusing about my new job. I can certainly ask him. He's an accountant, so he'll know if it's the right thing to do.'

'An accountant? Here in Barnmouth?'

'Yes, he's with Ponsonby's, next door.'

'You mean Peter Jackson?' No wonder John was such a fine young man. His father was the most upstanding partner in the firm.

'The very same.'

'Well, that makes it extremely simple. With him as guarantor, I'll be very happy to grant the loan. You better get off now and look for a suitable car.'

Invigorated by such a pleasant interview, but nursing his right hand following John's parting knuckle-breaking handshake, he now felt able to face Parker on his return from seeing Miss Harding. But Jane soon put a damper on that.

'He's not here,' she said, after he had called her into his room. 'He did come back, but then went straight out again – after talking to Richard and John...'

'Richard and John? Who on earth are they?'

'Mr Parker's assistants.'

'Oh, I see,' David replied, giving her a knowing look.

'That's not the case at all,' she protested, turning crimson at his teasing. 'Anyway, Mr Parker got back at just after eleven and, after about ten minutes, went out again. Richard – I mean his senior assistant – told me he'd gone off to Torquay.'

'Torquay? That's a bit odd. Did your Richard... sorry, did his senior assistant say when he'd be back?'

'No, but he said the matter was really urgent.'

CHAPTER 15

David was not surprised. Things seemed to be moving apace. Forty-eight hours ago, Parker, Broadman, Harding and Groves, let alone Dad, would not have warranted much of his attention – none at all in the case of Parker. Yet now they conjured up real or potential problems that seemed to be conspiring to ruin his cosy domain, never mind his career. At least he was not alone. At home, Sarah provided unstinting support, while Jane's progress was nothing short of startling. Before she left his room, he had heaped justified praise on her young shoulders and felt confident to leave his work in her hands while he was at the hospital. In making such a judgement, he was not insensitive to a subliminal image of her as his effective deputy, rather than Norman Charlton. *C'est la vie.*

Shut out the worries. That had to be the answer as he left for home. Clear his mind – give himself a break. What better way than to focus on his walk home, so often an effective antidote to the rigours of a morning's banking.

He approached the pier, which traversed the sea like a huge, horizontal hammer. The handle comprised walkways either side of a motley array of pinball machines, one-arm bandits and archaic contraptions that still showed penny-punters what the butler actually saw. If money was still available by the time trippers reached the head of the hammer, dodgem cars and galloping horses would provide further thrills and entertainment. At this time of year, these attractions lay dormant, the pier's only guests being a gaggle of fishermen, dangling their lines in the sea with an animation he felt was on a par with the supine crocodiles at Paignton Zoo.

The promenade was virtually deserted, enjoying a much-anticipated respite, particularly from marauding leather-clad youths on motorcycles and scooters, drawn to the town by a seafront inadvertently designed as an ideal racetrack and venue for two-wheeled altercations. Although he had no choice but to encounter such summer visitors on his walks to and from the bank, he studiously avoided the clubs and pubs which vied for the attention of these humourless helmeted visitors, not to mention the local girls of a certain disposition who seemed strangely attracted to flat vowels and an earthiness which lacked the warmth of the area's red Devon soil. He had sympathy for the elderly residents, originally drawn to Barnmouth's previous docile charms, and who tut-tutted throughout the summer months and bemoaned what the world was coming to. But he knew that the local traders had become tolerant of the new breed of visitor. They appreciated that the ringing of tills could encourage the arrival of their new cars to keep them amused during the winter months.

Not giving a second glance to the Esplanade Hotel – he must remain shut off – he made for the tree-lined roads which led to his house. He marvelled at how the trees could withstand the battering they had suffered these last few days. If only those on the golf course could be less resilient. Perhaps young John Jackson would be able to cure his slice; that would lessen the risk of encountering such hostile foliage.

Entering his front door, the aroma of simmering

vegetable soup and hot crusty bread wafted through the house and reminded him of how much he loved Sarah's home-made fare. He was thankful he did not have to settle for tinned soup, although this might be unavoidable should she return to work.

Sarah greeted him with a hug, her eyes twinkling.

He frowned. 'I didn't expect any levity this lunchtime.'

'Listen.'

And from the lounge, he heard it. The most evocative solo in his entire record collection – Coleman Hawkins's Body and Soul.

'It just seemed to sum up my feelings for you,' Sarah said, kissing him tenderly. 'I know I could have taken your Dad on my own...'

'No, I wanted to come. You've done everything, so far.'

'But you ought to be at work – what with the inspectors.'

'I was glad to get away.' Especially with Coleman Hawkins on the turntable.

'What happened this morning, then?'

He told her of the revelations about Miss Harding and her meeting with Parker who was now on some sort of mission to Torquay.

'I don't think she'll come back to work,' Sarah said. 'Not yet, anyway.'

'Is that female intuition?'

'Maybe. But she's clearly been up to something. Something she's ashamed of. No, she won't be back yet – not if her pride's been dented.'

He could only agree and suggested they got on with their lunch. He was relieved to find that Dad appeared to be philosophical about the hospital appointment and seemed to understand what it was all about. Lucky him. But the sooner they got on their way, the better.

He chose the route via Newton Abbot to get to Torbay Hospital, it being situated in the Newton Road, this side of Torquay. The first part of the journey aped an impressionist's landscape as the road meandered alongside the river, which tumbled down from the tors of Dartmoor to its estuary. Despite the onset of winter, colours abounded – though pastel, rather than the vividness of summer. Wild foliage and reeds sprouted from the river's banks and blended happily with the cultivated gardens that spilled down to the water's edge from their upland houses. Beyond the properties, a patchwork quilt stretched to the horizon, the fields occupied by sheep and cattle, the cereals having been harvested long ago.

It was a journey he had often made on the Saturdays when Torquay United were not playing at home. Newton Abbot, a major junction of the old Great Western Railway, sported an embankment at the western end of the station. It was a haven for groups of train-spotting youngsters, of which Mark had become a recent member. At his last birthday, he had been given the essential Ian Allan book containing the names and numbers of all GWR locomotives and he eagerly underlined each entry when a particular engine had been spotted. Even David became caught up in the excitement of witnessing a rare King-class monster heading the Cornish Riviera express to Penzance.

But there would be no train-spotting on this particular journey and all he saw as they crossed over the railway bridge was the signal gantry, which bestrode the four tracks of rails. Passing through the village of Kingskerswell, they went by the dog-racing track – a place he had no inclination to visit – and he soon turned his Hillman Minx into the drive of Torbay Hospital.

The previous time he had been in the hospital was for Mark's birth, but little had changed in the intervening eight years. Tiled walls, linoleum floors and antiseptic smells conspired to thwart bugs and disease, aided by a battery of doctors, nurses and orderlies, vying with each other in fervent activity. It did nothing to encourage his return.

Mercifully, the neurologist saw them straightway. He appeared to have been well briefed by Dr Edwards and kept his questions to a minimum, saying that his priority was the X-ray that he was putting in hand there and then. This was certainly good news. The process took half-an-hour and with the promise that the results would be sent to Dr Edwards within forty-eight hours, the three of them were soon on their way back to Barnmouth.

Two days was not long to await the outcome; it could well have been worse. Perhaps Aneurin Bevan's National Health Service was really beginning to work. But it was still long enough to dwell further on Dad's condition.

David had to agree with Dr Edwards. How could the problem be the onset of senility? Dad was not old enough for that. And he was simply not senile – he still had his faculties – it was his actions that had changed so dramatically. Wandering off, with no apparent motive or purpose, an inability to concentrate in stark contrast to the past and an increasing irascibility, for a man who could have invented the phrase "patience is a virtue".

Were these the products of brain malfunction? If so, what would the X-ray reveal? And would there be a cure for any evident defect? It was hardly like a car's engine failure – stick it in the garage for instant repair. He could not possibly equate remedies at Torbay Hospital with those of Blackstone Motors from where he had bought the Minx.

But there was no point in speculating. He did not have the wherewithal to hazard a valid opinion on the subject. They must rely on the medics. He took comfort in sharing Sarah's high regard for Dr Edwards who appeared determined to crack this particular problem.

CHAPTER 16

Jane's confidence was blossoming by the hour. If Mr Goodhart's complimentary words had been meant as an act of encouragement, they had certainly succeeded. Not since she had run the family home when her mother had been hospitalised had she felt more needed. She had now worked for three managers – at Torquay, St Marychurch and now in Barnmouth – and they were all quite different. The most senior, Mr Ramsbottom at Torquay, had been almost Edwardian in his attitude – to customers and staff. Silver haired and in his late-fifties, he was always immaculately clad in a dark pinstriped suit, wing-collared shirt and regimental tie, and his adversarial manner challenged all to question his authoritative presence. He had frightened her to death. It was only on her departure to St Marychurch, when he had presented her with a leaving gift of a cut-glass vase, that she had first seen him smile.

On the other hand, Mr Jevons at St Marychurch smiled incessantly and although she had already learnt to beware a smiling face, he was the exception, exuding good nature and jollity. He was also in his fifties, but still in his first appointment and showing no ambition to progress further, a view she felt was probably shared by the bank. He made it obvious that he had all he could ask for at St Marychurch. A small, undemanding business enabled him to spend a good proportion of his working week on his consummate pastime of sailing. To this end, he planned his day meticulously, making the most of the fact that he lived in the flat above the branch.

He would rise at seven, go downstairs to the office – sometimes still clad in his pyjamas – and open all the post before the arrival of his staff. He would then distribute it around their desks and return upstairs for breakfast. By the time he reappeared – between nine and nine-thirty – the branch was a hive of activity and well on the way to the shared objective of manager and staff – an early finish. To this end, Mr Jevons rolled up his sleeves in the afternoon, something that would have been abhorrent to Mr Ramsbottom, and helped tackle mundane matters such as listing cheques and adding up columns of figures. It enabled him to achieve his own personal target of sailing his yacht as soon as possible after the bank's closure at three o'clock. Jane felt that the regional manager would have preferred him to have more business-orientated objectives.

In her view, Mr Goodhart could not differ more from the other two. Apart from being much younger, he favoured contrasting objectives, shunning Mr Ramsbottom's authoritarianism for compassion and eschewing Mr Jevons's interpretation of a normal working day. She certainly respected Mr Ramsbottom – his position, anyway – and she had a high regard for the consideration shown by Mr Jevons to his staff, albeit not necessarily agreeing with his ultimate goal. After all, if this was adopted throughout the bank, National Counties might not have a future. No, the difference with Mr Goodhart was his dedicated work ethic, coupled with genuine compassion for both customers and staff. It was a combination to be admired and she only hoped he would not suffer a backlash from the unseemly events going on around them – particularly from Mr Parker and his team. She must do everything possible to support him.

After leaving his room, she sat down at her desk where Katie immediately joined her. The typist clasped a raft of letters for her to check before being signed by the manager, but the letters were clearly the last thing on her mind. 'Who was that gorgeous hulk you took in to see the manager this morning?' she asked, her eyes alive with expectation. Oh dear, the letters would have to be checked extra carefully; Katie's concentration could easily have waned over her typewriter.

'I don't know who you mean,' Jane replied, deciding to string the typist along. Just because Katie had the attractions she would wish for herself, did not mean she had the automatic right to put herself in the front line for any eligible man who might come into the bank. She already had designs on the inspector's assistants and now she seemed to be staking a claim on John Jackson.

'Oh come on, Jane, stop kidding. You know full well who I'm talking about. I saw you come out of the manager's room. You were red as a beetroot.'

Jane immediately blushed at the thought of it.

'There you go again,' Katie almost shrieked, a few heads turning their way and making her go an even deeper shade of red.

'All right, all right, keep your voice down,' she urged, wishing she were a manager with the privacy of her own room. 'If you must know, it was someone called John Jackson. His account's just been transferred from Loughborough.'

'What does he do, what does he do?' Katie demanded, unable to contain her excitement.

'I don't know. It didn't say on the PM card.' But unbeknown to Katie, she was just as eager to see the card once Mr Goodhart had dictated the content of the interview.

She always enjoyed reading the private memorandum cards that were maintained for every customer and were effectively a personal history from the day the account was opened. Everything of note was entered on the card, enabling any interviewer to have all relevant information set out concisely in one place. There was now only one problem for her. In the absence of Margaret, Mr Goodhart would dictate his notes to Katie who would be first to know everything about John Jackson. There was simply no justice!

'From Loughborough,' Katie digested, pursing her full, painted lips. 'I wonder what he's doing down here. And why do you think he wanted to see the manager?'

'I really have no idea,' Jane sighed, hoping an indifferent air would be shared by Katie. 'Anyway, what's it to you? I thought you had designs on Richard Allen.'

Katie grinned wickedly. How could this girl be so worldly-wise when she was four years younger than herself? 'Mustn't keep all your eggs in one basket,' she answered. 'Anyway, I was only thinking of customer relations. Must keep the customers happy, you know.'

Jane smiled and slowly shook her head from side to side. 'You're incorrigible, Katie. But I do envy you sometimes.'

'Envy me? Me? But you're Mr Goodhart's assistant. How could you possibly envy me?'

Jane smiled again, this time rather wistfully. 'But that's work. I was thinking of other things.'

'Men you mean?' Katie almost shrilled.

'Shh. Do keep your voice down. Yes, I suppose I do. Just look at me and then at yourself. I bet they're like bees round a honey pot with you. I've never had a boyfriend in my life.'

Her words came out before she realized what she was saying. How could she admit that to anyone – let alone Katie? She had effectively taken the girl into her confidence and must backtrack – immediately. 'You won't tell anyone that, will you? Just forget what I just said.'

It was now Katie's turn to smile, a gentle smile of such understanding that Jane felt like putting her arms around her and pouring her heart out. Instead, she simply looked down at the letters Katie had typed, shrugged her shoulders and said, 'I suppose we'd better get on.'

'I've got an idea,' Katie said, ignoring her last words. 'Why don't you come out with us on Saturday night? We're going to the Pavilion – me and Daphne. And Jilly might come as well. How about it? It'll be a great laugh.'

Jane could hardly believe what she was hearing. The Pavilion was a hall along the seafront, used for concerts, dances and even bingo in the height of the season. She had always avoided the place – especially on a Saturday night. 'The Pavilion? I couldn't go to a place like that.'

'Why ever not? It'll be great. It's the Saturday dance. Chris Barber's playing.'

'Chris Barber?' The name meant nothing to her.

'Jane! Where have you been? It's Chris Barber's Jazz Band. It's traditional jazz. You must have heard of him.'

She shook her head. 'Anyway, you say it's a dance. I've never danced in my life.'

'That doesn't matter. Oh, do come, it'll be wonderful.'

'But look at me. Can you really see me being the belle of the ball?'

'I don't see why not. You've such a pretty face and in your best party dress... Oh, come on, Jane, you really must come.'

It was surprising enough to receive such an invitation,

but she was astounded at Katie's last comment. Such a pretty face? Where on earth had that come from? Alongside Katie, Daphne and Jilly – in a dance hall of all places – she would be the wallflower of all wallflowers. It would be so embarrassing. She had to change the subject and decided to fend Katie off with a non-committal reply. 'You must know, Katie, it really isn't me. But I'll think about it. Now, I must check your letters.'

Katie positively skipped away to her typewriter. It was not hard to imagine her being the life and soul of any party – or of any dance at the Pavilion. But it would be a disaster for her. She preferred not to think about such a nightmare and after checking the letters – which were surprisingly accurate – she thought again about George Broadman and those credits that had been wrongly processed through his account.

He had been such a decent and likeable man. His larger-than-life personality matched his physique and it had so upset her that he had succumbed to such a fate, be it accident or suicide. It had been galling to break down in front of Mr Goodhart and she now felt her eyes moistening again, just thinking about it. But Margaret had clearly been even more upset. Surely, nothing had been going on between them? They would have been such an unlikely couple.

As for his crossfiring, whatever possessed him to do it? And what had Bernard been up to? He of all people should have known how to take in the credits. At least it was down to Mr Goodhart to take that up. Perhaps she would never know the outcome, but was it possible for Bernard to have blotted his copybook? She would not be the only one to be less than upset if that was the case.

It was now past twelve and she must take her lunch

break before Mr Goodhart went at one. She decided to stroll along the seafront and went to the ladies' cloakroom to get her coat. As she looked in the mirror above the hand basin, she thought of what Katie had said. No, it was simply not true. Why had she said such a thing? She took off her glasses to wipe away a smear from a lens, but before replacing them, looked again in the mirror. Perhaps her features were not so bad after all. A little gaunt, maybe, and her swept-back hair emphasised her high forehead. It seemed to dominate her whole face. Idly twisting a few strands of hair, she wondered if a new style might soften her features. Different frames might also be a good idea.

But this was nonsense. Putting on her coat, she left the office for her walk and to think more about George Broadman's account. She soon came to the Seaway Café and wondered what might have happened at Margaret's meeting with Mr Parker. It must have been serious for Richard Allen to be so concerned about the inspector having to dash off to Torquay. The café was now empty as it awaited its lunchtime trade, but not being hungry, she pressed on and soon reached an imposing building which she would normally have gone past in full stride. But today, she found herself drawn to it as if by a magnet and could not help but study an advertising photograph of a smiling, rather lean young man caressing a gleaming trombone.

CHAPTER 17

David awoke on Thursday morning with Sarah's arm gripping him around the waist like a straitjacket. She was in a deep sleep and he decided to lie still so as not to waken her – not that he could move anyway. He guessed the time was about six-thirty and although it was too dark outside to gauge the weather, he listened carefully for the sound of the wind that had dominated the week. Silence reigned. Perhaps the golf course would not be in its usual hostile state. When the wind blew, eyes wept, ears tingled, hats flew and umbrellas inverted. Problems quadrupled in the winter's cold and many a time the course would even be closed by low-flying cloud. Being the end of November, he had every right to speculate on what was happening outside.

But he still loved the ambience of Barnmouth Golf Club, which straddled the moorland above the town and boasted some of the finest views in Devon. To the east, the coastline extended beyond the estuary of the River Exe to the distant craggy cliffs of Dorset, while to the north and west, lay the wild beauty of Dartmoor, its many tors and acres of bracken breaking up the exposed homes of thousands of sheep, cattle and wild ponies. And to the south, far below in the valley carved into the abutting hills, the River Barn ambled down from Haytor to its firth in the heart of the town. The Great Western railway line followed the contours of the river and the regular whistles from the steam locomotives caused seagulls, ducks and other waterfowl to rise in protest at their disturbed repose.

Only the most dedicated golfers could ignore the surrounding scenery in their quest for ever-lower scores and for some, including David, the panoramic beauty could easily outshine the quality of the golf.

Sarah moved at last, loosening her grip to ease his threatening cramp. He encouraged her return to consciousness with a gentle dig in the ribs, and she drew herself away, yawned noisily and declared she had not slept a wink all night. He shook his head in wonder at a statement from someone whose comatose body had been shackled to his for the last hour. But he chose not to pick an argument, and simply leaned over to give his favourite wife a good morning kiss.

An hour later, he put his Hillman Minx into first gear and set off for the golf club, his clubs safely stowed in the boot. He had already donned his golf gear – tartan trousers, roll-neck shirt and two woollen jumpers – and his office clothes lay on the back seat of the car. He would change after the game, ready for his meeting with Parker, which had been postponed until the afternoon. Richard Allen had apologised for his boss having been detained in Torquay yesterday – why Torquay? – and said he wanted to see him at two-thirty today. The delay was so frustrating. What had Parker learnt from Miss Harding? Or had he gleaned nothing at all? Yet the trip to Torquay might, of course, be unconnected with matters at Barnmouth. He would have to be patient and only hoped he would not dwell on the outcome at the top of his back swing.

He pulled into the car park and eased into a space between a pale-blue Austin Devon and a green Morris Minor estate. As there was no sign of Stuart's Bentley, he removed his clubs from the car and went to the professional's shop to register for the Turkey Trot competition.

He immediately saw the tall figure of John Jackson taking down the details of a couple of golfers who were entering the event. The assistant professional smiled warmly when it was his turn. 'Morning Mr Goodhart. Your luck's in today – with the weather, I mean. I reckon it'll stay fine till lunchtime.'

This was more like it. What a difference from the dour professional who would hardly pass the time of day. 'I'm glad to see they've got you working,' he replied, hoping John's bonhomie would rub off on the pro. 'It's funny how a bank manager can get anxious about things like that.'

John grinned. 'There's no need to worry. I still haven't found a car, so I'm not in hock with you yet. Anyway, if I run short, we can always barter.'

'Barter?'

'How many golf lessons would you need to cover a month's loan repayment?'

David's eyes widened in mock alarm. 'If I knew you were a schemer like that, I'd never have agreed the loan. But I hope you're right about the weather. Have you seen Stuart Brown yet?'

'Stuart Brown? I'm sorry, I don't know many members yet.' He then scanned the list in front of him. 'No, he's not yet registered, but I'll keep my eyes open for him. Is he playing with you?'

David nodded. 'In a three-ball, with a guest, John English.'

'You know guests can't enter the Turkey Trot?'

'Of course, but Stuart and I'll mark each other's cards.'

As he collected his scorecard, he noticed the Bentley glide into the car park and he left the shop to meet his playing partners. Their cordial greetings augured well for a pleasant morning, but he was somewhat disconcerted by English's limp-wristed handshake, something he imagined Sarah would have expected. It was far different from Stuart's; his firm grasp betrayed his time as a senior army officer with a distinguished war record. It culminated in the award of the Military Cross and although Stuart had never discussed this with him, the locals believed it to relate to his selflessness in rescuing his men when under attack. David was thankful that opportunities to display such valour had not arisen for him, although he might have expected it in his role as a senior aircraftman in the RAF's fire service.

Ten minutes later, they stood on the first tee, cold and ill-prepared for their round. Unlike professionals, club golfers shun any pre-match preparation. Far better to get to the club at the last possible moment, have a couple of practice swings and then expect to hit the ball down the middle. David well knew it was more likely that the first shot would be sliced, hooked, topped or, in some cases, missed completely, thus setting in motion an unsyncopated rhythm lasting well into the round.

As it happened, he hit the best of their three drives on the long par five, which stretched to the western extremity of the course. Despite having the lowest handicap, Stuart struggled from the start, as if he had something on his mind. He and English were perfectly civil, but David sensed a palpable tension between them. It came to a head on the ninth hole when Stuart accused English of cheating. David could only agree. English's ball had lodged in deep heather and after lifting it for identification he replaced it in a more advantageous spot. David had seen him do it before and he had also spotted him improving the lie of his ball on the fairway. Perhaps he was not fully conversant with the rules, but Stuart did not seem to share that view by the way he castigated his guest.

The atmosphere progressively worsened and it was hard to believe the other two were friends and business acquaintances. Could this spat be symptomatic of something far more serious between them? Whatever, the tension had clearly affected the scoring over the first nine holes and David felt pleased to have risen above it and be in the lead. English, with the help of his sleight of hand, was not far behind, but he was not in the competition and his duplicity was a matter between him and his conscience. Nevertheless, it was most disturbing and he was clearly in danger of failing the three Cs test of any lending proposition – character, capital and capability. David would normally require a pass in each category, but a golfer who surreptitiously bends or breaks the rules is unlikely to confine such a lapse in character to one particular activity. A cheat is a cheat; a liar is a liar. And such transgressions need not be overt. Subliminal messages can swim in the minds of such customers and interviews with them could often end with the dreaded words, 'Don't worry Mr Goodhart, I won't let you down.' Talk about the kiss of death.

But he was anxious not to prejudge John English – even with that effete handshake. He would simply heed the warning signals – always to be ignored at his peril. For now, he would concentrate on his golf; there was a turkey at stake. But he would continue to keep his eyes and ears open.

By the end of the round, he had the best score – a respectable thirty-six points – though this was unlikely to win a turkey. Oh well, there was always next year. Once in the clubhouse, having showered and changed and munching a ham sandwich, he asked English about having a meeting.

'Yes, I'd like that,' the hotelier replied, glancing imperceptibly at Brown before continuing. 'The thing is, my bank's too small. And the manager doesn't understand the hotel business.'

David nodded – without agreeing. He had heard it all before. "My bank doesn't understand my business" was a common reason for customers wanting to change banks. It ought to be translated into "I went overdrawn without arrangement and the manager had the temerity to bounce my cheques".

'In what particular way?' he asked. A seaside bank manager not knowing about the hotel trade? Impossible. 'What doesn't he understand?'

'He doesn't have a clue about anything,' Stuart interrupted, not to English's liking, judging by the scowl that briefly etched his brow. 'He's wet behind the ears...'

'No, that's going too far,' English countered, then switching his attention back to David. 'He can't help being inexperienced, but the bank itself is too small. It's better suited to personal accounts – not business accounts like mine. Everything has to be referred to head office. At your bank, David, you'd be able to make a decision there and then. That's what customers really want.'

All right, this discussion was taking place over a convivial light lunch after a round of golf, but David was always wary when customers – especially potential customers – adopted an automatic air of familiarity. And he could well-imagine English always being presumptuous enough to assume the right to discard normal business protocol. 'No bank manager could promise you that,' he answered. 'So many things might have to be taken into account.'

'I'm sure you know what I mean,' English said, clearly aware of a bead of perspiration on his brow, but resisting any urge to wipe it away. David had noticed it appear shortly after Brown's interruption and was satisfied it was not the aftermath of a hot shower. English was nervous about something and it showed in his florid, rather flaccid features, which contrasted sharply with those of the debonair solicitor. No wonder Sarah had winced at the mention of the hotelier, especially if he had all but tried to paw the ladies at their coffee morning.

'How about Monday?' David asked, wanting to draw the subject to a close. If the conversation were to continue along these lines, it would need to be in the privacy of his office – without Stuart's presence. 'In the morning?'

'That'd be fine. Say eleven o'clock?'

After agreeing the appointment, they rose to leave and when English excused himself to go to the cloakroom, Stuart took the opportunity to have a quiet word. 'You will help him, won't you, David?' he urged, draping his arm around his shoulders.

'I'll do my best,' David replied, disturbed at the intensity of Stuart's aside. 'But it all depends on what he wants.'

'Oh, you'll have no problem with that. Just do it, please. Let's say as a favour to me. And by the way, I'll probably have some substantial new business for you before the end of next week.'

Five minutes later, David pulled out of the car park and made towards the long winding descent to the town centre. He dwelled uneasily on Stuart's last words. Had they been intended as a threat – or a bribe, for that matter? If so, it did not look good from the senior partner of the most prestigious solicitors in the whole area, never mind just in Barnmouth. No, it was not possible; he had simply made too much of the link between English's requirements and the additional new business being offered by Stuart.

It was quite normal for solicitors to introduce new customers to banks, particularly where the firm's own account was actually domiciled. Prior to John English, Stuart had introduced innumerable worthwhile accounts and David had been pleased to return the compliment by pointing his own customers towards the solicitor. The firm had been authorized to act on behalf of the bank in its affairs and those of its customers.

This two-way exchange of business was to everyone's benefit and David was proud of the relationship he had built up with Stuart. The solicitor seemed to relish having a get-up-and-go manager at the bank, as opposed to his predecessor – an admirable ambassador of the bank, but whose prime aim had apparently been to reach retirement without blotting his copybook. This meant an inevitable loss of new business contacts. But such opportunities abounded with Stuart, not just with new customers, but also with the vast sums passing through his firm's clients' accounts. David had soon learnt that he was no parochial solicitor and came to admire his skills at scouring the country – particularly London – in what seemed to be an unquenchable quest for new clients. The end result was the accumulation of abundant credit balances that significantly contributed to the bank's profitability. Yes, Stuart was a man to nurture, but that parting shot at the golf club was distinctly disconcerting.

He was still mulling it over as he walked through the front door of the bank. He immediately spotted an arm-waving Jane who rushed forward as he moved through the banking hall.

'I've been looking out for you for ages,' she cried. 'I wanted to...'

'Hang on a minute, Jane,' he interrupted. 'I'm not late.

You knew I wouldn't be back until one-thirty.'

'Yes, I know, sir, but... but I wanted to make sure I saw you before you got to your room.'

'My room?'

'Yes. Mr Parker's in there. He's waiting for you.'

'But I wasn't due to see him until two-thirty.'

'I know, sir,' Jane answered, looking round to the door of his room, as if to ensure it was still closed. 'But he said something's come up. And he hoped he could see you as soon as you got in. He asked if he could use your room. I didn't think you'd mind, so I said it would be all right.'

'Yes, that's fine,' he confirmed, his heart sinking at the prospect of further bad news. 'Yes, you did the right thing. I better get in there and see what he wants.'

As he entered the room, Parker was sitting upright at the desk, Gone was his familiar sprawling pose and he even rose to his feet.

'Ah, Mr Goodhart,' he said, as usual watching him intently, but this time with no hint of belligerency. 'I hope you don't mind, but Jane said...'

'Of course not. It's my pleasure.'

'It's just that I had calls to make – confidential ones. I know we weren't due to meet until later, but there's been a development.'

'With Miss Harding?' This is it. What is he going to reveal now?

'Certainly with Miss Harding. But since then I've been to Torquay. I've had a lengthy meeting with the police.'

'The police?'

'It was to do with your George Broadman. I'm afraid it wasn't an accident or suicide. He was murdered.'

CHAPTER 18

David's ruddy glow from the bracing golf course drained from his face. It had been bad enough that an accident or suicide had taken George Broadman's life, but murder was almost impossible to contemplate. Surely, Parker must be wrong.

'I can't believe it,' he said. 'Are you sure? How did you find out? Who told you?'

'Yes, I'm sure,' Parker answered, sitting down and motioning David to do likewise. 'It was the police – an Inspector Hopkins.'

'The police? But why should the police get in touch with you?'

'They didn't,' Parker replied. 'I went to them.'

'What?' Why would he go to the police about the death of a customer?

'Remember on Monday,' Parker continued, 'I told you I thought something was going on down here in Barnmouth? Well, since then so much more has happened.'

'You can say that again,' David acknowledged. He had never known a week like it.

'And there appeared to be a chain,' Parker continued, ignoring his interjection, 'with too many links in it for my liking – all of them involving your butcher. To start with, you bounced his cheques for the first time ever; then his dead body is found at the bottom of a cliff; and the next day, you established he'd been crossfiring – for months on end, without it having been brought to your attention. After that, your secretary flees the nest on the pretence of a migraine; and rather than talk to you about it, she demands to see me – not here in the bank, but at the Seaway Café, of all places.'

He paused, licking his lips, as if taking stock of his analysis of events, but then asked if there was a chance of a cup of tea. David phoned through to Katie and then waited for Parker to continue.

'And none of this seemed to relate to that other business we were concerned about. It was all very odd. But after seeing Miss Harding, I decided to pursue my dealings with the police.'

'Pursue? You were already liaising with them?'

Parker nodded. 'Because of that other business. But after what Miss Harding told me...'

The inspector paused and David wondered if he was to be taken into his confidence. 'Is it something you can tell me about?' he asked. It would certainly be awkward to be kept in the dark.

'Yes, indeed,' Parker replied, smiling – his first genuine smile since the start of the inspection. 'We need to get both our heads round this one. I think we should work in tandem.'

This was better, a joint effort. And had Parker's previous acerbity and bluntness only been an act? If nothing else, he had stopped jangling his keys and coins.

'The routine inspection must take its normal course,' Parker added, 'but I'll get my boys to do more than their normal share. And I'll have to verify all your overdrawn accounts – carry out the usual lending inspection. But as far as the Broadman affair is concerned, I think we should pool our thoughts and resources.'

'But what made the police say that George was murdered?'

147

'They didn't to start with. They were suspicious of my motives and interference, I suppose. But then I was shown in to see Inspector Hopkins. He was keeping his cards close to his chest, but became interested in my theories – about the chain of events. In fact, he grilled me quite hard; a case of role reversal,' he added, grinning at the irony. 'Then he let out what I had never contemplated – that Broadman's death was suspicious and was being treated as murder.'

'But what makes him think that?'

'Somehow or other, they got the wreckage off the rocks and carried out a routine examination. Even though it was smashed beyond recognition, they were able to check for possible mechanical defects. It seems they always look at the braking system – the hoses to be precise. And the telltale signs were there; the hoses had been cut with a knife. When Broadman applied the brakes, nothing would have happened. It could, of course, have occurred anywhere. But the police believe he had an assignation in the car park and the route from Barnmouth was up hill all the way – until he drove into the car park and had to stop.'

'So they've ruled out suicide altogether?' David asked, shocked at the revelation.

'It seems so, unless he fixed the brakes himself – to make it look like murder.'

'Do the police think that's possible?'

Parker shook his head. 'They've not known it happen before – not down here, anyway. No, they reckon it's murder, all right. And now they're glad I called. They're pleased to have the background from the bank – in their search for suspects.'

'And do they have anyone in mind – any suspect at all?'

'At this stage, they'd hardly let me in on that. But I'm

sure they've added Miss Harding to their list.'

'Miss Harding?' What was he on about?

'Yes,' Parker replied, now grinning, almost salaciously, 'George Broadman's lover.'

Of all the answers the inspector could have given him, this was the most unimaginable. 'She was his lover?' he could barely gasp, his eyes goggling in disbelief. 'Miss Harding? Oh, come on, you've got to be joking.'

Parker continued grinning, as if he had, indeed, cracked a joke, but then added seriously, 'The actual definition of the word "lover" may well be in doubt, but there's no doubting Miss Harding had been in love with George Broadman.'

'But how could you possibly know that?'

'She told me,' Parker almost cooed and actually rubbed his hands together, as if in relish at the unfolding story. 'Not straightaway. I had to gain her confidence before she could reveal anything so personal. At first...'

A knock on the door interrupted the inspector and at David's call to come in, Katie Tibbs entered the room, a tray of crockery balanced precariously on one hand as she used the other to open and then close the door. He feared the tray's contents might cascade over Parker's back and quickly rose to relieve the girl of her responsibilities as tea lady.

'Thank you, Katie,' he said. 'That's just what we need.'

'I hope it's all right, sir,' the typist replied, glancing rather impishly from one man to the other. 'I've never done it before. I mean I've never made a pot of tea for two. I like a mug, myself, and I usually have coffee. It's not so wishy-washy as tea. It's the milkiness I really don't like. I suppose I could have it without milk, but that doesn't seem right for tea, does it? I think they have lemon with it in

Russia, but I don't fancy that. Anyway...'

'Anyway, Katie, that's all for now,' David interjected. Her voracious appetite for chatting, if not for cups of tea, knew no bounds and he was anxious to hear more about Miss Harding's love life. He wondered if Katie knew about it, but immediately dismissed such speculation. In her hands, a powder keg of such information would have burst upon the gossip-sated Barnmouth staff, even reaching his own ears with any amount of luck.

When the typist had left the room, a quizzical smile touched Parker's lips as he slowly shook his head in evident bemusement. 'Quite a young lady,' he simply said.

'I think she's great,' David replied. 'She's always so bubbly – the life and soul of the branch. Talks too much, of course, and I'm always afraid she'll cross the line of acceptability. But she never seems to – and she's more intelligent than she leads you to believe. I also have the feeling that since Miss Harding went home, she's been drawing Jane out of her shell. That really would be a good thing. But talking about Miss Harding, can we get back to your meeting with her?'

'A good idea,' Parker agreed. 'I decided to get to the café first – to pick out a suitable table. As it happened, we had the place to ourselves. At first, it was extremely slow going. I chose not to say much and there was one pregnant pause after another. She was clearly nervous – and embarrassed. A few prods from me eventually drew her out and I tried to convince her I was a friend, not foe. She probably didn't think that on Monday.'

'Not unexpected on the first day of an inspection.'

'But I had to alter that view. Not so easy for an old codger like me, but I had to gain her trust. I needed to know why she wanted to see me, rather than you. It was so illogical. It seems it was all down to embarrassment. She's spent all these years trying to dominate a succession of managers – including you, of course. But it was all an act. She has one hell of an inferiority complex. Quite frankly, she couldn't face you – not at this stage, anyway. But she knows she'll have to sooner or later.'

Thank goodness for Jane's previous report of her visit to Miss Harding's house, otherwise the revelation of his secretary's inferiority complex would have been laughable. He recalled all the times she had tried to demean his position as manager. It had not seemed like an act then.

'It was all down to her mother,' Parker continued, getting up to stretch his legs. He even plunged a hand into his trousers' pocket, but appeared to resist the urge to chink his coins. Instead, he referred to his little black book as he returned to his chair. 'It went back to her school days. Her mother never gave her any encouragement, never attended school plays and always derided her efforts. Out of school – when she was in her teens – she had to be home by ten, at the latest. There was one time she missed her bus home and was called a dirty stop-out. As she got older, boys were forbidden, trips to the cinema had to be with her parents and she never holidayed alone or with a friend.'

'But why would a mother act like that?' David asked, appalled at such parental behaviour. Even his own mother-in-law had not gone to those extremes. As for himself and Sarah, he could not imagine them ever treating Mark in such a degrading manner.

'Jealousy. Her mother had always been jealous of her daughter's attributes. Looks, for instance.'

'Looks?'

'Miss Harding actually showed me a photograph – of

when she was about twenty. It was not a boast – more like the production of a piece of evidence. She was some beauty. Most striking. As were her results at school. She passed her matriculation with flying colours, went to college and landed a prestigious job in the bank.'

David pursed his lips and shook his head. A beauty? Impossible. 'But I don't see why this background should have turned her into something of an ogre at the office.'

'Her mother's illness was probably behind that – or should I say alleged illness. It started after her husband died. She was so frightened that a man would come along and whisk her daughter away. She would then be all alone. So she decided to become ill, in need of constant attention. Miss Harding didn't find it so bad at first, but as time went on... let's just say the metaphorical umbilical cord got tighter and tighter – through emotional blackmail.'

'That's strong stuff, although it does tie-in with office gossip about her home life. I mentioned some of this to you on Monday.'

Parker nodded. 'Miss Harding confirmed it all – and more. Her mother would constantly harp on at her. She'd say such things as "I don't know how I'd cope without you" or "I know you'd never leave me". Then she'd really hit home with "It's just what your father would have wanted, our being together, just the two of us". That sort of thing. It was like an incarceration. And when she was let out – to go to work – she simply rebelled. It was her way of letting out her anger.'

'I can see that's feasible, but how does George Broadman come into the picture?'

'Ah, George Broadman. He was Miss Harding's escape, the reason for keeping her sanity. It started at school. He was slightly older and she developed a crush on him. But it could never go any further – those shackles at home. They became friends, in a distant sort of way, but Miss Harding never made her true feelings known to him. Then their lives drifted apart until he opened a shop, at about the same time she came here. It rejuvenated her feelings for him and she had a ready-made excuse to see him each week.'

David smiled. 'And when I was about to bounce his cheques, she feared for her best cuts of meat.'

'She may have said that, but there was far more on her mind. About six months ago, they started dating.'

'What?' David exclaimed, and then remembered that Parker had described them as being lovers. But even if she had been a stunner in her youth, he could not imagine her on the arm of the big butcher now, never mind sleeping with him. 'But what about those shackles at home?'

'They never met in the evenings, just during the day. That way, her mother would never know. She knew her daughter was at work.'

'And she was at work.'

'Not all the time. Not during lunch hours, nor when she took her holidays.'

'You mean she went away on holiday with him? But her mother would never allow that.'

'No, she didn't go away with him on holiday and as far as her mother was concerned, she never took any holidays. Mother thought she was the dedicated bank secretary who didn't need breaks from work – something that suited her very well indeed.'

'But Miss Harding always took her full holiday entitlement – not necessarily in weeks at a time. She often preferred to have odd days off in the middle of the week – to break it up a bit.'

'And when is early closing day in Barnmouth?'

'It's Wednesday, but...' his words tailed off as it dawned on him. 'I don't believe it. You're having me on.'

Parker shook his head. 'No, it's true enough – right out of Miss Harding's mouth.'

'So they had secret trysts in the lunch hours?' And what did they get up to on Wednesdays?'

'I'm glad you're sitting down,' Parker replied, hardly able to contain his mirth. 'I'm sorry,' he then continued, becoming more serious. 'And bearing in mind the outcome, it's hardly a laughing matter. But they went racing – horse racing in Newton Abbot.'

'This is madness!' David exclaimed, yet again unable to believe what he was hearing. 'Miss Harding going horse racing? Gambling?'

Parker nodded. 'And that's the crux of this whole sorry business. Gambling. George Broadman was an inveterate gambler. Horse racing at Newton Abbot, dog racing at Torquay, casinos in Exeter and Plymouth – you name it, he did it. At first, Miss Harding knew nothing about it. But when he invited her to Newton races, she was flattered and, over a period, actually started to enjoy it.'

'But what made him ask her out in the first place? They weren't the most likely couple.'

'They were both single, not far off in ages and had started to get to know each other better on a butcher/customer basis. Then they started harking back to their school days. And after all those years, Miss Harding discovered she was still infatuated.'

'But what about George? What was in it for him?'

'He was probably more wily than anyone knew. I reckon he could see a possible source of finance. Perhaps not at first, but he then foresaw a potential way of financing his addiction. Like most gamblers, he lost more than he won and he got into debt. In a small way at first, but it then became difficult to control, so...'

'Hang on a minute,' David interrupted. 'This whole story has come from Miss Harding. Are you sure it's true? Isn't it possible there's a Walter Mitty element going on here?'

'A good question. And you're right; we can't get confirmation from Broadman himself. But it won't take much to check the gist of the story and the police are working on that. In any case, what about our own evidence?'

David raised his eyebrows.

'That crossfiring of his,' Parker added.

Of course! His gambling. That's what it was all about. And he was also in hock with his wholesaler. Thank goodness he had bounced all those cheques. 'But that doesn't explain his death.'

Parker pursed his lips. 'It depends on how much was involved. It's possible we've only seen the tip of the iceberg. That's something for me to work on. But what about your own enquiries? How are they coming along?'

Good. Confirmation that they would be working together. 'We're getting there. Jane's done a good job digging around. It seems the fault arose when George's credits were actually paid in. The finger's pointing at Bernard Groves and my next job is to see what he has to say about it. You're not thinking that Miss Harding might also be involved?'

'No, not with the actual crossfiring. When I broached the subject, she was genuinely stunned. She couldn't believe he'd been operating such a scam. She thought she'd given him all the financial help he needed.'

Oh no. Financial help? Had she been bailing him out? It had not been evident from her bank account and vouchers. In any case, her salary could not have supported his gambling debts. 'But I've seen no sign of that happening. Did she say how she'd helped him?'

'No,' Parker replied. 'She clammed up then. I hoped you might be able to help with that.'

Yet more investigations. 'I'll have to look into that. But I still don't see why the police might be treating her as a suspect.'

'It's because of her overall involvement. And if she's been financing him, was it a gift or a loan? Had she been demanding repayment, which was not forthcoming? Had there been a dramatic falling out?'

'That's fair enough,' David acknowledged, though hardly able to contemplate her tampering with the van's brakes. But did she have an accomplice? No, that was impossible. And what about her reaction to the news? 'But she was clearly shocked to the core when she heard of his death. I can't believe she was involved.'

'And how many times might that have been said of a trusted person – only to be proved wrong. And we're not just talking about a minor misdemeanour. Remember this is a murder investigation.'

CHAPTER 19

David well recalled his initial meeting with Miss Harding. He had arrived on his first day embarrassingly dishevelled; the weather had been worse than this week. His predecessor had joked about the deteriorating standards set by bank managers, but it was no laughing matter for Miss Harding who pointedly scrutinized him from top to toe. Only sheer strength of will prevented him from polishing the toecaps of his shoes on the backs of his trousers' legs, half expecting her to copy his war-time drill sergeant who delighted in scraping the sole of his own boot across those of his squaddies to emphasize their less than immaculate state. Instead, she had simply appeared disdainful, a look with which he would become painfully familiar as time rolled on. Now, two years later, she was a murder suspect. Unbelievable.

'Does she know she might be a suspect?' he asked Parker, then adding as an afterthought, 'For that matter, does she know George was murdered?'

'Yes, she knows he was murdered. I told her – in confidence. As for her being a suspect, I've no idea what was passing through her mind. But she was devastated. She couldn't go on with the meeting.'

No wonder. Whatever might have been going on in his secretary's life, murder was, surely, not an option. Having said that, this must be the first murder of a Barnmouth citizen in living memory and someone – no matter how unsuspecting – must be responsible.

'I had to let her go home,' Parker continued, closing his

notebook and putting it into his jacket pocket, 'but not before she promised to come and see you tomorrow. She's now terrified about her financial involvement. I think she wants to bare her soul.'

'To me? Why me, rather than you?'

'That was my doing,' Parker said, as he rose to leave the room. 'I pointed out her prime responsibility was to you, not me. Now I've broken the ice, so to speak, she needs to have a heart-to-heart with you.'

This really was now a team effort. And it was certainly a different side of the inspector from the one that grilled him on Monday. He was even starting to like the man and only hoped that Parker's change of attitude was not a double bluff.

With the inspector gone to pursue his own investigations, he now contemplated tomorrow's meeting with Miss Harding. Would she simply turn up at nine – as if on a normal working day? Or should he telephone her to arrange a specific time? And be harangued again by her mother? Definitely not. But any meeting would have to fit into his pre-booked interviews. As he considered the most appropriate action, a tap on the door announced the arrival of Katie Tibbs.

'Ah, Katie,' he said, beckoning her to take a seat. 'It's dictation time, is it?'

'If that's all right with you, sir. I'm not as quick as Miss Harding and...'

'I think you're doing splendidly,' he interrupted, 'and you seem to be teaming up well with Jane.'

'Oh, Jane... yes, she's lovely,' Katie replied, astonishing him with her choice of word. First of all, Miss Harding a beauty; now Jane lovely?' 'But she needs to come out of her shell a bit. I can't believe she's four years older than me. Well, I can, work-wise. She knows such a lot. Doing her exams and all that. She must be ever so brainy. And working for you, of course – being your assistant. I know I'm now working for you as well, but it's not the same. Shorthand and typing – that's different from actual banking. All that legal stuff. I couldn't get my head round that. But Jane...'

'You're quite the little chatterbox, aren't you, Katie?' Interrupting seemed to be the only way to stem her flow. At her age, he had been quite the opposite – taciturn in the extreme. Only a spell in the RAF had saved him from his own self-consciousness. On being called up, his banking background had singled him out as a potential pen-pusher and he had surprised himself at being forthright enough to shun the suggestion that he would be ideally suited in Pay Accounts or some other clerical role. Driving a vehicle held much greater attraction than wielding a pen and he became a fireman for five years. But having Katie's confidence would have enabled him to cope far better with such a change of employment and environment.

'Yes, quite a chatterbox,' he continued, then adding on seeing her look of concern, 'but don't change for heaven's sake. You're so refreshing – especially in the present circumstances.'

'You mean about poor Mr Broadman?' Katie asked, screwing her pretty face up in concern. 'Such a horrible accident.'

She clearly had no inkling of his murder, but the news would spread quickly enough. And when Miss Harding's involvement became public, he only hoped the likes of Katie would be discreet in their observations of such a dramatic and unexpected relationship.

'Yes, that and other things,' he simply answered, then

changed the subject. 'But let's get on with the dictation. And I'd like you to do me a favour. Miss Harding's coming in to see me tomorrow, but I'm not sure when. Would you please give her a ring and fix a time between my other appointments?'

He hoped that sounded natural enough and when she eventually left his room, Katie seemed pleased that he had enlisted her help, although a mite disappointed at Miss Harding's possible imminent return.

He now faced a problem he did not relish – Bernard Groves. He could not fault the general efficiency of his first cashier who ran the counter in immaculate fashion. The busy summer months in a seaside bank stretched workloads to the limit. Those customers who decried the banks' opening hours of ten till three as a sinecure for its under-worked clerks had no idea of the sheer volume of cheques, credits and cash which had to be meticulously sorted, counted and processed properly on to the accounts of those very same customers. Much of this work had to be dealt with after the doors had closed and many a time employees of other businesses would leave for home while he and his staff still pored over figures well into the evening. The problem was that everything had to be balanced to the penny. A difference of only that amount could lead to all his staff having to scrutinize every item in the day's work to discover the whereabouts of the miscreant item.

Not that Bernard Groves was ever the perpetrator of such misdemeanours. Painstaking to a fault, his errors were rarer than a honk in a Lester Young saxophone solo. On that basis, it was difficult to believe the cashier had taken in George's credits incorrectly. And it was impossible to relish discussing the matter with a man whose arrogance belied his position within the bank. Groves appeared to equate arrogance with wealth, something that he and Celia seemed to share in abundance. Parker had touched David's nerve in criticizing his apparent lack of knowledge of Celia's financial position, but with no bank account actually held in her name, how was he to know what she was worth? And it was not as if gossip prevailed. Instead, the citizens of Barnmouth seemed simply to accept that the Groveses were naturally affluent and relished any opportunity to attend their extravagant parties.

Thank goodness he had missed the latest – the cashier's fiftieth birthday thrash. He had wanted no part in the lavish event, everyone fawning over their opulent hosts, eager to have their glasses recharged with the expensive champagne which never graced their own tables. It was irksome – especially when Groves used his parties to flaunt his alleged standing in the town, in blatant detriment to that of his manager. And it was curious that George Broadman had been a regular guest. No doubt he supplied much of the food, but he was hardly of the social standing Groves normally courted.

Before calling the cashier into his room, David asked Jane to bring him the vouchers relating to George Broadman's account. He must be sure of his facts. It may well be there was a logical explanation for what had gone on, but it was apparent that Jane did not share that view when she sat down in front of him.

'I can't believe how the cheques in Mr Broadman's credits were marked cleared,' she said, as she spread the vouchers across his desk. 'I don't know who the drawers were, but the sorting code numbers all relate to those other banks.'

If that was the case, the true uncleared position could

not have been brought to his attention – by Jane, Barbara Bolton or the ledger clerks. Even Parker might now believe that earlier discovery of the crossfiring would not have been possible. With his softening attitude, the inspector might even have already suspected this. But what would be Bernard Groves's explanation? He now needed to find out and asked Jane to see if he had balanced his till and was able to come in and see him.

'I can't believe he could have taken his own life,' Groves said after arriving in the room and when David had raised the subject of George's demise. He even blanched at hearing the butcher's name, any trace of arrogance slipping from his countenance as easily as a snake shedding its skin. It was most disturbing. Further reptilian thoughts crossed David's mind as he surveyed the cashier's features across the desk: slippery as an eel, slimy as a snake, tears of a croc-odile. Could such analogies apply to Groves? Or was he wrongly letting unsavoury feelings infiltrate his thinking? Were such subliminal messages bringing to the surface his natural antipathy to the man?

'He wasn't the suicidal type,' Groves continued, breaking into his thoughts.

'So what type was he?' David replied, hoping to glean some further insight into the butcher. 'I thought I knew George well enough, but I've learnt a lot more about him these last couple of days.

Did he discern a glimpse of panic in Groves's eyes at that particular comment? If so, it quickly vanished as the cashier considered his reply. 'He was a pillar of respectability,' he eventually replied, apparently not wishing to elaborate on this character reference.

'In which case,' David said, having paused to let the cashier's words sink in, 'why has be been crossfiring?'

'Crossfiring?' Groves echoed, unable to disguise genuine incredulity at hearing such a revelation. 'He'd never get involved in anything like that.'

'You weren't aware of his other bank accounts?'

'Of course I was. It was common knowledge.'

'I didn't know. Wouldn't it have been politic to keep me informed?'

'I assumed you did know,' Groves replied indignantly, colour returning to his face. 'I thought everyone did.'

'Jane didn't know.'

Groves flushed even more at this apparent contradiction of his opinion. 'Well, she's only just arrived here.'

'Be that as it may,' David said, choosing not to pursue the point that Jane's two months at the branch hardly equated to just having arrived, 'George Broadman – going back for much of the year – has been regularly paying in cheques drawn on his other accounts – quite apart from his normal trade cheques.'

'But he's a tradesman. Of course he pays cheques into his account.'

'From other people, yes. But what about his own cheques? And those drawn by someone called Jack Stringer.'

'Jack? Well, that's his brother, of course.'

'His brother? How can he possibly be his brother?'

'Well, stepbrother, actually. So he said.'

'And have you ever met this stepbrother?'

'No... no I haven't, as a matter of fact. After all, he lives down in Plymouth.'

This was getting exasperating. Was Groves being deliberately obtuse, or was this the wrong line of questioning? He decided to grasp the nettle and asked why he had marked the cheques as cleared when they had been patently drawn on other banks.

'But they were as good as cleared,' Groves replied. 'Everyone knows – or knew – that George was good for the money. We never had a problem with his account.'

'Not with his account here, no. But what about his others? How could we possibly know about them? And what about the account of Jack Stringer?'

'Well, George was George, wherever his accounts were held. And he assured me his brother – his stepbrother – was all right. I trusted George and if you can't do that with one of the town's most respected...'

'Trusted?' David snapped, not believing what he was hearing. 'What has trust to do with it? You, of all people, should know that any cheque paid in and drawn on another bank must be treated as uncleared. It has to be cleared through the clearing system, for God's sake. How could you have deliberately marked those cheques as cleared?'

There, he could not have put it clearer than that. But it was a fact; this was what his first cashier had been doing. All because he trusted George Broadman. At the very least, it was getting to look like a disciplinary matter.

Groves shifted uneasily in his seat and seemed to shrink in size, all traces of bombast disappearing, as if he had been pricked like a balloon. Beads of perspiration appeared on his forehead and David imagined the jacket of his expensive three-piece suit shielded damp patches around the armpits of his tailored shirt. The air almost wreaked of his discomfort as he eventually replied, 'He asked me to do it.'

'He asked you to do it? And you simply complied – because he asked you to do it?'

Groves nodded forlornly. 'We'd known each other for

164

so long – not only through the bank, but also during the war. We were in the same regiment. And I did trust him. He knew the system and if he was technically overdrawn, he'd have to pay interest. He asked me to do it as a favour – in return for all the business he'd put the bank's way.'

'So we can now add bribery and corruption to his list of misdemeanours?'

'Misdemeanours?' Groves repeated, a look of panic now invading his eyes. 'What are you talking about?'

'I'm not going into that now,' David replied, choosing not to elaborate. 'But why was he paying those cheques into his account – those drawn by himself and by Jack Stringer? Did he tell you what it was all about? They were hardly trade cheques.'

Groves simply shook his head, as if deciding he had said too much already.

'Well?' David persisted. 'What did he say? He must have given you a reason for what was going on.'

'No, he didn't. And I didn't need to ask. I trusted him. Can't you understand that?'

It was fast approaching five o'clock, high time for the cash to be locked away in the strongroom. And with Groves choosing not to elaborate any further, David decided to call a halt, ending the interview with the parting shot that the inspector would be his next inquisitor.

But it was all most disconcerting. Was Groves a deliberate accessory in George's crossfiring? Or was he simply naive? More and more questions seemed to be arising from the whole affair. And he could not forget it was a murder enquiry.

CHAPTER 20

Sarah grinned wickedly as she shook in the extra helping of pepper. 'That'll teach David for saying it wasn't hot enough last time,' she muttered under her breath. Because of the weather, she had chosen his favourite dinner tonight – Lancashire Hot-pot. They both preferred it spicy and the big test for David was whether it induced an involuntary hiccup. They had no idea why spicy food should have such an effect on his digestive system, but her last hot-pot had been noticeable for the absence of any tracheal eruption.

As she placed the finished dish in the oven, her mind drifted back to Torbay Hospital and she prayed that the results of the X-ray would reach Dr Edwards quickly. Would anything be revealed and, if so, what? Was it a mental problem? Surely not? David's Dad had always been mentally alert and still was. He had the highest IQ of them all and was able to complete the Telegraph's crossword with sickening regularity. Yet, he had wide mood swings and his fuse was far shorter these days, but the tragic accident would account for that, particularly if he harboured guilt feelings. And his other traits of forgetfulness, disorganization and the inability to taste or smell hardly added up to mental malfunction. As for his childish behaviour, was this not something that happened to older people? Shortly before her grandfather's death, he had bemoaned the fact that he had started life in nappies and was now finishing in them. This might not be an apposite example of reverting to child-like behaviour, but it was symptomatic of the reversal process that could afflict the aged.

No, he was certainly not asylum-bound, but there was something seriously wrong with him and they must rely on Dr Edwards to decipher the problem and find a cure. In the meantime, she would force herself to be more tolerant of his unpredictable actions. He did not deserve the anger she had fired in his direction.

With the dinner safely tucked away in the oven, she prepared to collect Mark from school. It was only a short walk to St James's Primary, but although the sun was now shining, she would need to wrap up well against the continuing Arctic wind. At least David had enjoyed calmer weather in the morning and she was eager to learn whether he had won a Christmas turkey. Throughout their married life, budgeting had never been easy and even since his appointment as a manager, money had continued to be tight. A free turkey would be more than welcome to ease the festive season's expenditure.

She knew he would do everything possible to win, but his golf could be unpredictable. Despite being talented and competitive, he often responded to her after-match enquiries with a wistful shake of the head, bemoaning those couple of holes where it had all gone horribly wrong. It was such an infuriating game and with her own impatient streak, she could never contemplate taking it up herself. But it was certainly good for David and she always encouraged him to play on such a bracing, healthy course.

She stepped out briskly for the school's gate and was soon among the other mothers awaiting the mass exodus, which caused temporary mayhem on the adjacent pavement. Although some mothers shared escorting duties, it did not suit her. Far better to glimpse Mark's smiling face in the throng and then hear first-hand his animated descriptions of the excitements of the day as they strolled home, hand in hand in that unique bond between mother and child.

At such times, she counted her blessings, Mark's arrival having defied medical predictions about her childbearing ability. But a difficult birth had decreed he should be an only child. It did not bother them, David joking that quality outweighed quantity, but having an only child was not always easy. How many times had others supposed that he would be horribly spoilt? Yes, they did spoil him, as any child should be by loving parents, but he was not cosseted and was expected to play his part in their close-knit family life.

Not that he eschewed boyish humour, excitement and infatuations – his newfound love affair with Torquay United being a prime example. Rather him than her! David had taken her to two matches at United's beloved home of Plainmoor. The first was on the 8th March 1952. How could she forget that date when David never stopped talking about it? And all because Torquay had beaten Swindon Town 9-0. At the time, she had thought nothing of it. Was this not what was supposed to happen at football matches? It was not until two weeks later when she had sat through a tedious 1-1 draw with Walsall that she realized the Swindon match was a little unusual.

'Only two days to go,' Mark cooed, skipping alongside her as she strode home as quickly as possible. She had left David's Dad listening to the wireless, but after Monday night, he was not to be trusted alone in the house for long. 'Do you think there'll be anyone famous in the directors' box? Any film stars?'

'Film stars? Whatever makes you think there'll be film stars watching Torquay United?'

'Directors make films, don't they? It always says so at

the end.'

'Oh, Mark,' she replied, smiling. The innocence of youth. 'They're film directors, not football directors.'

As she explained the difference, it seemed this treat might become something of a let-down. No doubt Mark would have preferred Stuart Brown to be a film director, but with his debonair good looks Stuart would more likely see himself as a matinee idol. At their coffee mornings, she and the girls certainly shared that view, in marked contrast to their distain of John English. It was strange that David had played golf with the two of them this morning.

'Do you think we'll beat Southend, Mum?' Mark then asked, apparently wanting to get back to the subject of the actual match.

'I really have no idea,' she replied, as they reached the front door. 'But before you get carried away any further with this football match, I want you to tidy your bedroom. You left it in a right mess this morning.'

When they were inside the house, she was relieved to hear the wireless and find David's Dad engrossed in the latest episode of Mrs Dale's Diary. Why he should want to listen so avidly to a serial aimed at bored housewives, she would never know and he simply raised a hand in acknowledgement of their arrival, clearly not wanting any conversation to interrupt the activities of the doctor's wife.

Sarah shared David's antipathy to his father's incessant use of the wireless. He would tune it to any conceivable station, no matter what programme, but being averse to loud noise, at least he kept the volume down. Not that she was against loud music, having been introduced to David's love of jazz by way of a concert at Torquay's town hall by the Stan Kenton Orchestra. He had explained what a treat it was to see such a band, not only in the unlikely venue of

Torquay, but in England itself. He said the musicians' union would not countenance Americans playing over here because it would take away work from its own members. Yet fans like David were eager to have sight and sound of stars known to them only through records. He was not the only one to think unkindly of what was seen as a dictatorial trade-union standoff. But a compromise was made; Americans would be allowed to play over here on an exchange basis, with the same number of British musicians touring the States.

And thank goodness for that. The concert had been exhilarating; a far cry from some of the rock and roll bands now coming into vogue. She had a sneaking regard for Elvis Presley, but worried as to where this music would lead. Even in Torquay, hooligans had used Bill Haley as an excuse to cause wanton damage to the cinema showing "Rock Around the Clock".

With Mark ensconced in his bedroom – would he ever be able to keep it tidy? – and Mrs Dale still in full cry, she took out her embroidery to continue the latest sampler which she hoped would eventually join her previous efforts now adorning their bedroom wall. It was such a therapeutic hobby, but she always felt pangs of guilt whenever she settled into it during the day. Yet running a household was not like a nine-to-five job, so why not take an occasional break?

It seemed no time at all before the front door opened to David's two-tone "arrival home" whistle. 'Hello, darling,' she called from the kitchen, quickly putting her sewing away. 'How did you get on?'

'Get on?' he queried, stepping into the room and giving her a hug and a kiss.

'Yes, your golf. Are we going to eat at Christmas?'

'Oh! I'd completely forgotten about that. And it was only this morning.'

'That's not like you, darling. But how did you get on?'

'Thirty-six points, but I doubt that's enough. A couple of dodgy holes again. Bunker trouble. On the other hand, I beat the other two and we had the best of the weather. A fierce wind blew up for those starting later.'

'So when will you know?'

'I could go up to the club now.'

'Darling! You've only just got in. And what about your dinner? It's your favourite tonight.'

'Hot-pot? Thank heavens for that. I could do with a boost.'

'But thirty-six points is good, isn't it?'

'I'm not thinking about the golf,' David replied, letting out a world-weary sigh. 'It's everything else.'

'So what's happened now?' she asked, concerned at the furrow between his eyebrows.

'Let me get some drinks first. And how's Dad... and Mark?'

'They're fine. Your Dad's in the sitting room listening to the wireless and Mark's in his bedroom. I'll get him down and we can all have a chat together.'

'No, don't do that,' David replied hurriedly, turning back from his mission to get them a drink and motioning her to sit down opposite him at the kitchen table. 'And let's forget about the drinks for a moment. I just want to get everything off my chest. After all, you're the best sounding board I know.'

Sarah could count on the fingers of one hand the number of times David had been sufficiently concerned to open out his heart to her about problems at work. He had clearly been bothered on Monday evening, what with the inspectors and George Broadman, but since then, he had not elaborated much, probably because he was more preoccupied about his Dad and their visit to Torbay Hospital. But as he stretched an arm across the table and took one of her hands in his, something was clearly troubling him.

'I can't believe all I've heard this afternoon,' he opened up, his eyes almost pleading for the support she had always tried to give him throughout their marriage. 'Let's start with the bare facts. One: George Broadman's death was no accident; he was murdered. Two: for years, he'd been a compulsive gambler. Three: he's been dating Miss Harding, of all people, and she's somehow been financing his addiction. And four: Bernard Groves has been deliberately mishandling his credits, so we couldn't have been aware that George had been crossfiring for the last six months. There's no hard evidence that all these things are linked up, but it looks that way. I really can't take it all in.'

Sarah was dumbfounded, moving her lips, but with no sound emerging. She simply did not know what to say. Instinctively, she rose from her chair and walked round the table to put her arms around him and hug him tightly. The poor darling. What a combination of events. As for George Broadman's murder, that was unbelievable. But apart from his death, what about his gambling? Who would have thought it? And as for his going out with Miss Harding, how could that possibly be true? And Bernard Groves? If he had been found out doing something wrong at work, that would be his come-uppance. She had never liked the man. But even he could hardly be linked with a murder. Surely not?

'I can't believe what you've just said,' she eventually replied, clasping David even tighter. 'It's simply not possible – none of it.'

'I'm afraid it is,' he said. 'I can't start to grasp what's been happening at the office this week.'

'Well, you needn't say any more. You're home now. Let's have that drink and put it all to the back of your mind. Dinner won't be long.'

'No, hang on a minute. I just want to get it all off my chest.'

And he elaborated on all the background: the interviews with the inspector and with Bernard Groves; the problems he encountered with Mrs Harding and her daughter's revelations to Jane; and how the police had assessed George's death as murder and all the implications surrounding his crossfiring activities. Sarah was only thankful that his Dad and Mark must have been engrossed in their own activities not to enter the room. It certainly allowed David to open up.

Half an hour later, she felt he was far more at ease with himself as they all sat around the dining table tucking into their hot-pot. He now seemed totally unburdened as he chatted to Mark about Saturday's football match and even showed interest in the programmes his father had been listening to on the wireless. And she smiled in satisfaction when he delivered the not-unexpected hiccup.

CHAPTER 21

The next morning, David left home for the office half an hour earlier than usual and he felt guilty about withholding the reason from Sarah. Throughout their marriage, they had harboured no secrets and the continuing strength of their union was testament to their shared philosophy. But before going to work, he wanted to make a short trip and feared that by telling Sarah, she would accuse him of being melodramatic and persuade him otherwise.

Whenever confronted by an unpalatable truth, he needed to question its veracity. The more he thought of George Broadman's murder, the less likely he felt the butcher could be the victim of such a violent end. George may well have been an inveterate gambler – even having a relationship with Miss Harding – but he was single and free to carry out such activities should he so wish. On the other hand, his crossfiring could not be condoned, yet it hardly constituted a reason for being murdered. Could not suicide still be an option, his state of mind having been disturbed?

To satisfy his own curiosity, he had decided to re-trace George's route on that last fateful journey. The distance would have been about three miles and if, as the police claimed, the van's brakes had been tampered with, he felt it inconceivable that George could have travelled that far without once having to put his foot on the brake pedal.

He turned his Hillman Minx into the High Street and made for the shop from where George probably started his journey. He then pointed his car towards the seafront, going past his bank and the amusement arcades, before taking the road to the River Barn, which divided Barnmouth from the hills stretching towards Torquay. Traffic was light and he was surprised to reach the river without having to use his brakes. Admittedly, his normal driving style was to use gear changing to slow the car down, or to negotiate sharp bends or junctions. Not all drivers adopted the technique he had learnt when driving fire tenders in the RAF, but George's military training could easily have led him to drive in a similar manner.

He crossed over the bridge, entranced, as always, with the beauty and tranquillity of that stretch of water; home to a flotilla of yachts, dinghies and rowing boats. The vessels shared their abode with a variety of ducks and waterfowl, while the numerous swans included the black breed, which were so prevalent in the area. It was one occasion when it was easy not to concentrate on the road ahead, but strict speed restrictions reduced the likelihood of mishaps. He reached the sharp corner at the end of the bridge and still found no need to brake, having changed down to first gear ready for the incline towards Torquay.

Then it was uphill all the way to the top of the hill, the road twisting and turning around a series of hairpin bends that followed the contours of the coastline cliffs. Drivers coming the other way would be constantly braking, but his own progress relied solely on the accelerator until he changed down a gear to enter the car park on the left. Once off the road, the main parking area sloped down to the barrier at the cliff's edge and for the first time since the start of his journey, he had to brake – and quite sharply at that.

In that instant, he went cold from fear. It was quite clear that if he had not braked, the car would have sped towards the cliff-top barrier – with the dire consequences now known to all. After stopping the car, he pulled on the handbrake and switched off the ignition, beads of perspiration peppering his forehead. He was thankful he was seated, and remained motionless as he tried to gather his thoughts.

It was patently clear that if someone had tampered with the van's brakes, it would have been perfectly feasible for George to have driven from his shop to the car park, blissfully unaware of the impending catastrophe.

But any killer would not have been able to guarantee the chosen route, nor the non-use of the brakes. If George had braked in Barnmouth itself, or across the bridge, the most likely scenario might have been a gentle shunt into the car in front, a major let-down if murder had been planned. And the risk would not have been worthwhile unless the killer knew that he was heading for that particular car park from where the wreckage on the rocks below might never be recovered to reveal the tampered brakes.

There appeared to be too many flaws in such a plan and it made him wonder if George might, indeed, have planned his own suicide to make it look like murder. But why would he do that? If the balance of his mind had been disturbed enough to carry out such an act, why would he wish to inflict the blame on others? David had never come across anyone who had taken his own life, but it must be a last desperate act, probably accompanied by a suicide note by way of explanation. But it seems there was no such missive from George.

All these unanswered questions suddenly made him realize that this was a police matter, not one for him to theorize over. Yet he was glad he had made the journey and just wondered if his forthcoming meeting with Miss

Harding might provide clues for Parker to pass on to the police. But before proceeding to the office, he had another destination in mind.

How could he have forgotten to check if he had won a turkey? The result would have been posted on the club's notice board yesterday, but he had been so preoccupied on leaving the office that it had not crossed his mind. Some golfers were not bothered about the outcome of a match or competition. How often he had heard a competitor opine at the end of a less than successful round that the important thing was taking part and that "it beats being at work". It was so typically English, being a good loser. But entering a competition was about winning – without, of course, forsaking the traditional British sporting spirit.

Driving back from the car park, he passed through the town and steered the Minx up the hill to the golf club. It would only be a ten-minute diversion, but he was delayed by meeting John Jackson.

'Just the man I want to see,' the assistant professional said, shaking his hand. 'I was going to phone you this morning. I've found a car – a Hillman estate. Can I come down and see you to finalize the loan?'

'A good choice,' David replied. 'I've been very pleased with my Minx.'

John smiled in appreciation. 'And an estate will give me all the room I need for my clubs. Would this morning be all right?'

'It isn't actually,' David answered. If only he could have a day just dealing with car loans. 'My diary's full already. But you don't have to see me; I've already agreed the terms. Come and see my assistant – Jane Church. I'll tell her to expect you. Would late morning be all right?'

'That'll be fine,' John replied, a quizzical look on his

face. 'Another round of golf, is it?'

'Cheeky. I've only come up to see if I've saved myself a few bob on our Christmas dinner.'

This young man was definitely going to be good for the club and David's smile was even broader when the notice board confirmed that he had, indeed, won a turkey with his thirty-six points. He felt positively light-headed as he drove down the hill to the bank, hoping that the result would be a good omen for what lay ahead.

He reached his office at eight-thirty and noticed Jane already at her desk. Good – he needed to see her early in case Miss Harding came in first thing, and after checking his diary for appointments, he called her in. She arrived quickly, clutching the files he would need for his interviews. But was this really Jane? Where was the grey cardigan? And her dowdy skirt? And what had happened to her hair? As for lipstick! He would not normally notice such things – as Sarah so often bemoaned – but today's contrast was striking. Jane immediately flushed and he realized he had been staring. But he could not let the moment pass without a fully justified compliment. 'You're looking very smart this morning.'

Jane turned even redder. She cast her eyes down to her blue and white striped blouse and then to the documents in her hand, which she placed on the desk. 'Thank you, sir,' she managed to say, clearly bemused at how to respond to such praise and immediately changing the subject. 'These are the files for your interviews. But Katie says Miss Harding's coming in at nine. Why would she know that?'

David winced at the question, detecting a tinge of professional jealousy. Had he dropped a clanger? It had seemed natural enough to ask Katie to contact Miss Harding, but there was now a definite air of pique wafting across his desk. Of course... Jane was now Miss Harding's buddy. They were on intimate terms – Margaret and Jane. No wonder she might be feeling miffed that he should have asked Katie to make yesterday's follow-up call. He cursed himself for not having properly thought it through, not having considered possible sensitivity between his two young assistants.

'I asked Katie to contact her last night,' he said. 'I didn't want to trouble you. You've enough on your hands as it is. And it seemed logical as Katie's doing Miss Harding's work.'

He knew it was a weak explanation, but was relieved that Jane appeared to accept it at face value, her eyes softening as the next question formed on her soft-hued lips. 'Shall I let you know when she arrives? I presume you want to see her straightaway. I suppose it's about her meeting with Mr Parker?'

David agreed.

'I feel so sorry for her,' Jane said. 'How do you think she got on with him?'

'I'll find out this morning – her side, anyway. It seems she really opened up to him.' He grinned, as he added, 'I think it must have been because of his natural charm and sensitivity.'

'I'm not really surprised,' she replied, not sharing his levity. 'Richard and John told me he's quite a sweetie under that tough exterior. Well, they didn't actually call him a sweetie... that's my word. I think they said something like warm-hearted. But I think he's a sweetie-pie, myself.'

Sweetie-pie? Parker? He might be warming to the man, but a sweetie-pie? 'I can't say I've thought of him like that,' he said, smiling and pleased that the atmosphere between them had lightened. 'But I'll have to keep an eye on you two.'

Oh dear. That flush again. Had he overstepped the mark? He enjoyed casual working relationships with most of his staff, but it could lead to occasional flippancy, either way. It was a tricky balance that depended on mutual respect. But he need not have worried about Jane. She seemed to relish hearing a comment which might associate her with the opposite sex and she returned his smile, something she would have found difficult a few days ago.

'You better get on, now,' he said, 'but before you go, I saw John Jackson this morning. He's found a car and wants to take up the loan I agreed. I told him to come in and see you to sort out the paperwork. I suggested late morning. Is that all right?'

'Of course, sir,' Jane replied, proving again that rouge need form no part of her newborn make-up bag.

She left the room, almost bumping into Katie who was waiting outside to come in. David could see that Katie was even more animated than usual and overhead her whispered aside to Jane, 'She's arrived.' But it was clear that Miss Harding was not the main cause of her excitement as she sat down opposite him.

'What do you think?' she exclaimed, her eyes sparkling like diamonds. She could hardly contain herself as she awaited his reply.

'I'm sorry,' he answered, yet again impressed by the sheer vivacity of his young typist. 'What do I think?'

'You must have noticed, sir. You must have.'

'Noticed?'

'Yes, Mr Goodhart. Surely, you noticed. Jane – the change in her.'

He leaned back in his chair, shook his head slowly

180

from side to side and smiled benignly. 'Yes, I noticed.'

'And what do you think? What do you think?'

'Katie, it's hardly my position to express an opinion on how you girls look or what you wear. So long as it's suitable office attire...'

'But you've got to approve?' Katie interrupted, clearly disappointed at his apparent disinterest. 'I worked so hard on her.'

'If you must know, I did compliment Jane on her appearance. But come on, then. Tell me what's been going on.'

'I had to do something. We couldn't let her be a wallflower. Me and Daphne... we're taking her to the Pavilion tomorrow night. To see Chris Barber.'

'Chris Barber? I didn't know he was playing.'

'You've heard of him, sir?'

Did he seem that much of an old fogey? Why was it the young so often felt they had a monopoly on current fads and fashions? No doubt Katie would be astounded if she knew her manager could rock 'n' roll with the best of them. 'Of course I've heard of him. He plays my favourite form of music. I saw him in Brixham last year.'

'You've seen him? Mind you, it's Lonnie Donegan I'm wanting to see. Have you heard his Rock Island Line? It's skiffle.'

He knew only too well the current craze of skiffle. He might even have missed out on fame and fortune. In his youth, he played the banjo, strumming along to his Louis Armstrong records, but gave it up when the instrument became unfashionable. Now the tide had turned, traditional jazz taking it to its heart. My God, he could have been a rival to Lonnie Donegan. 'Yes, I know all about skiffle, but these days I prefer modern jazz to trad.'

'I must admit I don't know much about jazz,' Katie

181

said, 'but I do love dancing and it'll be a great night, so I persuaded Jane to come with us. She wasn't keen at first. But last night she said she'd come. I don't think she's ever been to a dance before. Actually, between you and me, I'm not sure she's been anywhere before. It's such a shame, because she's so pretty. I told you that yesterday, but I don't think you really agreed. But what about today? Isn't that blouse lovely? It's one of mine, but don't tell her I told you. You won't tell her, will you? She looks so nice in it. And isn't her hair lovely? I'm going to give her some nail varnish today and...'

'Katie! As much as it might be of vital importance to you, this really isn't the time and place to be discussing your social life. Now, what about Miss Harding? Has she really arrived?'

'Yes, about five minute ago,' Katie replied, becoming serious for a moment. 'I spoke to her last night and she wanted to see you as soon as possible. So we thought nine would be right – before you got involved with your interviews.'

'Yes, that's fine. I can do my dictation later. Ask her to come in, will you?'

'Of course, sir. But do you think she's all right? I'm so worried about her. I can't think what might be wrong. It's such a mystery.'

'We'll just have to wait and see,' David said, touched that young Katie was so concerned about someone with whom she would normally have no affinity. 'Just ask her to come in, please.'

When she had left, he braced himself for what was to come. This had the makings of a most awkward interview. Miss Harding may have displayed her alter ego to Jane and Parker, but would she open up to him?

CHAPTER 22

Two women; two changed demeanours. And what a contrast as Miss Harding sat opposite him. Whereas Jane now exuded an air of vitality and warmth – even joie de vivre – his secretary exhibited all the signs of a broken woman. It shook him to the core.

Sunken bloodshot eyes told the story of grief-stricken restless nights, with anguished days providing no respite. Lank hair, sallow features and unkempt apparel completed a sorry picture. Gone was the apparent self-assurance, which had dominated a succession of bank managers.

How could he break the almost palpable silence as Miss Harding stared down at her hands, her fingers idly twisting themselves into shapeless patterns? This was not like an interview with a customer who wanted facilities or advice. On such occasions, opening gambits fell easily from his lips, but now, with the prospect of personal humiliation usurping this once-proud purveyor of power, he felt uncomfortably hesitant as to what to say. In the end, it did not matter.

'I expect Mr Parker has told you about our meeting,' Miss Harding said, breaking the ice, but with eyes remaining averted from his. 'I mean he's told you what I said to him?'

'I certainly saw him yesterday afternoon,' he replied. 'He told me certain things, but whether...'

'He may not have told you everything. In any case, I didn't put him fully in the picture. I meant to, but in the end, I was too frightened.'

'Frightened?' David could not help himself exclaim, her words reminding him that George Broadman's death was being treated as murder and fearful of what might be lurking in her mind.

'Yes, I was too scared about what I'd done. I'm so ashamed.'

An air of foreboding swept over him as the import of her words sank in. This was not his role – to be subject to such a confession. It was not Parker's role, either. This was surely a matter for the police. He had better stop what was happening before it properly started.

'Miss Harding, is this really what you should be doing? I mean talking to me like this?'

'But who else should I tell?' she replied, raising her head and, for the first time, looking him in the eye. 'In the end, I couldn't open up to the inspector. It didn't seem right – going behind your back. It really has to be you. I know you'll be fair. And you'll advise me of what I should do.'

'But what about the...?' But before he could mention the police, Miss Harding put up her hand to stop him in his tracks.

'No, Mr. Goodhart, please... let me continue. And I think I'd like to start right at the beginning. That way, I hope you'll understand. I know I'll have to face the consequences, but I'd like you to try and understand.'

As her story unfolded, he listened in silence, not wanting to interrupt for fear of curbing the flow. It was an extraordinary account of a life, of which, until yesterday, he had been mostly unaware. It was all he could do not to gawp as he heard of his secretary's youth, her schooldays mixed with success and humiliation. Her mother had eschewed all parental support and encouragement, never attending open days, concerts or prize-givings when Miss Harding had been a regular recipient. The account must have been the same as that given to Parker, even the production of the photograph that had so smitten the inspector. David was astounded at the beauty of the girl in the picture, so different from the woman sitting opposite him. Yet such attraction had been laid to waste, her mother refusing the girl any social life outside the confines of her family. It seemed her father had little say in the matter. His wife had dominated him, consumed by jealousy and wanting to deny her daughter any of the opportunities she, herself, had missed out on through the years of depression and then war.

But she could not deny her daughter of thoughts and feelings. Boys would occupy the minds of most schoolgirls and she was no exception. But whereas other girls would seek out such friendships – openly or not – she could only view from afar, the occasional crush never materializing into anything more than a figment of her imagination. And so it was with George Broadman.

According to the inspector, they had been at school together, but this was not strictly true. Their schools were not co-educational, but lay adjacent to each other, leading to frequent fraternization by pupils after lessons. George was in a group of boys more interested in sport than girls, but this did not prevent Miss Harding from singling him out for her wishful attention. But it came to nothing. Her mother saw to that. And it was not until she became secretary at the Barnmouth branch of National Counties that she came across him again at the butcher's shop.

Over the years, weekly visits to the shop cemented her feelings for the youth of her dreams and his continued single status drove her hopes along roads of unimaginable contours, but to an unattainable destination, her emotions being unrequited by the brawny butcher – until six months ago. He then started taking an interest in her, enquiring about her life, her job and even reminiscing about their school days. Then he actually asked her out, inviting her to a lunchtime drink and sandwich at the Three Bells towards the top of the High Street. She had never entered a pub before, nor had alcohol passed her lips, but she accepted the invitation with almost shameless alacrity, as if in defiance of everything her mother stood for. During her continuing widowhood, her mother had cocooned herself in her house, feigning one infirmity or ailment after another to deny her daughter any social life. At first, Miss Harding had doted on her grieving mother, only later recognizing the assiduity of her intentions. But by then she had been driven into an existence from which she could see no escape – until the introduction of George Broadman's attentions.

As the story unfolded, David felt desperately sorry for his secretary, wondering if this case was exceptional, or whether such parental selfishness was more prevalent than he might imagine. Who really knew what went on in family life unless one was part and parcel of it?

Miss Harding continued and for a moment her tired eyes actually shone as she recalled those opening weeks in the company of George. They were halcyon days indeed, but she was grateful he had wanted their relationship to be kept strictly under wraps. That suited her admirably. Her mother must never find out and by taking her holiday entitlement mainly in individual days, she was able to be with George while her mother believed her to be at work. There were tricky moments at the office, particularly at lunchtimes, and she felt really proud that all her subterfuge had successfully prevented Katie, in particular, from having any inkling as to what was going on.

The visits to Newton races started in June and continued throughout the summer. At first, she assured David, it was just a thrill to be taking part in an activity so alien to what she had done before. George was a gentle, charming companion and she loved the way he affectionately referred to her as Peg, but as the weeks passed, she became increasingly concerned at the size of his wagers. It also became obvious to her that such gambling was a foolhardy activity, especially when he confided in her about his regular visits to betting shops and casinos.

But she had become besotted and when he enquired apologetically if she could possibly help him out when he had taken a particularly heavy loss, she duly obliged, not wanting anything to sour this wonderful burgeoning friendship.

And that was the start of the rot. One request led to another and at no time did his winnings cover his accumulating losses. In itself, this did not worry her too unduly. With her lifestyle, on what else would she spend her money? But behind the scenes, an ominous cloud threatened their relationship. She did not know any of the details, or who else was involved, but George admitted he had become entangled with unsavoury company. Suddenly, his needs far outstretched her own resources, yet somehow, she had to help. At last, she had a friendship that had lightened her life. She cared so much for this first man to enter her sheltered world and the miracle was that he seemed to care for her. She knew they were an unlikely couple and she accepted his wish that their relationship should remain platonic, the steel bond between them forming more of a brother and sister partnership, rather than lovers. And she could never let him down in his hour of need.

As David listened, he could not decipher which way this plot was unfolding. Parker may well have thought the police would have her name on their list of suspects, but from what he was hearing, it seemed she would have done anything to help this now-revealed sad figure of a butcher. How could murder have been on the agenda? But why was she feeling frightened and so ashamed? And he was more than a little concerned to hear about unsavoury characters being involved.

'It's all quite extraordinary,' he said, as his secretary lapsed into contemplative silence. And there was clearly more to come. 'I had no idea George was a gambler. It certainly explains his crossfiring activities.'

Miss Harding's eyes focused on his and he thought she was going to burst into tears. Instead, she bit on her bottom lip and leant forward earnestly. 'You have to believe me,' she pleaded. 'At the time, I knew nothing about that. He was so stupid. There was no need for him to do it. He knew I'd always help him out.'

'That's what's puzzling me,' David said. 'How were you able to help him? From what you've said we're talking about large sums of money.'

Miss Harding shook her head in despair. 'A huge amount. And for what? Clearly, he wasn't the only stupid one.'

Whether from self-incrimination or self-pity, the floodgates now opened. At first, the tears tumbled silently down her cheeks, but heartrending sobbing quickly followed. Yet again, his top-drawer handkerchief was needed and he pressed it into her hands. She simply squeezed it into a tight ball, but then unfurled it and mopped her face dry as she eventually managed to stem the tears.

David surveyed the scene with a disturbing detachment and contrasted his impassive response to his concerned reaction to Jane's tears earlier in the week. On that occasion, he was touched by her genuine distress at hearing of George's death, yet now, even though Miss Harding had clearly enjoyed a much closer relationship with the butcher, her compassion appeared to be self-serving.

He might well be doing her an injustice, but the more she said, the more disturbed he had become. What had it really been all about? And she had still not answered his question about the money.

'I'm so sorry,' she then said, apparently back in control of herself. 'How embarrassing. But I think I might have been duped by George. Yet now he's dead, I'll probably never know.'

'What do you mean by duped?' David asked, thinking this had been a one-way affaire de coeur.

'Looking back, I wonder if he had planned it all – deliberately. All those years nothing happened and then, six months ago, he starts showing an interest in me. I really did think he was attracted to me, but on reflection, I think it was because I worked in a bank. But I'm not sure. I'll never be sure.'

'But why would he be more interested in where you worked?'

'Because of our business – money.'

'Money?'

'Yes. The way he saw it – this is what I'm thinking now – he sold meat, we sold money. In his shop, he could always put his hands on meat and here, well...'

'You can't be serious,' David exclaimed, aghast at the

implication of what she was saying, made worse by the reddening of her face and her contrite expression. 'I think you'd better answer that question I just asked. How did you actually help him? How did you manage to finance his gambling activities?'

Miss Harding concentrated again on her hands, finger nails digging deeply into the palms. She seemed hypnotized by her actions, before eventually looking up at him as he awaited her answer with bated breath.

'At first I used my own money. You probably wouldn't have noticed – looking at my vouchers on a daily basis. I only cashed small amounts at a time, but I did it frequently. Unless you totted them all up, I guessed you wouldn't cotton on to what I was doing.'

David groaned inwardly, knowing this was the case. He had to examine and initial all such vouchers, but provided there appeared to be nothing evidently unusual, individual cash withdrawals would not have appeared suspicious. And there would normally be no need for him to look at them collectively on a weekly or monthly basis.

'But my own money started to run out,' Miss Harding continued. 'I told George and he was distraught. It was those other people – those I mentioned earlier. I didn't know who they were, but George was terrified of them. They seemed to have some sort of hold over him.'

She paused, as if in despair at her unfolding story, a feeling shared by David as he harked back to the concerns expressed by Parker back on Monday afternoon.

'It was then that I realized he needed much more from me than my company. But I tried to dismiss it from my mind. I simply didn't want to believe it. Then he started asking about banking systems and what checks were in operation here. Perhaps that's when he got the idea about crossfiring. But I swear it wasn't the result of anything I said. He then talked about my mother and whether she'd be able to help. But that was impossible. The last thing I wanted was for her to know about our friendship. That was when he said she didn't have to know.'

David could hardly believe what he was hearing, especially from this particular member of staff. Was nothing sacrosanct?

Miss Harding gulped deeply before continuing. 'Anyway, I'm ashamed to say I went along with him. Mother's quite wealthy and George pointed out that it would all come to me eventually. There are no other beneficiaries. So he persuaded me I would only be borrowing something that would eventually be rightfully mine. I know it was wrong, but he assured me it would be all right. Like a fool, I believed him.'

'You mean you took money out of your mother's account?' This was madness. Yet she was already nodding her head and pursing her lips in obvious affirmation. 'But she must have found out. She'd have seen the entries on her statement. And what about the balance? She'd notice how low it was getting.'

'No,' Miss Harding replied, now totally deflated, all remaining colour drained from her face, 'she wouldn't have known. I re-typed all her statements and destroyed the originals.'

'You what?'

But there was no need for her to repeat her confession; her expression said it all. When she had entered the room, she had looked a broken woman, but now she was not simply broken, her whole bearing and demeanour had collapsed like an imploded building. She sagged in her chair, eyes closed and taking in short sharp breaths as if the room was devoid of oxygen. He feared the first-aid skills he had acquired in the RAF were going to be needed, but any sympathy he may have felt for her was now a thing of the past.

Internal theft in banking was abhorrent – no matter what self-justification might be put forward by the perpetrator. Fortunately, it was infrequent, but its very rarity could breed complacency – in the adherence of basic rules and regulations. This could lead to flawed codes of conduct by apparently trusted employees. The only example David had personally come across was a manager at a branch on Dartmoor. This man had been treasurer of the local branch of the National Farmers' Union and over a period of some weeks had "borrowed" monies from the Union's bank account. He had experienced a temporary personal cash problem and when this had been resolved, he duly repaid the money. No one would have known, except that he had subsequently confessed to a visiting inspector who immediately suspended him. But for his voluntary confession, he would still hold his job. Even though nobody had lost anything, the bank could not afford to continue to employ someone whose trust could not be relied upon.

The same outcome must surely now apply to Miss Harding. She might claim it was a family affair – that her mother's estate would, indeed, devolve to her at some time in the future – but such reasoning was immaterial. Mrs Harding was a customer of the bank in her own right and premeditated forgery and deception had taken place. There was no defence for her daughter. An affair of the heart had shorn her of all the ethics and principles she had embraced in her career. She now faced suspension, humiliation, shame and legal action – something the bank normally instigated, if only as a warning to other would-be miscreants. But even worse might be to come. The key element to this sorry saga was George Broadman – murdered George Broadman. David was certain the police would want to interview Miss Harding as soon as possible and what would they make of her story?

As he contemplated this, he was relieved to see his secretary open her eyes and sit up in her chair. She looked at him as though she had been reading his mind. 'I suppose I'll have to see Mr Parker again,' she said, almost under her breath.

There was no doubting that. And being in residence, the inspector would want to initiate the first stage of disciplinary action. He would also need to liaise with Inspector Hopkins and it could well be that separate bank and police charges would be made against her. But whatever the outcome, it was clear that Katie Tibbs would continue to deputize as his secretary for some time to come.

CHAPTER 23

Saturday mornings were never David's favourite time at work and he was thankful it was Norman Charlton's turn to be in charge of the branch today. Friday had been draining – emotionally. As expected, Parker had taken over the "Harding Case" – as it would no doubt now be known – but David had been impressed with the compassion the inspector had shown his secretary who had though, been suspended and sent home. Perhaps Jane's assessment of Parker was not far off the mark.

It was not so easy to view Miss Harding so favourably. At the start of yesterday's interview, he had felt sorry for her and could not believe she might have been involved in George's murder. But he could not forgive her sheer criminality. To re-type her mother's bank statements without the forged entries was no impulsive action; it was patently premeditated and would derive no sympathy from judge or jury. If she was capable of such underhand action, of what else might she be guilty?

Although he had shared these thoughts with Parker, he desisted from making any such inferences within the office. Yet rumour would be rife and he and the inspector had agreed that he should address all his staff before they went home. That way, they would all hear the same message from his lips – namely the bare bones about Miss Harding's suspension. It ought to lessen any counter-rumours, although these would probably still persist. He also chose to tell them that George Broadman's death was being treated as murder, the police having advised Parker that they had now passed this information to the Herald Express local newspaper. It would have to be seen whether the news would reach the national press.

It had been an uncomfortable occasion, with not one word of response from his staff. But he was subsequently comforted by the reaction of Jane and Katie when he discussed future working arrangements with them in his room. Both had accepted the situation with a maturity beyond their years and he was touched with their assurances of giving him their full support. Jane was especially upset for Miss Harding – though not knowing the specific charges made against her – while Katie made it clear she would do her utmost to be a capable deputy for the departed secretary. Thank goodness for such tangible support at this difficult time.

But now it was Saturday and after spending the morning pottering around with his thoughts, the afternoon was soon upon him when he had no option but to switch off. Mark's excited babbling saw to that as they made their way towards Plainmoor.

He had supported Torquay United since before the war. It had never been a glamorous team, forever lingering in the 3rd Division (South), alongside their nearest rivals, Exeter City. The only other football league club within a hundred miles was Plymouth Argyle who tended to laud it over their neighbours because their fortunes occasionally flirted with the 2nd Division. Until now, he had seen no indication that Torquay would follow suit, but last season the team finished fifth in the league and this season hopes were riding high. Only four games had been lost of the twenty played so far and, for the first time, he and his fellow supporters had genuine aspirations for 2nd Division football.

How the team would cope in a higher division was questionable. Until now, competing with the big boys had been restricted to cup games, the pinnacle being two years ago when the stars of 1st Division Leeds United – including the world-class John Charles – were soundly beaten 4-0. But the team was brought down to earth last year when high expectations over a home tie with Birmingham City were dashed by a comprehensive 7-1 thrashing. Perhaps it might be better to be satisfied with 3rd Division football. He was philosophical enough to appreciate that it was far more satisfying to follow a winning team in a lower division than suffer the frustrations of losing most matches in a higher league.

As for Mark, he was revelling in his first season of support, having not yet seen the team lose. But he was still unsure of watching the match from the directors' box. 'You mean I can't take my rattle?' was his anguished cry when the invitation arrived. In the end, the issue became theoretical following the last home match against Reading. Their chosen position at matches was on the rail to one side of the goal at the cowshed end of the ground. In the second half, Torquay's centre forward, Ted Calland, bore down on goal in an exhilarating run before unleashing a pile-driver. But the ball deviated in flight, and in horror – more perhaps at the missed goal than his own safety – Mark threw up his rattle-bearing hand in self-defence, only for the ball to crash into it, sending the brunt of the rattle far into the stand behind them and leaving an impotent handle clasped between his fingers and thumb. David had assumed the resultant tears were caused by physical pain and he had blanched at what might have happened if the cannonball shot had hit Mark full in the face. But the boy's angst related solely to the unseemly demise of his cherished rattle.

Now, his main concern seemed to relate to his Mum who had urged him to be polite and respectful in the company of such important people. 'But I can't just sit there doing nothing,' he moaned, as they neared the ground. 'It's bad enough not having my rattle, but if I can't stand up and shout either...'

David smiled, but had some sympathy for the boy. Mothers did not always understand when it came to sons and sporting occasions. He recalled being selected for his school's junior cricket team and, not having his own whites, asked his mother to shorten his older brother's trousers for him. Instead, she made them into shorts and it took him years to get over the humiliation of wearing them.

He had arranged to meet Stuart Brown at the ground. Plainmoor had been the home of Torquay United since 1910 and was situated between the suburbs of St Marychurch and Babbacombe. It was a compact ground with a wooden stand situated along one side of the pitch, but much of the terracing was in the open and with gates averaging 8-9000, many spectators had to put up with the vagaries of the West Country weather.

It was approaching two o'clock as he swung his car into a side road adjacent to the ground. Having parked the vehicle, they made their way to the stand where he saw Stuart waiting in the entrance that would take them up to the boardroom.

The solicitor welcomed them warmly, ruffling Mark's hair in a way that always annoyed the boy – especially when doing his best to be adult. They then followed Stuart up a wooden staircase, which led to a room far too small for the number of people occupying it. Was this going to be a big mistake? Mark always liked to spend the time before a match digesting the programme and taking in the atmosphere around the ground. In this claustrophobic room, the only thing he might be able to digest was likely to be a biscuit and glass of orange squash, while the smoke-laden air was in stark contrast to that outside.

Yet, surprise, surprise – Mark was soon tugging at his coat, looking up at him, his eyes sparkling. 'Dad,' he urged, in his best stage whisper, 'over there – it's Sammy Collins. And look, Don Mills is with Ted Calland...'

But before he could go any further, half the men in the room moved towards the door, making for the stairs. It then dawned on David that their destination was the dressing room. If it had not been for Mark, he doubted he would have recognized the players in their unfamiliar suits, especially as the boardroom was the last place he would have expected to see them.

'Surprised?' Stuart asked, noticing his bemusement. 'The players don't normally come up here before a match, but it was the chairman's idea. He wanted to recognize their unbeaten run. They'll be back up here after the game. Let's hope it's not with their tails between their legs.'

David grinned. 'At least there's a bit more space now they've gone.' And it also enabled him to see a familiar face across the room – John English. What on earth was he doing here?

'Come on,' Stuart then said. 'Let me make some intro-ductions.'

He started to usher them around the room to meet the chairman and other directors, some of whom had brought guests, but none recognizable. If there were any famous people in Torquay today, they clearly had better things to do than attend a football match. They then reached John English who smiled broadly and also ruffled Mark's hair.

Why do these people do that to the boy?

'This is getting to be a habit, David,' he said as they shook hands. 'You'll start to think of me as a sports nut, rather than an hotelier. But the truth is I know nothing about football. I can't think why Stuart invited me.'

You can say that again. What was it about Stuart and English? They were such an unlikely couple. He only hoped their apparent enmity on the golf course had been resolved. And thank goodness it was Mark and not Sarah who had come with him today.

'I thought you might appreciate a familiar face,' Stuart said, as if by way of explanation. 'We'll have to get young Mark to show him the ropes about football, eh sonny Jim?'

David winced at Mark's likely reaction. The boy abhorred that expression as much as he detested having his hair ruffled. He must be craving their normal position behind the goal. But at least Stuart was including him in the conversation.

'Anyway, young man,' Stuart continued, 'what do you think the score will be?'

'3-1 to us,' Mark replied, successfully hiding his likely feelings. 'I think Sammy Collins will score and Don Mills will get at least one of the others.'

'Good man. That's what I like to hear. Positive thinking. What about you, David?'

'I'll go along with Mark. So long as we don't lose our unbeaten run...'

The rest of his sentence tailed off as they heard applause and cheering greet the teams out on the pitch. Mark tugged at his sleeve as they went outside to find their seats. 'We haven't got a programme, Dad.'

His obvious disappointment at not being able to browse through the programme in the run-up to kick-off was now compounded by the prospect of not getting a programme at all. Heaven forbid that the one omission from his collection would be for this particular match. But relief was at hand as the chairman arrived, clutching programmes which he passed along the row to his fellow directors and guests.

The match looked like turning out how Mark had predicted, two goals by Sammy Collins and a third by Don Mills giving Torquay a comfortable 3-0 lead. But there was to be a sting in the tail. With only ten minutes to go, Southend scored, only to compound their impertinence by scoring again. 3-2... and as the crowd bayed for the final whistle, they scored again to share the points. Disaster! How could the team possibly let go a 3-0 lead?

A shell-shocked atmosphere pervaded the boardroom in the aftermath of the game, but it was tinged with relief that the unbeaten home record remained intact. Even John English had been caught up in the drama, now claiming to be a convert to professional football. But his presence still disturbed David. Was he being softened up prior to Monday's interview? There was no need for anything like that; a straightforward borrowing proposition was being put to him, with ample security. In any case, Stuart would not proffer an introduction unless it was cast-iron. He was too professional to do otherwise.

As they enjoyed the club's post-match hospitality, such thoughts continued to preoccupy him until, once again, he felt Mark tugging at his sleeve. The arrival of the team, freshly bathed and Brylcreemed, but looking a mite uncomfortable in the formal surroundings of the board-room, was quickly dissipating any disappointment Mark may have felt at the result and the absence of any famous guests. For his part, David was always surprised that footballers appeared far younger when met face-to-face, compared to when watching them from the terraces. Now, some of them seemed fresh out of school, but this was clearly not Mark's perception as he took the opportunity to thrust his autograph book under the noses of his heroes.

Stuart used the moment of Mark's new focus of attention to guide David to an unoccupied corner of the room, moving close to him confidentially.

'You're still seeing John on Monday?' he asked.

'Yes,' David replied. Here we go. Is this what the invitation's been all about? 'He's coming in at eleven.'

'Good. I just wanted to have a quiet word,' the solicitor said, almost surreptitiously. 'You probably noticed a bit of an atmosphere between us on the golf course. It was nothing really. John was a bit embarrassed I'd made the arrangement. He thought I was being too pushy. But that's the trouble with some people. They want to go it alone. Yet they don't have the wherewithal to take the plunge.'

'But he doesn't give me the impression of being slow to come forward,' David answered. To where was all this leading? He could do without any outside prejudices before his meeting. On the other hand Stuart was a good friend of the bank and it would be unwise not to let him have his say. 'And I'm not sure why he needs to see me. I thought he was making a success of the hotel. His bank must be perfectly happy with him.'

'Yes, they are,' Stuart hastily acknowledged. 'And he is successful, but he's too conservative. He needs to take advantage of his success – to expand – in a big way.'

'But wasn't it just the bar area he wanted to expand? Isn't that what you told me?'

'Yes, but that's just the start. He needs more beds. And I reckon he could manage those within his existing overheads. That can only help his margins. Anyway, next door's coming on the market. I think he could get it for a snip. It would make a great annex to the hotel. But he'd need to borrow the lot.'

'The lot?' David exclaimed, making a few heads turn in their direction.

'Shh,' Stuart urged. 'I know this isn't the ideal place. But I wanted you to meet John again. You can see he's all right. And I really want you to do this, David...'

He stopped abruptly as the club's chairman came up and asked him to join him and the other directors for a brief board meeting. David remained in the corner, alone with his thoughts, knowing they would infiltrate his mind throughout the weekend. Whatever the cost of the next door premises, the bank could not be expected to stump up the full purchase price. The customer's own stake should be at least a third or even fifty per cent. After all, it was the entrepreneur who should shoulder the primary risk. In this case, if the bank put up all the cash, the property might as well be called the National Counties Hotel, rather than the Esplanade.

But why was Stuart pushing so hard? And as for John English being "all right". What would Sarah think about that? The whole thing was making him feel decidedly uncomfortable.

CHAPTER 24

Jane Church had never experienced such a Saturday. She gazed intently at her reflection in the rectangular wooden-framed mirror, which adorned the rather functional dressing table in her small bedroom. This spot of privacy might well be minute, but at least she had her own room in her parents' terraced council house – something youngsters of larger families in the street could never hope to emulate. Being an only child had some advantages, but many a time, she had yearned for an older brother or sister to look up to, or a younger sibling to keep an eye on. But it was not to be and she had led an existence others might equate to loneliness. She certainly enjoyed her own company, but was never lonely. How could she be, with her heroes and heroines – created at first by Enid Blyton and then by Lewis Carroll, Robert Louis Stevenson and Jonathon Swift? Even Dickens and Shakespeare provided her with great enjoyment once she had adjusted to the challenge of such notable wordsmiths.

But now, murder? Here in Barnmouth? It was almost as if she were living within one of her beloved novels. How could Mr larger-than-life Broadman possibly have been murdered? Who could have done such a thing? And why? And why had Margaret been suspended? None of it made any sense at all.

Nor did her own extraordinary action this morning. Had it been a calamitous mistake? It was as if a stranger now stared back at her. The fringe had altered the whole shape of her face, while her mousy locks had been straightened and drawn back into a pert bobtail. Could it really be her? Yet she was beginning to like what she saw.

It was so confusing. Should she reproach or acclaim Katie? Joining her and the other girls who had decided to go to the Pavilion was one thing, but agreeing to a full-scale makeover was another matter. No, she should not have succumbed to Katie's pressure and as for allowing her to make the appointment at the hairdresser... Thank goodness she had resisted the girl's ideas about full-painted lips and mascara. Yet she could still get to like this new face in the mirror.

But those glasses; they looked so incongruous. After sixteen years, she still recalled the "four-eyes" jibes at primary school – made worse when she also wore a patch to correct a lazy eye. But the teasing soon waned and she came to accept her glasses as an obligatory accessory – essential for her studying and reading. And until now, they had proved to be no social obstacle; how could they be when socializing had been virtually non-existent? But the Pavilion now beckoned and her self-consciousness would be acute alongside Katie, Jilly and Daphne.

Yet an extraordinary thing had happened this morning. As she left the hairdresser, she took off her glasses to investigate a speck in her eye, when a minor, distant road accident grabbed her attention. It was astonishing. She could see details of the contretemps quite clearly, yet the wording of a nearby street sign was a blur until she put her glasses back on. She remembered her mother saying how her distance vision had improved as she got older; could this now be happening to her? On her way home, she could not resist removing and then replacing her glasses with no detrimental effect, so much so that for the last few hundred yards to her house, she left them off altogether.

She felt strangely naked as she approached the property and was grateful neither to meet anyone, nor that her parents were in the garden to greet her. She had to replace the glasses to unlock the front door and mount the stairs to her bedroom, but as she now sat at her dressing table, she pondered on whether she should dare venture out to the Pavilion with her spectacles tucked safely away in her handbag.

Three hours later, before stepping out to meet the girls, her parents' response to her enquiry as to how she looked clarified the decision for her.

'You look as pretty as a picture,' her father said, visibly glowing with pride at her changed appearance and, despite her new image, making her blush. 'I love your hair and you haven't worn that dress before, have you?'

'No, Dad,' she replied, hoping such approval would be echoed by her mother. 'Katie lent it to me. I didn't have anything to wear.'

'It's perfect,' her mother said. Thank goodness for that. 'But what about the Pavilion? Are you going to be all right there?'

'Katie says it's really respectable. Chris Barber's playing...'

'Chris Barber?' her father interrupted. 'I love his band.'

'I didn't know that, Dad. I'd never heard of him.'

'That's your mother's fault,' her father replied, grinning. 'As soon as he comes on the wireless, she tells me to turn it off. Pop rubbish she calls it.'

'Oh, come off it,' his wife said. 'But more to the point, what time does it end? We don't want you traipsing the streets late at night.'

'I really don't know. But I'll be all right. I am twenty-two, you know.'

'Where's all this new-found confidence come from?' her father asked, getting up from his chair and giving her a hug. 'Just remember you're the most precious thing in our lives. We couldn't bear it if you came to any harm. Anyway, what's happened to your glasses?'

'I thought you'd never notice,' Jane answered, drawing away from him. 'It sounds silly, I know, but I only realized today that I probably only need them for reading and close-up things.'

'Oh, yes?' her father countered, winking slyly at his wife. 'I smell boys on the horizon.'

'Dad! Please don't tease me. I'm being serious. But if I don't really need them to...'

'I think you should give it a try,' her mother interrupted. 'I always hoped that one day you might not need them. I've never told you before, but when I was your age, I ought to have worn glasses, but I put off getting them for years...'

'I didn't know that,' her husband butted in.

'You probably wouldn't have asked me out if I'd worn glasses. No, love, give it a try. If you find you need them, you can always put them on later.'

And with such a ringing endorsement, she left the house, almost light-headed in anticipation of the evening ahead. She had eventually agreed that her father should meet her at the Pavilion's entrance at eleven o'clock and was actually relieved at not having to walk home alone at that time of night.

As she made her way along the seafront, she could not help but contrast her emotions with what it must be like in the Harding household. The speed of Margaret's suspension was shocking. Mr Goodhart had not elaborated on what had been going on, but it must have been serious to suspend her. The whole office had been agog and some had speculated about a link with Mr Broadman's murder. The news had particularly shocked Bernard Groves whose face had drained of colour. Was it all somehow linked to the crossfiring? But Margaret would not have been involved in that. Her suspension must be unrelated. Yet, what had she said in her bedroom? She was embarrassed and humiliated, but "it was much worse than that". Could she have been an accomplice of Mr Broadman? No, that was impossible. How she wished she could go and see her to offer some form of comfort, but Mr Goodhart had forbidden any such contact.

Her arrival at the Pavilion brought her back to the present and she paused at one side of the entrance wondering if the other girls had already arrived. They had agreed to meet outside, but she could imagine Katie going straight in, eager to get into the action. But she need not have worried, spying the girls skipping along the promenade, chattering excitedly as they approached the Pavilion. But as she made to join them, they went right past her, mounting the steps to the foyer, before turning back to stand at the other side of the entrance, looking from side to side as they continued their animated conversation.

What was going on? Why were they ignoring her? She was tempted to turn tail and return home. Instead, she moved across to join them, only to receive blank stares when she greeted them

'Jane?' Katie suddenly said, frowning. 'Jane! It's you. Daphne, Jilly, it's Jane!'

It was then that she realized the girls had not recognized her with her new hairstyle and without glasses.

'You look lovely,' Katie exclaimed, Daphne and Jilly nodding their heads enthusiastically. 'That hairstyle... it's great. And where are your glasses?'

'In my handbag,' Jane replied, failing to suppress a blush. 'I decided to try and get here without them. For some reason, my long sight seems to have improved.'

'Well, don't put them on yet. We've got to get used to your new look. Come on, let's get inside.'

And with that, the four of them waltzed into the building, arm in arm. It seemed the most natural thing to be doing; yet it was the first time she had been inside the Pavilion – let alone any dance hall. And even though the music had not started, the general hubbub made her spine tingle.

The musicians were making their way to the stage and at the other end of the hall, lines of young men, pints in hand, congregated in the area around the bar, sizing up the girls who had adopted one side of the hall for themselves. Katie ushered them all to this particular area, introducing her to other girls, all of whom studiously ignored the men at the bar. She could see that this standoff might last for some time, presumably until Dutch courage eventually spurred the men into action.

The music suddenly burst out around them to spontaneous cheers from the crowd. She recognized Chris Barber from his picture and was enthralled at his easy manipulation of his ungainly trombone, its deep sound blending in close harmony with the trumpet and clarinet. Behind this front line, the drums and banjo provided a pulsating beat that set her feet tapping and she could not prevent herself from jigging around. No wonder Dad liked this music so much.

'Isn't this great?' Katie shouted to make herself heard.

She nodded enthusiastically and then followed Katie's eyes which had strayed to the bar area. Katie! Leave them alone for now. Just listen to the music. But even before she could return her own eyes to the stage, she could not help but notice one man standing out, almost head and shoulders above the others. It caused her to look away quickly, her heart missing a beat. She did not need her glasses to recognize the distinctive figure of John Jackson.

CHAPTER 25

By Monday morning, David felt well refreshed from his weekend away from the office. He always found football therapeutic and the dropping of a home point had hardly made a dent in United's unlikely push for promotion. It certainly did not spoil his Saturday evening, spent playing family board games until Mark's bedtime when three landings on a hotel-occupied Mayfair had sent the boy upstairs in a huff. It was an opportune moment to encourage Sarah into the complexities of chess, but with only two previous lessons behind her, it was already looking beyond her. He would have to rely on Mark for future competition.

He had sometimes pondered on how the cut and thrust philosophy of chess could apply to lending interviews, the endgame reflecting his final decision on whether or not to grant a loan. But he resisted any urge to issue the challenge of "Check Mate" when he had destroyed persuasive, but flawed, arguments put forward by a potential borrower. At other whimsical moments, he also curbed any temptation to adopt a play on words by inscribing Cheque Mate, rather than Refer to Drawer, on cheques that he bounced. The alternative words would certainly be a fitting riposte to those customers' deliberate indiscretions.

Apart from tinkering in the garden, Sunday had been a day of rest. He had devoured the papers and also a good helping of topside, Sarah's choice this week for their traditional Sunday roast. A slightly-strained atmosphere had prevailed between them, attempts at overstated bonhomie failing to disguise their shared anxiety about their next visit to Dr Edwards. With some foreboding, they viewed the outcome of last week's X-ray, even if Dad exhibited no such concern, being blithely oblivious to events that might affect the cosy insularity of his day-to-day way of life.

It was as if outside influences had no bearing on him at all. Not for the first time, David compared him to a child. Perhaps it was a matter of trust. A sick child would accept without question a mother's call for medical assistance. Dad was the same. He had not demurred at either the visit to Dr Edwards or the subsequent trip to Torbay Hospital.

Now, at about mid-morning, shortly before the arrival of John English, Sarah telephoned to say the doctor had just rung, asking them all to visit his surgery at six-thirty that evening. He had given no indication of the outcome of the X-ray, but the apparent urgency caused David some disquiet. He still did not fully understand what the X-ray might reveal, nor what remedial work might be possible, should this prove necessary. He could grasp the significance of an X-ray diagnosing a broken bone in a leg, with its subsequent setting and mending, but he could not relate this to such a sensitive area as a person's brain. With such confused signals dogging his mind, he would need to exercise full concentration during the forthcoming interview and he was relieved when Jane ushered John English into his room. He must now pit his thoughts on the primary job in hand – banking.

After the usual salutations and obligatory views on the current state of the weather, he asked the hotelier how he could be of help, even though he had been forewarned by Stuart Brown of his likely future plans.

'I need to expand, David,' English answered, his hearty informality continuing to sit uneasily on David's shoulders. 'I'm having to turn away business – through lack of space. And I can't afford to do that. The season's too short as it is – far too short to sacrifice additional turnover when it's there for the taking.'

Oh dear. That insatiable drive to increase turnover. So many business people saw it as their prime requisite, quite overlooking possible attendant cash problems. Increased sales normally led to mounting overheads and English would not be the first enthusiastic entrepreneur to become too busy wooing new customers to the detriment of keeping an eye on cash resources. It was only last month that an apparently profitable building company had gone bust. The directors had failed to realize that increased sales did not equate to instant cash. Credit has to be given, but actual cash – not profits – is needed for the payment of outgoings such as wages. If cash runs out, together with any line of credit from the bank, trouble looms with a capital T.

'I gather you wanted to expand the bar area, but...'

'The bar area? Oh, yes... yes, of course. That was my first thought. But something much better's come up. Next door's on the market.'

'The Red Lion?' David asked, momentarily forgetting the name of the other pub that flanked the hotel.

'No, the Chalk and Cheese – on the other side.'

'But why would you want a pub as well as a hotel?'

'I wouldn't,' the hotelier replied, a smirk causing his flaccid jowls to wobble like one of Mark's favourite jellies. 'There's not enough business for two pubs so close together – especially with the hotel in between. So, the Chalk and Cheese is being closed down. If I can get the building, I'd use it as an annex to the hotel. It wouldn't take much to convert the bar area to bedrooms, nor the floors upstairs. From then on, the sky's the limit.'

Another ominous trait – over-optimism. Far be it for traders to be pessimistic, but David and his fellow bank managers always sought a generous helping of realism. So many times he had seen overt optimism materialize into failure, only for the blame to be pinpointed elsewhere. Far better, in the first place, to have considered the hundred and one things that could threaten what might otherwise be a viable proposition. It was all about budgeting and forecasts. Putting pen to paper, rather than simply keeping figures in the head, or written on the back of a hand. It was a great discipline – not to mention confidence inducing.

'That makes it all sound rather simplistic,' he replied, good-naturedly, not wanting to appear too cynical so early in the interview. 'But before even thinking of the conversion, what about the cost of the building? A property like that wouldn't come cheaply.'

'Ah, but it will,' English replied, smirking again in unconcealed self-satisfaction. 'I'm getting it for nothing.'

'For nothing?'

English nodded, beaming broadly. 'I've made a deal with Austin Bentley.'

'Austin Bentley?' David queried, his mind flitting between thoughts of motorcars and the potential nightmare of the word "deal".

'Yes, the owner. Well, he's not the actual proprietor – more of a front man for the company that owns the pub. But he's effectively run it for the last five years.'

'You mean you've made a deal with someone who isn't the actual owner?'

'Yes, but he's the owner's representative and he's going to be my partner.'

David's heart plummeted. Partnerships could so often be the kiss of death. All might be well when they start out, friends getting together for a common cause, but in time, obstacles often led to a dramatic falling out. As with a failed marriage, personal trauma mixed easily with financial grief, shared all too frequently with a partnership's bankers.

But this sounded much worse. Austin Bentley did not own the pub, yet he was going to be a partner in the hotel? Directors of a company might well take a back seat in the actual running of the business, but the legal transfer of its title and assets was quite another matter. Bentley would have no say in this at all. If such a transaction was to go ahead, the legal expertise of Stuart Brown was going to be essential.

'We've got to know each other well since Austin took over the Chalk and Cheese,' English continued. 'You could say we're good drinking mates. It goes with the trade, of course. But between you and me, he's a bit naive. As soon as I suggested a partnership, his eyes positively gleamed.'

'But how can he agree to a sale and become a partner when the business and property belong to a company? Who owns the company? And who are the directors?'

'That's all hush-hush. For tax reasons, I suppose. But Austin assures me they want to merge the business with mine – the property, that is. And they're happy with a straight transfer, provided they can share in future profits. And provided Austin's a partner as their representative. But I'm only agreeing a 20% share. By getting the property for nothing in exchange for that, I'm laughing all the way to the bank – if you'll excuse the pun.'

This was madness! A partnership with the representative of an unknown company, never mind with someone who's a drinking mate. If anyone was being naive, it was John English. But even if everything was open and above board, the 20% arrangement would make it a restrictive partnership. Would that apply to liabilities as well as gains? Unlimited liability was normally the case in partnerships. Anything else was fraught with danger.

'I really can't see how this will possibly work,' he replied, 'but even if it could happen...'

'Stuart says there's no problem.'

'Stuart? You've been through it all with him?'

'That's his job, isn't it? He said leave it all to him and he'd sort out the legals.'

The legals? A can of worms, more likely. But why had Stuart not tipped him the wink? He had been anxious enough for him to help, so why had he not explained the background?

'Even if that's the case,' he answered, as English continued to smirk, 'and even if, somehow, Austin Bentley can become a partner, does he realize that with only a 20% stake in the partnership, he'll still be deemed to be a full partner, legally?'

'Pardon? How can he be a full partner with only a fifth share in the business?'

'It's the law – the Partnership Act of 1890 to be precise. As far as debts are concerned, each partner is jointly and severally liable. And that means to the full extent of his private resources. Are you sure Austin Bentley under-stands this?'

'Austin Bentley? I'm not sure I even know what you're getting at.'

'Well, let's start with the bank mandate. Banks – and this applies to all banks, not just mine – banks require all partners to undertake joint and several liability for any borrowing.'

'Meaning?' English asked, frowning and pursing his

lips in puzzlement, the crease lines of his jowls extending up to his cheeks. How could this man believe himself to be a womaniser?

'Meaning that if the partnership – jointly – could not repay any indebtedness, the bank could then call upon each individual partner's assets. So, if the business failed...'

'Failed?' English interrupted, a look of astonishment shining from what David now realized were rather beady eyes, set a mite too close for comfort. 'You think my business is going to fail?'

'No, no, not at all. I'm setting out the facts that could apply to any business. If it failed – owing the bank money – our initial action would be against the partnership itself, picking up the business's assets. In your particular case, I assume that this would primarily mean the hotel itself. In other words, the bricks and mortar of the building. Then, if the sale of the property failed to clear the indebtedness, the bank would be entitled to look to each partner individually. That means looking to their private assets until the borrowing is repaid completely.'

'You must be joking! I couldn't let that happen to me, never mind Austin.'

'But isn't that the effective situation you're in at the moment? I assume you own and run the Esplanade as a private operation. There aren't any partners, are there?'

'No, it's just me – always has been.'

'So, you're personally liable for everything – should the unforeseen happen and the business folds up,'

'Not at all. The bank only has a mortgage over the property. I've not lodged any other assets with them.'

This was now heading for trouble. Security to cover bank lending could often be a vexed topic, but it was disconcerting to hear English's apparent understanding

that a bank could only look to pledged assets to clear any borrowing on an account. He would need to be assured that a customer is always liable, irrespective of whether or not security may have been lodged.

Taking formal security by way of a charge or mortgage over a specific asset clarifies the position, but even without this, a bank could still seek redress through the courts should a customer choose not to repay voluntarily.

As he developed this explanation, he watched with disquiet English's face turning a shade of puce, anger apparently building up inside in anticipation of an imminent eruption. When it came, words spewed from his mouth like intermittent bursts of lava from an active volcano, any heartiness at the start of the interview having evaporated in the heat of the moment.

'That's outrageous. It's obscene. How could you... no, I can't believe it. But if you tried that on me, Mr Goodhart, I'd fight you. Court action, indeed. I'd get Stuart to take you to the cleaners...'

'If you don't believe me,' David countered, as English drew breath, 'just ask him. It's the law, I'm afraid.'

At that, English sprang from his chair. 'You banks,' he spat out, 'you're all the same. Stuart told me you were different. But you're not. Goodness knows what his reaction's going to be.'

And then he was gone, the interview ending in the most unsatisfactory way, without even getting to the point of discussing the required facility. David sank back into his chair and sighed. It was a no-win situation. He had given English sound advice about the implications of partnerships, but knew he would be castigated for his troubles. Yet he felt mightily relieved. He had seen sides of English's character that were decidedly questionable and felt no loss at having failed to acquire the hotelier's banking business.

The man had patently failed to pass one of the three Cs, which constituted the core of any lending proposition. C for Capital was no problem; the value of the hotel supporting a case for facilities, while C for Capability had been proved by his successful running of the hotel over so many years. But C for Character was a massive stumbling block.

English was not a man he could like or trust. All manner of weaknesses threatened to break out of his eggshell façade. His duplicity on the golf course had been compounded by his boastful ruse to dupe the owners of the Chalk and Cheese into swapping the value of their property for only a 20% return of the hotel's future profits. And he had hardly been complimentary about Austin Bentley's apparent naivety. It did not auger well for a business relationship between the two men.

Then there was his totally unwarranted angry outburst, which sat uneasily with his limp-wristed handshake. He was a complex man, indeed; not someone with whom a harmonious banker/customer rapport could ever be forged. Sarah's assessment of him had been spot on.

Yet one thing was particularly bothersome. Why would Stuart Brown be involved with the man and what would he make of this particular episode?

CHAPTER 26

David opened the bank's front door to make his way home after a day of contrasting emotions and immediately bumped into Mrs Smithers who was waiting to come in.

'What on earth are you doing here?' he asked, surprised at seeing the cleaner who normally worked in the morning.

'I hope you don't mind, love, but I've swapped my jobs around. It's only for today and Mr Charlton said it was all right.'

'Of course,' David agreed, smiling at the cleaner's natural informality. Far better to be called love than sir! 'But why the change?'

'There's a big conference going on next door, love. Mr Brown's still got his London clients down here. They've normally gone by the end of the weekend, but something special's going on and they asked me to change.'

'It makes no difference to us, but you'll have to work round some of the staff. They're a bit behind because of the inspectors.'

'Don't worry, dear, I won't get in their way. Is Jane still here?'

David nodded, looking over his shoulder. They ought to be having this conversation inside. 'Yes, she's still around. But come inside. We'd better get this door closed.'

'Of course, love,' Mrs Smithers agreed, stepping into the banking hall as he made to shut the door. 'It's just that I wanted to have a quick peek. I've been hearing all sorts of rumours.'

David could not help but grin and was still smiling as he left the office for home. Jane had caused quite a stir. And her changed appearance and demeanour had certainly been compensation for his unsatisfactory interview with John English. Her eyes had positively sparkled when they had both dealt with the incoming post that morning.

'What's got into you today,' he had not been able to resist asking as she confidently dealt with his queries. Was this the same girl?

She had just smiled – and blushed – in acknowledgement, leaving him to hope that Katie might shed some enlightenment on the change.

'It was Saturday night,' the typist had subsequently cooed as she took his dictation. She needed no encouragement to share her excitement. 'But don't let her know I've said anything,' she quickly added as she regaled him of their evening out. She could not have enthused more about Jane's new look, made even more dramatic by dispensing with her glasses. He could understand that, having had a glimpse of the effect when she had temporarily removed them in his room last week. She was wearing them again today, but they did not detract from her changed appearance. She even looked glamorous. But he was curious as to why, two days after her night out, her eyes were still glistening like those of a besotted teenager.

He pondered on this as he reached the promenade and approached the hotels and guesthouses that stretched away from the pier towards his own house. His eyes soon locked on to the Esplanade Hotel and then took in the adjacent Chalk and Cheese. He had never really taken much notice of this particular pub, but it did not seem suitable as an annexe to the hotel.

Unlike the four-storey hotel, it only had two floors

and its fabric needed considerable attention to bring it up to the standard of the hotel. It seemed to him that the amount needed for renovations would be far too excessive in relation to the return that might arise from the conversion, especially as no more than six bedrooms would probably be squeezed into the existing accommodation. The building could never be worth 20% of the combined premises and he was becoming even more suspicious of the motives behind the deal being hatched by English and Austin Bentley. He was only too thankful that he and National Counties would not be associated with this particular venture.

He was involved with enough other matters as it was. What was going on in Barnmouth? Winter should be providing respite from its summer excesses, but all hell had let loose this week. Murder, fraud, deception – where would it all end? At least George Broadman's death was a matter for the police, but what about his crossfiring and Miss Harding's involvement? These were banking problems, through and through. Could he have forestalled them? Had he slipped up? Would it all get sorted out?

Yet he tried to shelve such thoughts as he continued to his house. They now had Dr Edwards to contend with. Despite Sarah's high regard for him, he still seemed too young. As with policemen – and bank managers for that matter – there was no accounting for experience. On the other hand, who was he to talk, having only been in his own post for two years?

He reached the corner of his road and could already hear the repetitive thump of ball meeting foot. He wondered if Mark had reached the target of twenty "keep-ups" he had set the boy a week ago. Ball-juggling had started to appear in football, his favourite practitioner being Len Shackleton, dubbed as Sunderland's "Clown Prince of Soccer". But Torquay also had a ball artist in Don Mills and Mark had aspirations to match his hero's sleight of foot, practising daily with the heavy leather football he had been given on his last birthday. So far, he had managed to bounce the ball on his instep twelve times before its inevitable descent to earth and from the groans coming from the garden, David knew that his target of twenty was not yet under threat.

'How are you doing?' he asked as he stepped into their front garden.'

'I haven't even done six,' Mark replied, picking up the ball and booting it at the door in frustration.

'Hey, mind that door. The last thing I need is to re-paint it – never mind repair a panel.'

When he got inside, Sarah looked at the end of her tether. 'If he doesn't stop kicking that ball, I'm going to go out of my mind. Why you ever gave it him, I'll...'

'Hang on a minute,' David countered, having not even been given the chance to say hello. 'It was our present, not mine.'

'But it was your idea. You chose it.'

'But you agreed. It was a joint present – from both of us.'

'Then I must have been out of my mind. What with your father's wireless blaring out all day, and now the thump, thump, thump of that football. As soon as he got in from school, he started it. And my apple sponge hasn't risen. Goodness knows what's wrong with the gas...'

As her frustration tumbled out, he took her in his arms and slowly, but surely, the tension eased from her body. For half-a-minute, they stood in silence, the only sound coming from the front garden, Mark's kicking of his football synchronizing curiously with the beating of Sarah's heart against his chest. Dare he mention this? No, that would hardly be politic. Instead, he moved back from her, smiled into her moist eyes and kissed her gently on the lips. 'Welcome home, darling,' he then mimicked. 'Had a good day?'

'It's all right for you,' Sarah bemoaned, but now in better humour. 'It's just that you go off in the morning... and I know you have a busy job and it's not easy. But you're meeting people. There's so much variety in your day. I'm just stuck at home, doing the same old things and... and I'm bored. I need some sort of outlet. Let's face it, I need a job.'

It was hardly the appropriate time to suggest she already had a full-time occupation – managing the home and looking after him and Mark, let alone keeping tabs on Dad. He also appreciated that he could never cope if their roles were reversed, but he did not have a satisfactory answer to overcome her obvious frustration. 'Perhaps the time's come for you to get a part-time job,' he offered, but without conviction. The available positions were unlikely to give her the mental stimulation she sought.

'I tried that, didn't I? With the bank. But they didn't want to know. They'd somehow forgotten I was good at the job and they'd spent time and money training me. Surely, I could have given something back?'

'Bank policy, I suppose,' David answered, leading her into the lounge and steering them towards the drinks' cupboard. 'How about a pick-me-up?'

'I could do with something – what with Dr Edwards coming up. I think I'll have a gin and orange.'

David mixed her drink and poured himself a light ale before sitting down next to her on the sofa. 'The bank did offer you a full-time job.'

'But how could I do that? Not now, anyway. No, I'll be all right. It's just that every now and again frustration boils over and...'

The sentence tailed off as Mark bowled into the room. 'Dad, Dad, I've done it. I just did twenty-one.'

'Thank God for that,' Sarah blurted out. 'Now you can come in and do something worthwhile.'

'Mum!'

'All right,' David said, anxious to play the role of peacemaker. 'Mum's only joking. But well done and what's your next target going to be?'

'Oh, David,' Sarah pleaded, 'let's give it a rest for the moment. Mark, go and get yourself tidied up. We've got to go to the doctor's soon.'

'The doctor's? I don't have to go, do I?'

'You can't stay here on your own. No, we're all going. But we won't be long. We must get back for supper and I don't want you staying up late. You've got school tomorrow.'

When Mark had gone upstairs, muttering under his breath, David broached the subject of his father. 'How's Dad been? Apart from his excessive use of the wireless.'

'His usual self, I suppose. But he did tell me something. And it's quite scary.'

Oh, no. Whatever next?

'I asked him again what made him go into town last Monday night. He didn't seem to have any real answer – just said the usual reasons. When I asked him what he meant, he said he'd gone out the night before – and on other occasions.'

'He what? How could he have done? We'd have known.'

'That's why I said it was scary. He said he always went out when we were asleep in bed.'

'And you believed him? He's just imagining it. He must have been dreaming.'

'You tell me. But I know I'm not going to be able to sleep at night now. Just in case.'

'The sooner we get to Dr Edwards the better. Let's hope something positive comes out of it. Dad seems to be getting weirder by the day.'

Half-an-hour later, they sat in the doctor's surgery, having left Mark deposited in the waiting room seeking out a magazine which might be suitable for an eight-year-old boy. David had warned him of the likely range and age of doctors' reading material and as a precaution, the boy had brought along his football programmes, even though he must know their content word for word.

David's first impression of the doctor echoed Sarah's high regard for the man. A firm handshake accompanied good eye contact, without it being disconcertingly penetrating. A clear desk and tidy room depicted an orderly man, while an abundance of textbooks and medical journals adorned shelves and bookcases. It was evident that the doctor sought greater challenges than curing the common or garden ailments which must dominate his working day. This was a man whose judgement he could respect.

'I know Mrs Goodhart has already told me quite a bit about Albert,' Dr Edwards said, once introductions and some small talk were out of the way, 'and I hope you don't mind my calling you Albert,' he added, smiling at the older man, before turning back to David, 'but I should be grateful if you would go through the sort of things that have concerned you since his car accident.'

For the next few minutes, David described as best he

could the traits that Dad had increasingly exhibited over recent years. He gave examples of his childishness and short-term memory problems together with their concerns about his inability to concentrate and his total lack of organization. Although this might be age-related, he suggested that if Dad had been younger, it would be impossible for him to hold down a job. And he had become particularly stubborn, with irrational behaviour leading to his night-time escapades.

'And what about any aversion to noise, or a prevalence towards swearing... and yawning, for that matter?'

'Yes, he hates noise,' David answered, grinning at Dad as he added, 'and, thankfully, his addiction to the wireless is tempered by its low volume. He doesn't swear – never has done, but, yes, he yawns all the time. And going back to noise, he can't cope with a mixture of sounds – as when several people are talking at the same time. Is there anything else, Sarah?'

'The only other thing,' she added, 'is that he seems to have lost his senses of taste and smell.'

Dr Edwards listened intently to all of this and then withdrew a set of X-ray pictures from a large envelope on his desk.

'I'm not an expert on these,' he said, 'but I've discussed them with the consultant. Although they aren't conclusive, they do reveal what might be a broken blood vessel – right here at the front of the brain.' David and Sarah leant across the desk as the doctor pointed out a slight mark, which they would not have noticed unless it had been highlighted for them. 'But the trouble with X-rays is that they're one-dimensional. That's fine for detecting fractures, but when it comes to identifying internal bleeding, a three-dimensional scan would be preferable. The only problem is there's no such thing at the moment.'

'But I'm still not sure what you're getting at,' David said, frowning. 'I get the impression this all harks back to the car accident, but if Dad hit his head on the windscreen, couldn't that show up on the X-ray as a fracture?'

'It could have done at the time, but I gather no X-ray was taken then. And if there had been a fracture, particularly a small one, it could have healed itself over the years since then.'

'So if any fracture might now be healed, what would a scan reveal?'

'That's difficult to predict,' Dr Edwards answered, smiling sympathetically, 'because we'd be into unknown territory. But since Mrs Goodhart's first visit, I've been researching my journals. It does seem that a three-dimensional scan is in the offing and if it came about, it ought to detect internal bleeding in the brain far better than a simple X-ray.'

'But this bleeding in the brain – what does that actually mean?'

'In a nutshell, a head injury – or brain injury to be precise. Albert experienced a traumatic car crash – head-on, I gather. That means his head almost certainly hit the windscreen. The only physical evidence at the time was probably a state of concussion, but when a car comes to such an abrupt halt – like Albert's must have done – the brain is thrown against its shell. This can rupture its arteries, causing blood to be pumped into the brain itself.'

David and Sarah winced in unison at the thought, but chose not to interrupt.

'Now, none of this can be seen,' the doctor continued, 'and once the effects of concussion have worn off, Albert would have appeared all right, physically. But unbeknown to everyone, internal bleeding might have taken place. If that happened, he was extremely lucky, because he could have died. Any such bleeding must have stopped of its own accord, but by then, irreparable damage could have been done.'

'Irreparable?'

'I'm afraid so,' the doctor confirmed, nodding his head sadly.

'And if this actually happened, would such brain damage be causing Dad's irrational behaviour?'

'That's what I believe. I'm certainly no expert, but damage to different parts of the brain can lead to different problems. That's why I asked you about Albert's behavioural pattern. Many head-injured people can't stand noise and certainly can't cope with discussions involving more than one person...'

'Like now,' David interrupted. 'He's not making any contribution, because he's confused by the signals coming from different directions.'

'A typical reaction. But people with head injuries are also affected in so many other different ways. I mentioned swearing earlier. In that respect, some people can change character dramatically – much to the consternation of their loved ones.'

'At least we don't have that problem,' Sarah said, probably sharing David's relief that such a scenario was not being inflicted on Mark, let alone themselves.

'No, Albert's problems all seem to stem from what might arise from a head-on car crash. But again, I must stress that I'm only surmising. I'm certainly no expert and you now need to go and see the neurological consultant.'

'But after all this time since the accident, do you think he would be able to do anything for Dad?'

'I really can't prejudge that. And he might disagree with what I've been saying. But would you like me to fix an appointment?'

'Of course,' David replied, pleased to see Sarah nodding her assent. 'And I must say we're most grateful for all you've done yourself.'

'That's my pleasure,' the doctor replied, smiling and then addressing Albert directly. 'But don't you go off on any of those jaunts again. You've already given your son and his wife enough to worry about.'

Albert smiled benignly, as he had during most of the consultation, but David was not convinced he would do as he had been heeded.

CHAPTER 27

With heavy heart, David awoke the next morning from a fitful sleep. Events at work and now at home dogged his natural optimism as never before. But Sarah's steadfast support knew no bounds. She was so positive.

'We're actually getting somewhere,' she had said on their return from Dr Edwards. It was not a view he shared. The doctor might be excellent, but he had described any possible brain damage as irreparable. It was difficult to be positive about that.

'We know he's physically all right,' Sarah had continued, 'and that's got to be good news. And if he does have a head injury, the consultant should be able to confirm it. Then we can move forward, knowing the problem – and understanding it.'

If only. But as he set off to work, he would try to share Sarah's confidence. As for the bank, his staff had worked late last night and it was only fair for him to arrive first today and get them off to a good start.

The town was almost deserted as he approached the bank. Being so early, it was still not light and he was surprised to find the bank in darkness until he recalled that Mrs Smithers had done her shift last evening, rather than this morning. She would normally let in the first staff to arrive and he fumbled in his pocked for his bunch of keys, which included those for the front door. He immediately found that the door had not been double locked by the last person to leave – presumably Mrs Smithers. More front door problems! Thank goodness Parker was not around to witness another misdemeanour. But why the omission? Deadlocking the front door was the automatic procedure and there could be no possible excuse for such negligence.

Moving inside, he switched on the main lights and closed the door behind him, slipping the security chain in place. After a fleeting concern that something might be amiss inside the bank, he was relieved to find everything appeared normal until he saw Mrs Smithers's bucket and mop nestling on the floor at one end of the counter. Walking to the back office, he then noticed the broom cupboard stood wide open with a brush and dustpan outside, and he could also hear a tap running gently in the adjacent cloakroom.

Irrationally thinking that someone might be in there, he hesitated about pushing the door open, but then found the courage to ease it ajar. The cloakroom was empty. Turning the tap off, he went to his own room and hung his coat in the cupboard.

It was all very odd and most unlike Mrs Smithers. Perhaps she had felt unwell and gone home early, but even then she would have tidied up first and left a note. If only he could ring her, but he knew she was not on the telephone. Someone had better call round and Jane was probably the best person as she lived on the same estate.

Trying to put his concerns to the back of his mind, he collected the incoming mail from the post-box and was halfway through opening it when the front door bell sounded. He went to open the door, keeping the security chain in place to identify the new arrivals, who turned out to be Jane and Jilly Sheffield.

'Mr Goodhart!' Jane exclaimed as he opened the door. 'What are you doing here so early?'

'You're not the only ones to put the hours in,' he

answered, grinning, and pointedly looking at his watch as if they were late for work. 'But once you've got your coat off, Jane, I'd like you to come to my room straight away.'

'Is something up?' she asked, a few minutes later as she sat opposite him.

'I hope not, but I'm worried – about Mrs Smithers.'

'Has something happened to her? She was all right when I left last night.'

He explained about his arrival and how he had found her cleaning equipment around the branch and that the front door had not been deadlocked.

'It sounds as if she left in a hurry,' Jane said. 'But that's not like her. She's always so meticulous.'

'I'd like you to go round to her house – to see if she's all right. It won't take you long, will it?'

Jane shook her head. 'Only about ten minutes. Shall I go straight away?'

'Please. If only for peace of mind. I'm sure everything must be fine, but it's better to be safe than sorry.'

When she had gone – her faced etched with worry – he turned his attention to the post, though finding it difficult to concentrate. It was a particularly heavy mail and included five requests to open new accounts; various loan applications for items as diverse as a new Vespa motor scooter to a second-hand fishing trawler for sale near the estuary of the Barn; two notices of customers' deaths; and numerous end-of-year returns to be completed for Head Office. He would delegate most of these items to Jane when she returned, because he had agreed to see Parker who wanted to get on with his basic branch inspection.

It reminded him of how his concern for Dad had put to the back of his mind the events of last week, any one of which would normally have dominated his thinking, day and night. A branch inspection had sufficient import in itself, but when this was accompanied by a case of cross-firing, the suspension of a trusted employee and the murder of a valued customer, he could not help but wonder if the gods were conspiring against him. And now he had Mrs Smithers exercising his mind. Where would it all end?

Jane then broke into his reverie by bursting into his room. She must have knocked, but he had not heard. 'There was no answer when I rang the doorbell,' she blurted out, panting hard as if she had run all the way back to the bank, 'and I couldn't get in. Both doors were locked and the curtains were drawn. I think she might be ill in bed. The neighbours weren't around and I didn't know what else to do.'

'We must call the police,' David exclaimed, reaching for his telephone. 'If she's ill, it could be serious. And if she's not in the house...'

He did not want to contemplate the alternative, but two matters now worried him. Clearly, the well being of Mrs Smithers was paramount, but security might also be a serious factor if she had disappeared with the bank's keys. Locks could certainly be changed, but he hoped not to have to undertake such an extreme measure. Come on, come on, why don't they answer? 'Is Mr Parker in yet?' he asked Jane, cupping his hand over the receiver.

'Yes, I spotted him in the back office when I came in.'

'Good. Ah, at last,' he said, as the police finally answered his call. He explained all that had happened and was relieved that the officer seemed to share his concern, promising to send a car round to the house immediately.

'Not much more we can do now,' he then said to Jane, 'but I must put Mr Parker in the picture. And Jane... many thanks for all you've done. You've been a great help.'

He had been due to see Parker at ten, but he could not delay telling the inspector about Mrs Smithers. He only hoped the thaw in the man's demeanour would continue. He needed all the support possible; any contrariness would only be counter-productive.

But such concerns soon proved unfounded. Parker's appearance was little changed – crumpled suit, shop-soiled tie and an overall resemblance to a wartime refugee – but his eyes had lost their previous intensity and they actually radiated care, something that had been denied the apparel worn by this inscrutable man.

'I understand,' he said, before David could raise his concern about Mrs Smithers, 'that apart from all that's been going on here, you've a problem at home.'

David was almost as surprised at the inspector's words as at the look in his eyes. He was rarely one to broach troubles at home within the confines of the office and he had certainly not mentioned anything about Dad to Parker. But it was Mrs Smithers he wanted to talk about, not Dad.

'It was Jane,' Parker added, not giving him a chance to butt in. 'No, she wasn't telling tales out of school. I wanted a quiet word with you last night, but you'd left. Jane said you had a doctor's appointment – for your father. I didn't press her, but she was very worried. You've got a good girl there. Most loyal.'

'Mm,' David agreed, glad the inspector was seeing Jane in her new light. It was also interesting that she had not enquired about the doctor's visit this morning, quite rightly concentrating on their concern over Mrs Smithers. He only wished he could do the same now with Parker. 'Yes, it seems my father might have a head injury going

234

back to a car crash six years ago.'

'A head injury? Does your doctor know about such things?

'Not really, but he's done some research. We've now got to see a consultant.'

'I know the feeling,' Parker said, surprising David yet again. 'We've been through the same thing with my family. A nephew of mine – my brother's boy. He crashed his car two years ago.'

'And he has a head injury?'

'That's what the doctors think, but they can't be sure – not without a full-scale scan of his brain.'

'Yes, that's what we've been told.'

'The thing is,' Parker continued, 'he looks completely normal, but he certainly acts strangely.'

'Like a child?'

'Yes, but also in other ways. I suppose it's a general naivety – or gullibility. For instance, he can't refuse requests from beggars in the street and if he passes the same beggar again, he'll give him more money – even though he can't afford it. And when he's driving, he'll offer anyone a lift – no matter where a hitchhiker wants to go. He went to Bristol a couple of weeks ago.'

'Good heavens!' David exclaimed, thankful that Dad had stopped driving. 'At least we don't have that with my father. But he's started wandering off. I suppose that's the same sort of thing. We went out last Monday night to celebrate our wedding anniversary. Trust you to arrive on that particular day,' he added, grinning at the inspector who clearly acknowledged the irony of starting his inspection on such a day. 'Anyway, my father agreed to babysit, but when we got back home, the front door was wide open and there was no sign of him. The police eventually brought him home after I'd reported him missing. That's when they told me about the vehicle on the rocks. We thought it might have been Dad...'

His words tailed off, as the emotion of that awful moment threatened to overwhelm him.

'But where had he got to?' Parker asked, encouraging him to continue.

'Only into town,' David replied, back in control. 'The police found him wandering around aimlessly, muttering about trying to find a black baby, of all things.'

'How extraordinary.'

'Yes, but it's worse. He says he's done it before. He even went out the previous night – without our knowing it.'

Parker had been listening intently and now shook his head sadly. 'It's not quite like my nephew, driving off as he does. But it's the same sort of trait – like going off on a wild goose chase. I reckon they're both head injured. But where do we go from here?'

'I don't know, but something else has come up.' At last, he could get on to Mrs Smithers and he told Parker all that had happened that morning. The inspector's frown deepened as the story unfolded, but he then confirmed his full support.

'You've done very well,' he said, 'and so has Jane. Are the police going to report back to you?'

'I certainly asked them to.'

'Has anything like this happened to Mrs Smithers before?'

'Never. I don't think she's ever been ill. She's a tough old bird – in the nicest possible way.'

'Well, let's hope the police ring soon,' Parker said, getting out some sheets of paper from a file he had brought into the room. 'Now, before we get round to the branch inspection, I wanted to have a word about those other accounts of George Broadman. Once the managers of the other banks knew what had been going on, they were most co-operative. And apart from Broadman's crossfiring, some mighty strange things had been happening on his accounts.'

He looked down at his first sheet of paper, tracing his finger over the entries at the top of the page. 'Believe it or not, it goes back to 1953 – significant transactions which seem to have nothing to do with his business.'

'Gambling?' David queried. 'But Miss Harding reckoned that only started this year.'

'According to the other banks it was gambling. Quite frankly their action – or I should say, inaction – left much to be desired.'

'What sort of transactions are you talking about?'

'Cash. Large cash credits. Then, some days later, Broadman issued his own cheques for similar amounts to other people.'

'But wasn't this all tied up with his crossfiring?'

'No, these were cash credits. It's not like manipulating cheques through the clearing system. Broadman was actually quite clever. He openly admitted he was gambling. He said he kept having lucky streaks. That's unusual, because compulsive gamblers normally keep quiet about their activities – never mind their winnings. I reckon it was a deliberate ploy on his part. And it worked. It all started in a small way, regular cash credits going into his account. The novelty then wore off as far as the cashiers were concerned. It became a regular routine of taking in larger amounts of cash as the weeks and months went by – no questions asked. It was all about his plausibility. He simply lulled them into a false sense of security. It didn't cross anyone's mind that occasionally – just occasionally – he might hit a losing streak.'

'And you say the credits got larger and larger? What amounts are we talking about?'

'£500, £1000. Even up to £20,000.'

David closed his eyes at the enormity of what had been going on. Could it have been happening at his own branch? But Jane's investigations had revealed nothing like this. 'And the other cashiers – and managers – never questioned such amounts going into his accounts?'

Parker shook his head in genuine despair. 'And they also showed no apparent interest in where the money subsequently went. Bearing in mind we're talking about several hundred thousand pounds, you'd imagine someone would have thought something funny was going on.'

David could only share Parker's concern at what looked like blatant acts of complacency. In so many ways, banks must be put on enquiry when unusual transactions pass through a customer's account, whether cheques or cash. Unusually large cash credits must be queried. He recalled reading about Al Capone operating a cash scam in the 1920s. The mobster used a string of cash-operated laundromats scattered around Chicago to disguise his revenue from prostitution, racketeering and violation of the Prohibition laws. It was a way of cleaning what was essentially dirty money, because once such money was inside the banking system, its original ill-gotten source could not be identified. And what starts off in America often finds its way across the pond. So banks must be on their guard. The paying-in of unusual large cash credits was a classic case of when banks must be put on enquiry, something that George's other banks would appear to have patently ignored.

'And where did the money go?' he asked, with bated breath.

'Broadman made out his cheques to a variety of payees,' Parker replied, studying David carefully, 'but there was one particular recurring name...'

The shrill ring of the telephone interrupted him and David stretched for the receiver, mouthing the word "police" as he started to listen to the caller.

'Bad news,' he said, after putting down the telephone. 'Mrs Smithers is in hospital. But it could have been worse. The police found her in her sitting room armchair, apparently asleep. But they couldn't wake her and they thought she was dead – heart attack. They then detected a slight pulse and rushed her to Torbay Hospital. She's in a coma, but they hope she'll recover consciousness soon.'

Parker shook his head. 'It sounds very odd. Why would she leave the bank so suddenly and then end up at home with a suspected heart attack? Things just don't happen that way.'

'You're right. It doesn't make any sense. I just wish I could talk to her and find out what happened. But we're going to have to wait. The police are staying at her bedside until she comes round. Until then no one can see her.'

'I don't like the sound of it at all,' Parker said. 'Too many coincidences for my liking. And here's another one. I was about to tell you about Broadman's cheques. The most regular payee was a certain firm of solicitors – Ducksworth Brown and Sargeant, would you believe?'

CHAPTER 28

Yes, there were too many coincidences and Parker's chain of events seemed to be adding links by the day. As for Mrs Smithers, David still had no news by Wednesday lunchtime. He sat at the kitchen table with Sarah, not having much appetite for the cheese and pickle sandwich she had prepared. He was also bothered that there was clearly something on her mind, but having first been told about Mrs Smithers last night, her spoken concern now was for the cleaner. 'I still don't like the sound of it at all,' she said, frowning. 'She would never leave the bank like that – especially if she was able to get home without help. And if she was that unwell, she'd have told her neighbours.'

'I couldn't agree more,' David acknowledged, still not having got over the shock of the cleaner being in hospital in a coma. 'But what did happen, then?'

'I don't know, but I bet the police think it's fishy. When will you be able to go and see her?'

'Tomorrow, I hope – provided she's regained consciousness. It also depends on how my day pans out. But I might get Jane to go instead. I could then go on Friday – or tomorrow evening. What about you coming?'

'That would mean your father babysitting. It'd be too short notice to get anyone else. And I'd be worried if your Dad did it. He's wandered off too often already. I don't want the police round again.'

'You mean like last Monday?'

Sarah shook her head and looked a little shamefaced.

'No, I'm sorry, David, I'd have said straight away, but what with the worry about Mrs Smithers, I...'

'Sarah? What's happened?'

'They came round this morning,' she said, getting up to put the kettle on. 'To see your Dad.'

'What? Why would they come to see him? What happened, Sarah?'

'It was about ten o'clock,' she replied, having filled the kettle and got out a couple of cups and saucers. 'I was vacuuming upstairs and thought I heard the doorbell. I wasn't sure, but you know what a racket our vacuum makes. Anyway, I switched off and the bell rang again. I was in my pinny, but whoever it was would have to take me as I was. When I opened the door, there were these two tall men...'

'Why didn't you say anything about this earlier?'

'I didn't have the chance,' Sarah replied, indignantly. 'We were talking about Mrs Smithers. Anyway, the men said they were police...'

'I hope you identified them properly.'

'Of course I did, David, and stop interrupting. They were from Torquay C.I.D. and wanted to speak to your father. They wouldn't say what it was about and they wouldn't let me in on the interview.'

'But they must have given a reason.'

'No, they didn't, but after about twenty minutes, they came out of the room and said how helpful he'd been. They then said they were getting somewhere at last.'

Was this yet another link in the chain? Whatever, the cheese and pickle sandwich now seemed even less appetizing. 'What did they mean by that?'

'I don't know. But they left looking very pleased with themselves.'

'What did Dad say?'

'That's the annoying thing,' Sarah replied. 'When we got back from Dr Edwards on Monday, I promised myself I wouldn't get cross with him again, but this morning, he was infuriating. As soon as the police had gone, I asked him what it had been all about and he just tapped his finger against his nose – all secretive-like. He then went up to his room with a knowing smirk on his face. It was maddening.'

'It sounds like he was enjoying being the centre of attention. But who were these policemen? Did you get their names?'

'Yes, the younger one was Pound, because I thought of him pounding the beat. The other one was Hopkirk or Hoskins... something like that.'

'Not Hopkins?'

'Yes, that was it. Inspector Hopkins.'

So there was a definite link – and it went back to yesterday. 'I think Parker's behind it.'

'Your inspector? What does he know about your father?'

'Not a lot, but we did talk about him yesterday – when we had a meeting about the inspection.'

Sarah looked askance at him. 'But what's your Dad got to do with your inspection?'

David grinned, despite his concern. 'Nothing at all. But Parker had heard about our visit to Dr Edwards – from Jane. He wasn't prying – quite the opposite, actually. He was genuinely concerned that I might have a problem at home – on top of all that's going on at the office. In fact, he knew what we were going through. A nephew of his has also had a car crash. They now think he sustained a head injury – just like Dad.'

'But why would that make the police come round and see him?'

David shook his head. 'I've no idea. But I did mention that Dad had gone on walkabouts. And I told Parker about that black baby episode.'

'But that still doesn't explain why the police came round here.'

'I still think it's down to Parker,' David replied. 'When we'd finished our meeting, he said he'd arranged to see the police in the afternoon – about George Broadman. There have been some extraordinary things happening on his other bank accounts – in addition to his crossfiring activities.'

'But your Dad can't be tied up with that?'

'No, I'm not saying he is, but there must be a link. Hopkins is dealing with the murder investigation, so why else would it be him who came round here this morning?'

CHAPTER 29

A surreal air prevailed at the branch the next day. Once again, Parker was nowhere to be seen and news was unforthcoming about Mrs Smithers. By the afternoon, David had had enough and called Jane in to see him.

'We can't hang around doing nothing any longer,' he said, taking note again of how she now looked the part of a management trainee. 'I'd like you to go to the hospital and find out what's going on with Mrs Smithers.'

Jane's eyes sparkled at his instruction. Of all his staff, he knew she was the closest to the cleaner and she had been mortified at what had happened. It would also be less dramatic for her to be his emissary, rather than go himself.

'You mean now, sir, or this evening?'

'Straight away, please. It's bank business and I haven't any more work to give you this afternoon. You shouldn't have any trouble getting buses, but if you get delayed coming back, go straight home.'

Jane positively glowed at being given such a task and almost ran from his room to get her coat. It was certainly the right decision and would now give him the opportunity to sit quietly and reflect on all that had been happening.

He would definitely try and see Mrs Smithers tomorrow and he would also have liked to have called on Miss Harding. Whatever would become of his secretary? He visualized her at home, imprisoned with her mother who might still be unaware of what she had done. If so, he could well imagine her mother's outrage at the bank's temerity to suspend her daughter, no matter for what reason. But if her mother did know, was she the sort of person to condone such dishonesty – especially as she was the actual victim? Would the Harding blood be thicker than water? Whatever, the bank had an open and shut case against his secretary and he feared the worst for her eventual outcome.

He also harboured disturbing concerns about Bernard Groves, now drawn into his spider's web of thinking. Not being able to rely upon the integrity of his head cashier would be untenable. Admittedly, his only apparent crime had been his mishandling of George's credits, but did such sleight of hand extend to other areas? He was a man of obvious wealth, common thinking being that it arose from his wife's side of the family. But there was certainly no proof of this. And he had clearly enjoyed a close rapport with George, a man now proved to have been the perpetrator of unmitigated skulduggery. David now found himself questioning his head cashier's actions and lifestyle in a way he could not have previously imagined. The fact that neither he nor Sarah particularly liked him only increased his concern over what this ostentatious man might have been up to.

And was it a coincidence that, at this of all times, John English – one of the least attractive men he had met in Barnmouth – had come on the scene? He would have liked to dismiss Sarah's overt antagonism of the hotelier, but he had always respected her unfailing character assessments. She had called English "slimy" and although it was not a term he would normally associate with a fellow golfer, he knew what she meant. Golf was a game where high standards of sportsmanship were strenuously maintained, as opposed to some other sports where acts of stealth and cunning might be used to gain advantage and influence results. But English's behaviour on the golf course left much to be desired. He was also one of those men who oozed charm and bonhomie when things were going their way – when they were in control – but whose veneer would crack at the sign of any unpalatable resistance. The proposition to finance the next-door premises simply did not ring true, but his response to questioning smacked of a desperation that did not inspire confidence. Whenever a customer flounced from his room, David always felt confident that he had been safe in turning a proposition down. But on this occasion, he had not even been given the chance to say no.

But what bothered him further was the relationship English seemed to have with Stuart Brown. There was some bond between them that was particularly odd. Why would Stuart be so anxious for him to help the hotelier? There was nothing untoward about a professional relationship between a lawyer and his client, but accountants would normally be more involved in the funding requirements of a business. Perhaps the link was the hotel itself and David suddenly blanched at recalling that the Esplanade was the venue for Bernard Groves's extravagant parties when George Broadman supplied the meat during the austere post-war years of rationing. Could there be a link between the lot of them?

As for George's other activities, he could not contemplate what else the butcher might have been up to. Manipulating the cheque clearing system might well have provided some temporary financial respite, as would encouraging Miss Harding to dip into her mother's account. Parker's discoveries at the other banks were quite another matter. The huge sums involved could not possibly arise from profitable nights out at racetracks and casinos. In any case, why would George have paid in such large amounts, only to withdraw the monies soon afterwards by issuing his own cheques to other parties – including Stuart's own firm?

He switched his thoughts back to work and after he had carried out a few clerical tasks and signed his letters – typed admirably by Katie – the time was approaching five o'clock when a tap on his door heralded Jane's return to the branch.

'What are you doing here?' he asked, looking at his watch. 'I said you should go straight home.'

'I thought you should know right away. Mrs Smithers has come round.'

'Thank God for that. How did you find her?'

'That's the problem. I couldn't see her. They wouldn't let me go into her room.'

'They?'

'The police. They were everywhere.'

'So how do you know she's all right?'

'There was a friendly young constable on the door,' Jane replied, blushing. 'He told me what was going on.'

'Which was?' This was like drawing blood out of a stone. Come on, Jane, get on with it.

'She recovered consciousness in the middle of the afternoon and the policeman at her bedside called his station. Hoards of police then descended on the hospital. There's an Inspector Hopkins in charge and he's been with her ever since. She can't have any visitors yet, but we can probably see her tomorrow.'

Inspector Hopkins! So the coincidences were being proved right. But what link could there possibly be with Mrs Smithers?

They would clearly have to await the answer to that

and he was still pondering on the possibilities throughout a fitful night's sleep. By mid-morning on Friday, with no further news from the hospital, he decided to telephone about visiting, but was forestalled by Parker's sudden arrival.

'I'm sorry I've been so elusive,' the inspector said, a look of triumph accompanying his words. For one moment, David feared someone had slipped up on another branch security matter, but he need not have worried. The routine inspection appeared to be the last thing on Parker's mind. 'I was with the police for much of yesterday – and this morning. And do you know what? They've made an arrest – for George Broadman's murder.'

CHAPTER 30

David could hardly believe his ears. It was one thing knowing that George had been murdered, but he had not contemplated who might have carried out the actual act. So many things had been going on – so many coincidences – but he had not dwelled on the likely perpetrator, if only because he could not believe it to be anyone he knew. It could, of course, be a stranger, but one thing for sure; it was not Bernard Groves – thank God. He had duly turned up for work this morning and, right now, was busy cashiering.

'I feel almost too stunned to respond,' he eventually said. 'Are you sure it's true?'

'There's no shadow of doubt. I've been liaising closely with Inspector Hopkins and he made the arrest himself. And you'll never guess who the catalyst was in the investigation.'

Parker was clearly enjoying holding court and David sensed that he would be withholding that particular titbit for now.

'But we'll come to that later,' Parker continued, proving the point. 'Many questions still need to be answered, but a major piece of the jigsaw was filled in last night. You could say, a second catalyst turned up.'

'But who actually killed George?' David asked. A direct question might be the best way to stop Parker's apparent desire to prevaricate with this catalyst business.

'Ah – they're still working on that.'

'But you said they'd made an arrest.'

'And so they have. But at this stage, it's as an accessory to the actual murder. Having said that, a full-blown murder charge could still follow. One thing's for sure, the Barnmouth community will be rocked by the news when it gets out.'

'But who is it? And when will it...'

'It'll probably be in tomorrow's Herald Express – and the nationals, possibly. As for who? None other than that pillar of the community – Stuart Brown.'

'Stuart Brown?' David could hardly echo Parker's words. This was shocking. 'That's impossible. It can't possibly be right.'

'I'm afraid it is,' Parker replied. 'It seems there's much more to your Mr Brown than meets the eye.'

'Is there enough evidence to charge him?' David asked. If not, they could be in big trouble. If anyone were able to level a charge of false arrest against the police, it would be a lawyer – particularly one with the wherewithal of Stuart Brown.

'They certainly think so. And they've definitely learnt enough about his activities to level further charges against him. Much of this they've gleaned from Broadman's bank accounts. That's why I've been so involved. It's been quite exciting.'

That certainly showed. The inspector was like a child in a sweetshop. And no wonder. Liaising with the police on a murder case would be far more exciting than carrying out the humdrum routines of a branch inspection. David only hoped the powers-that-be in Head Office had properly authorized Parker to divulge privileged information about a customer to the police. The rules of confidentiality could not be abandoned without good reason.

'Let me give you some background.' Parker continued

in a more confidential manner. 'But this must remain within these four walls – and I'm talking about your room, not the overall bank itself. After all, certain staff here – to one extent or another – have been caught up in the affair.'

'You don't mean...'

'No, hang on a minute,' Parker interrupted, opening up a large folder he had brought with him. 'You'll see as the plot develops.'

David settled back in his chair. What on earth would be revealed? It did not look as if it would be a straightforward case of murder. Would those links he had been contemplating yesterday become pertinent? And he was also mindful of normal branch routines. Had they been flawed in some way? Had individuals fallen down on their duties? After all, this was still a branch inspection, even if Parker had apparently banished that particular function for the time being.

'A most significant aspect of the whole affair,' Parker eventually said, after getting his papers in order, 'is that there's been a long-standing relationship between Brown and Broadman. It started in the war when they were in the army together. Broadman was a corporal in the Catering Corps and at some stage Brown was his senior officer. Hopkins hasn't yet established what exactly happened between them, but he's absolutely certain that Broadman became beholden to Brown in a major way. He thinks it's tied up with Brown's Military Cross. He's doing his research now, but he believes Brown saved Broadman's life on the battlefield. That might sound far-fetched, but if it's true, it could well have given him a hold over Broadman – enough to draw him into his nefarious activities.'

'Nefarious activities?' David's eyes widened. This was madness. 'You mean of Brown? Just a minute. Is that what you meant last week about something untoward going on in Barnmouth?'

Parker nodded and turned over a page. 'We knew something was going on – something tied in with a London mob. But we had no idea what the connection was down here. Then you mentioned about Brown's London clients and it got me thinking. Do you know much about them?'

David shook his head. 'Not really. There's never been a need. They don't have specific accounts with me. Any transactions relating to them go through the clients' accounts in the firm's name.'

'And on the face of it, there's nothing wrong with that. But the amounts have been huge. And this is one reason you've been doing so well. Most branch managers would die for the credit balances you've held here.'

David was becoming unnerved at the way this conversation was developing. For some time, he had been congratulating himself on the credit balances held at the branch, believing that the close business rapport he had nurtured with Stuart Brown had encouraged the solicitor to put more and more business with him. Could this now all start to backfire?

'But don't worry,' Parker continued, as if sensing his unease. 'As far as I can tell, you've handled the accounts properly. As for Brown's actual clients, you might not know much about them, but Hopkins has certainly made some discoveries. Ready to be shocked? A good part of those credit balances stem from armed robberies.'

If it was Parker's intention to shock, he had undoubtedly succeeded. What was going on in Barnmouth, never mind the branch itself? It was bad enough knowing that a respectably-thought-of customer had successfully hidden his ill repute and that seemingly efficient and upright members of his staff had bent rules and manipulated accounts. But now it seemed the branch had been harbouring the illicit gains of London's underworld.

'And Stuart Brown was involved in all of this?'

'He certainly was. Not in the actual robberies, of course. And how he got involved in the first place isn't yet known. But they're working on it.'

'And these robberies... are we talking of banks?'

'Banks, post offices, bullion vans. Anyone handling cash. They weren't interested in things like jewellery, gold or silver. Just hard cash.'

'And this cash is turning up on accounts here? Isn't that a bit far-fetched?'

'Is it? I was sufficiently concerned to get my boys to go through the firm's clients' accounts. The last thing I wanted to see was thousands of pounds of cash being regularly paid in here. That would not have augured well for you at all.'

David knew that only too well. It had happened at George's other banks. They had blindly accepted large sums of cash into his accounts and that was asking for trouble. The cashiers must be put on enquiry when such money was paid in. Surely, Bernard Groves had not slipped up like that? 'But there were no such credits,' Parker continued, not allowing him to finish such a potentially damaging train of thought. 'And that's where George Broadman comes into the picture.'

'George? Was he part of the London mob?'

'No, not directly. But don't forget he had that indeterminate link with Stuart Brown. And what about his accounts at the other banks, and those of Jack Stringer? We now know that Stringer was a concocted alias. And I told you it wasn't just crossfiring going on at those other banks.'

David shook his head sadly as Parker continued.

'Remember how he deposited increasingly large sums of cash – under the guise of his gambling winnings? As time went by, those banks got beguiled by the man and became lax to the point of outright negligence. They should have been asking him what it was all about, yet they did nothing. Heads are certainly going to roll for that.'

'And then George issued his own cheques to other parties,' David added, 'including some to Stuart's own firm. I suppose they were paid into the clients' accounts here.'

'Not necessarily – not directly, anyway,' Parker answered, his eyes sparkling at the unfolding drama. 'I think they were too clever for that – or thought they were. They used a network of accounts. The tracing back of specific items would then be nigh on impossible. Having said that, we'll do our best to disprove that particular notion.'

David closed his eyes as he marshalled his thoughts, which kept throwing up the age of prohibition. 'So, the banks were robbed around London; the actual cash found its way down here and was deposited in a variety of bank accounts; and cheques were then issued and paid into differently-named accounts at other banks. The dirty cash had been well and truly cleaned – like with Al Capone's old laundry operations.'

'Capone may have started such a ploy,' Parker added, 'but it's now a growing concern over here. Yet the criminals wouldn't get away with it if the banks did their job properly. In time, I'm sure some specific laws and regulations will have to be introduced. If not, this type of fraud will become a major problem.'

'But I can't imagine Stuart Brown actually handling the cash. It'd be too big a risk for him. But if he did, how did he get hold of it?'

'Don't forget those regular meetings down here with his London clients. We now know that "clients" is something of a misnomer. He was effectively their partner. They brought the cash down and he handed it over to Broadman who then got it into the banking system.'

It was now looking horribly feasible – if still unbelievable. Why else would London clients need to come down here each month? And he and Sarah might well have rubbed shoulders with them in the Royal House Inn. The men in the bar on their anniversary night out were certainly from London.

But there was clearly more to come. Parker had not yet got round to dealing with the actual murder and its catalysts.

CHAPTER 31

'But why would Brown get into this sort of thing?' David asked Parker. Goodness knows the man was not short of a bob or two. And he had a notable position in town.

'Why does anyone get involved in criminal activities? Greed, normally. The allure of money – and power. Is he that sort of person?'

'He's always been rather self-important,' David replied. 'And a bit of a ladies' man, but he's pleasant enough – and generous. I suppose his Bentley's a form of status symbol, but I can't see any reason for him to get involved with criminals. He's successful in his own right without taking risks like that. But what about George Broadman? What was in it for him? And why was he killed?

Parker turned over his pages before looking at him intently. 'Those are the imponderables. At present, the police are keeping an open mind. But they have their theories – and they're sure they know how he was killed. As for the reason, it probably goes back to the war. The police think it's blackmail. Remember, they believe Broadman owed Brown something and the solicitor subsequently got to know all about his gambling addiction. It doesn't take much to put two and two together. And the police think Broadman eventually had enough of it and tried to exert some form of pressure on Brown.'

'Stuart wouldn't have liked that,' David said. 'Not if it might affect his status in town. But would that have justified Broadman being murdered?'

'It could have – with the villains we're talking about. I don't think they'd have much truck with someone like him – particularly if he started to make things awkward for them.'

'And the London lot were down here at the time. I might even have seen them on the evening of your first day here. They were also around last weekend.'

'Yes, I know,' Parker replied, checking his notes. 'But how had you heard?'

'From Mrs Smithers. She normally cleans Brown's offices in the evenings, but was asked to change her hours – because of their visit. So she swapped her duties around. She cleaned here on Monday evening, rather than the next morning. It was all agreed by us. That was the evening she went home ill.'

'I'll come back to that in a moment,' Parker said. 'Unwittingly, you've jumped the gun.' Not for the first time, Agatha Christie's novels crossed David's mind as Parker paused, as if to gather his thoughts.

'First of all,' he continued, 'you need to know about that all-important catalyst I mentioned earlier. Believe it or not, it was your father.'

'My father?' David exclaimed.

'I told Inspector Hopkins about his walkabouts – not only on the Monday night after Broadman's car went over the cliff, but also the night before. That's why he went round to your house on Wednesday. He was anxious to hear about that black baby story.'

'You must be joking.'

'Mr Goodhart, you might find this difficult to believe, but without our realizing it – and that means you, me and, indeed, your father – his recounting of what he saw on Sunday night was the all-important breakthrough for

Hopkins.

Extraordinary! It was difficult to believe anything now. How could Dad have any bearing on Stuart's arrest?

'That Sunday night,' Parker continued, 'or, to be more precise, in the early hours of Monday morning, your father was in the High Street. Remember how horrified you and your wife were? He'd left the house when you were both asleep. Anyway, he was approaching Broadman's shop when he saw someone lying in the road, half under the butcher's van. He thought the man had been run over. But then a big car drew up alongside, the man jumped in and the car sped away.'

'So?' David queried. How could this be significant?

'So, it was a big car – a big black car. Would you believe, a Bentley? And your father couldn't forget the registration plate – BAB 1. Get it? The black baby.'

David closed his eyes in disbelief at Dad's infantile interpretation of Stuart's personalized number plate. Whatever would Sarah say? Even with her raw grasp of chess, "Check Mate", perhaps?

'And your father's curiosity was such that he went out again on the Monday evening – when you were out celebrating – specifically to look for that "black baby" again. It might sound crazy, but that unlikely scenario convinced the police that one of Brown's London cronies doctored the brakes on Broadman's van. The man was then driven away by Brown himself. And before you suggest that this is all a figment of your father's imagination, the police wouldn't agree. They've found enough evidence in the "black baby" – by way of fingerprints and other items – to justify the arrest of Brown. And by now, they should have nicked the man who actually fixed the brakes.'

'But that brake tampering,' David said, trying to push

258

Dad's involvement to the back of his mind, 'I still don't understand why Broadman should have driven to that car park in the first place – especially with the weather being so foul.'

Parker smiled the smile of a man who had all the answers. 'Brown had agreed to meet him there – to deliver the next tranche of cash. It was their normal meeting place. But one thing bothers me. He couldn't have guaranteed Broadman making the assignment – not with his van's brakes having been put out of action – and...'

'But hang on a minute,' David interrupted, 'getting there would have been entirely feasible. Last week, I retraced his entire journey. I suppose I was trying to play the private detective. It was just that I couldn't believe he was able to travel from Barnmouth to that car park without once using his brakes.'

'And?' Parker asked.

'And I found it no problem at all. Nor would any driver who used his gearbox for slowing down. Perhaps Brown knew Broadman used that technique.'

'But there was one thing Brown probably didn't know,' Parker said. 'Hopkins thinks that Broadman had intended to kill him.'

'What?'

'When the police recovered Broadman's body, they found one of his shop's knives on him. That's hardly the sort of thing he'd normally have on his person.'

Was this possible? Stuart trying to kill George when, at the same time, George was trying to murder him?

'And there's more evidence against Brown and his gang,' Parker continued. 'Remember I mentioned a second catalyst?'

David raised his eyebrows. What was coming now?

'It was Mrs Smithers. And this is where Brown and company really slipped up. But when you go to see her, be prepared to find her distraught.'

'I'm not surprised with what she's been through,' David said, amazed at such an unlikely combination of apparent witnesses as Mrs Smithers and Dad. 'Such a sudden illness must be frightening.'

'But she's not been ill – not in the sense you mean. They tried to kill her.'

'They what?'

'And she's distraught at what you and I are likely to say. It certainly won't happen, but she thinks she's for the high jump.'

David had suffered enough shocks already, but this was getting beyond all reason. 'Why would they try to kill her? And why does she think she's in trouble with us?'

'We just have to thank God she came out of her coma. If not, none of this would be known. As it is she's been able to give Hopkins the full story.'

Parker studied his notes, as if to ensure his certainty of the facts and then recounted what had happened. In the middle of her evening's cleaning, Mrs Smithers – now alone in the branch – had heard the front door bell ring. Moving to the door, she looked through the spy-hole and, seeing the friendly face of Stuart Brown, decided there was no need to use the security chain. But as soon as she opened the door, a stranger emerged from the shadows, Brown having disappeared from view. The other man bundled her into the building and then threatened her on pain of death to act naturally as he forcefully escorted her home. Once inside her house, he shoved her into her sitting room chair and rammed a cushion in her face. He made it clear he was going to suffocate her, to make it appear she had suffered a heart attack while sleeping in her chair. But the villain had been careless on three counts. He had removed the cushion too soon, wrongly assuming she was dead; he had failed to ensure the banking hall and back office had been cleared of her cleaning receptacles; and he had not known that on leaving the bank, it was the invariable practice to double-lock the front door.

'But why did they do this to her?' David asked, as Parker drew breath.

'We know because the man was so confident of the end result that he actually told Mrs Smithers as he pressed the cushion into her face. They thought she'd heard something incriminating when she'd been cleaning Brown's office the previous evening. But not according to her. She told Hopkins she'd heard nothing. So it was a botched murder attempt all for nothing.'

'And she believes she's in trouble for not using the front door chain?'

'Exactly.'

Dear Mrs Smithers. Nearly murdered, yet her main concern related to the bank's rules. But it would certainly be a salutary lesson for everyone else. That door chain would now be invariably used. Yet he had a sneaking sympathy for the cleaner; she could hardly have expected such dire consequences upon seeing the town's most prominent solicitor standing on the bank's doorstep.

Parker then rose to go, as if deciding it was the end of the story and it certainly seemed to be an open and shut case against Stuart. 'But by the way,' he said, turning back as he reached the door. 'I gather you saw the Esplanade's owner last week.'

'Yes, John English. He wanted help in buying the premises next door. I didn't like the sound of it at all.'

'Quite right,' Parker said, nodding his head. 'He might also be implicated. It seems he was in the Catering Corps with Brown and Broadman. Hopkins thinks the London gang wanted to use the new building as their base down here.'

When he had gone, a mixture of relief and incredulity hung over David as he contemplated all he had heard. But it was now past noon and although he did not feel in the mood to start tackling the day's work, he needed to see Jane to find out what had been happening in the office. He picked up the telephone, but before he could speak, there was a knock on the door and Katie Tibbs burst into the room, her eyes alive with excitement.

'Ah, Katie,' he said. 'I was just about to get Jane...'

'She's just gone to lunch,' Katie blurted out. 'She went early because you were tied up. I said you wouldn't mind. But, Mr Goodhart, come outside – quickly – or we'll be too late.'

As he rose from behind his desk, he was astounded that Katie should reach across and grab his hand, tugging him towards the door, like an excited child hastening a parent to witness some extraordinary childish feat.

'Come on,' she urged, dragging him from the room towards a window that overlooked the High Street. 'Come on, quickly, or you'll be too late. Look – up the street – you can just see them. It's so exciting.'

He had no idea what he was supposed to be looking at, but followed the direction of Katie's pointed finger and suddenly saw the objects of her attention. He could not help but smile and shook his head slowly from side to side in disbelief. But he had to admit he felt almost as pleased as Katie, who could hardly contain her excitement. Jane was strolling up the road, casting a casual eye in the shop windows, but it was clear from her glances in the opposite direction, that her main attention was focused on the tall well-built young man at her side. Hand in hand, they sauntered towards the top of the town until they reached the corner by the church and passed out of sight.

'There!' Katie shrieked. 'What do you make of that? Isn't it just wonderful?'

He could only agree, but having extricated himself from her grasp, he ushered her back to his room. Some routine dictation might be the best way to bring her back to earth. But she had more to spill out.

'And there's another thing,' she said, before he could broach the subject of work. 'Your wife telephoned – while you were with the inspector. She didn't want to interrupt you, but asked me to give you a message. She seemed really excited – you know, pleased excited, not the worried sort. A bit like me just then, I suppose. Anyway, she...'

'All right, all right, Katie.' Would he ever be able to shut the girl up? 'Just give me the message. What did she say?'

'Oh, it was only a short message. And I'm not sure what it actually meant. Your wife just said the bank had telephoned. At first I thought she meant it was us. But it couldn't have been anyone here, because it'd been so busy. We've been up to our eyes this morning...'

'Katie!'

'Oh, sorry, sir. Anyway, whoever it was, they asked if she could do mornings at Newton Abbot. I can't think what that might be all about, but she said you'd understand.'

Yes, indeed. Of all he had heard that morning, it was the one thing he could really understand. At last, the bank had relented – a part-time position at Newton Abbot would be perfect for her. When he arrived home that evening, he knew Sarah's eyes would be sparkling as brightly as Katie's. After dictating a few letters and then dismissing Katie to her typewriter, he reflected on how different the circumstances of his family were from those who had been caught up in the Broadman affair. Although he could not condone Miss Harding's actions, he actually felt some sympathy for her – a victim of a sheltered upbringing and dragged into the mire by an unscrupulous rogue who had been her knight in shining armour, but who had feet of clay. Was it possible that the bank – and the police – might adopt an understanding attitude towards her plight?

The affair might also change Bernard Groves's philosophy for the better. Parker had still to see the cashier about the way he had mishandled George's credits and a formal reprimand might well result. Thank goodness no one had so far implied that he had been in league with the butcher, or any of the other protagonists, for that matter. Yet he had been in George's regiment. Was that a worry, or a coincidence?

As for English's possible involvement, that was not a surprise. He definitely had a link with Stuart and the meetings on the golf course and at the football ground now looked to have been engineered. Time would tell as to their wartime association, but his reasoning behind the extension of the hotel was looking increasingly dodgy. It was good fortune that it had not proved to be a valid banking proposition.

But Jane's scenario was much happier and he had no concerns at all about her boyfriend. She could easily have grown into another Miss Harding, her lack of confidence thwarting her development as a person. But during these last two weeks, she had blossomed out of all recognition from her inglorious start at the branch and John Jackson was just the man to take her forward.

He smiled as he thought of her blossoming relationship and at the excitement it had caused Katie. As for Mrs Smithers, he must see her this afternoon and put her mind at rest. Then home to Sarah. Although the eventual outcome of the branch inspection would soon be dominating his mind, such thoughts would have to wait another day. For now, he wanted to share Sarah's joy at receiving the bank's eventual offer of part-time employment.

And what about Dad? His part in Stuart's arrest was amazing. Perhaps the head-injury would not be the lost cause he had feared. There might well be difficult times ahead, but he would do his utmost to ensure that Dad would get the best possible quality of life. He deserved nothing less.